A GATHERING OF MONSTERS

A MONSTER ROMANCE COLLECTION
VOLUME I

WINTER RANDALL

A Gathering of Monsters

A Monster Romance Collection Vol. 1

Winter Randall

Author's Note

All of the stories in this collection include graphic sexual content intended only for adults. Almost all of them also include one or more of the following:

    Blood/Gore
    Physical Violence
    Emotional Abuse
    Attempted Sexual Assault
    Anxiety Disorder
    Depression

If any of these might be triggers for you or difficult subjects, please proceed with caution.

—W

Contents

My Best Friend's Mate

My Best Friend's Mate

I've been in love with my wolfman best friend since we were teenagers. But we're not kids anymore, and now it's time for his body to choose a mate.

I know it won't be me, and that thought is enough to make me wish I had never met Eli James. How can I watch him mate and fall in love with someone else?

Tonight is the mating, and there's a wolf with red eyes tapping at my window.

CHAPTER ONE

Ten Years Ago

"Class, this is our new student, Eli James. Eli has just moved here from Boston. Everyone, please say hello."

"Hello, Eli," everyone in class chants, unenthusiastic.

Eli James is a wolf. Wolfman? Wolf-person? I'm not sure of the right word. I'm new to this. I guess we all are, especially in Amber Hills. It's been less than a decade since humans figured out there are non-human people on the planet, like wolf-people. And in all that time, there's never been one living in Amber Hills. Which is why, when Eli starts down the aisle toward one of the few empty seats, everyone in our 7th grade English class sends him dirty looks. Amber Hills isn't exactly known for its inclusivity, wolf-people included. I hate this town.

He's coming toward me, his feet shuffling on the linoleum, and I get a flutter of nerves in my stomach. I've seen wolf-people on the news, but I've never seen one in real life. He's...tall. Way taller than everyone else in the room, and even though he's wearing totally normal clothes—jeans and a t-shirt —they fit him oddly, sort of wrinkling in places.

He starts to move right past me without a glance in my direction, but our teacher calls out, "Eli, there's no reason for you to be all the way in the back. Please take one of the empty desks closer to the front."

I twist in time to see the look on Eli's furry face, a look of annoyance. I'm fairly certain I hear him growl softly. I bite back a smile and watch him come back up the aisle. There are a few scattered seats, but from the look on Eli's face, I get the feeling he'd rather chew his own arm off than take any of them. I wonder if he's having a hard first day here.

"You can sit by me," I say, nodding at the chair beside me that's empty.

Eli hesitates, his eyes finding mine, and I hold in a gasp. They're black, his midnight irises taking up almost all the space in his eye. When he moves, it isn't to speak. Instead, he bends forward just a little and sniffs the air around me. The gesture seems to be involuntary, and this time, I can't hold back my smile. He comes closer, fitting his big body into the seat beside mine, and I decide to return the favor. As subtly as I can, while Eli is digging through his backpack, I give the air around him a sniff and get that flutter in my stomach again. He smells like citrus, and a blush splashes its way across my cheeks when I imagine him in the shower, scrubbing every inch of his dark, thick fur the way I have to scrub my own thick hair.

The world continues on as before, our teacher going back to her discussion on *The Lion, The Witch, and The Wardrobe*, and just when I've managed to get myself re-focused, a low, gruff voice beside me says, "I don't need your pity."

His voice sends a shiver up my spine. I turn my head, trying not to be obvious, so our teacher doesn't notice. "I don't pity you."

He doesn't look like he believes me. His eyes scan over my face, and his mouth moves gently, until one of his shiny white fangs flashes.

His face seems to soften at that, and I wonder at his defense mechanisms. Does he have to have his guard up at all times? That must get exhausting.

I turn back to the front of the room, but when I feel a puff of air against my neck, I spin around quickly. Eli is leaning toward me across the aisle, those black eyes so close to me that I startle.

"What's your name?" he asks.

"Jessa."

His mouth parts, pulling into a wide, toothy grin. "Nice to meet you, Jessa."

And at the young age of twelve, I fell in love.

Chapter Two

Present Day

I absolutely detest the office where Eli works. It's stuffy and quiet, and every time I come to visit Eli, his boss stares, like he's personally offended by humans and wolf-people being friends.

Eli still has an hour on the clock, but I'm bored, so I brought him coffee. "Here you go," I say, setting the paper cup down beside his keyboard. The lobby of the office is empty, so I hop up onto the edge of the reception desk, even though I know Eli will probably get in trouble if his boss sees me.

Without taking his eyes off his computer, Eli reaches out and peels the label off his coffee cup.

I roll my eyes. "You know, it doesn't make you less masculine if you like peppermint lattes. Someone's going to smell it on your breath one of these days."

"Thanks for bringing it to me," he says, sipping at it while he types with his other hand. I watch the movement of his throat and the careful way he holds his cup so that his claws don't puncture the cardboard. I shift and feel a rush of satisfaction when Eli's eyes shoot over to me, going straight for my chest. I purposefully left quite a few buttons on my blouse open, and I wore my pleated skirt, the one that always rides up high on my thighs when I move. I love it when Eli can't keep his eyes off me. I love the way his lips always curl up above his teeth when he looks at me that way.

But then I remember what today is, and all the excitement inside me vanishes. I look down at the coffee in my hands. I don't even want it anymore.

"Do you really think tonight will be the night?" I'm barely able to speak above a whisper.

Eli finally stops working, no longer clicking away at his mouse, typing away at his keyboard. He sighs and sets down his coffee. "I think so. I can feel it."

"What does it feel like?" I lean back on one hand, until our faces are close together. Eli and I have never been very good at physical boundaries. I always want to be close to him, and he never seems to mind.

He wrinkles his nose. "Come on, Jessa. I don't want to talk about this stuff with you."

"Eli, we've been best friends for ten years. Just fucking tell me."

He chews on his bottom lip, his cute little fang sticking out. He seems to be intentionally avoiding my eye. "It's sort of like I have a beehive under my skin."

I push closer, until my arm is pressed against his. I love feeling his fur against my skin. It feels...decadent. "I don't know what you mean."

He sighs. "It's like there's something buzzing all the time. And every day, it gets louder and more uncomfortable. I don't think there's any way it could get any...worse. Or...well...worse maybe isn't the right word. It's not *bad*. It's impossible to explain. But it has to happen soon. I'm already a year older than my brother was when he mated."

Just hearing him say that word sends a shiver down my spine. The extent of what I know about wolf mating, I learned in Health class, freshman year of high school. We learned first about the human body and then about wolf bodies, and seeing as how Eli was the only wolf in school, it was a humiliating experience for him. Our teacher clearly chose to include wolf anatomy just for him. I remember the day we learned about the mating—when a wolf is compelled by their biology to take the mate of their body's choosing in order to come into maturity—and how Eli buried his face in the hood of his sweatshirt through the whole class.

"Well, congratulations on puberty, I guess." I slide off the desk and sling my purse up over my shoulder. "I need to get back to work." This is a lie. I spent the weekend fulfilling all the orders for my art business, which I sadly run out of my childhood bedroom in my parents' house, and until someone purchases a new commission, my schedule is wide open.

But I don't need him to know that. Let him think I'm so busy that I'm not dwelling on him mating some totally random wolf-woman when the moon rises tonight.

"Okay," he says, his black eyes watching me as I fix my skirt. "I'll see you tomorrow."

I shrug. "Maybe," I mutter.

His hairy eyebrows bow in. "What do you mean, maybe?"

I shake my head. I can't talk about this with him or I'll start crying, and crying in front of my best friend because he might find his soulmate tonight would be humiliating, to say the least.

"Jess, nothing's going to change, even if the mating does happen tonight."

I throw my hands in the air. "You don't know that. Look at your brother. The second he met his mate, it was like nobody else existed. He totally stopped hanging out with his friends."

Beside him on the desk, Eli's phone starts to ring, that boring corporate *ring-ring-ring* that drives me crazy. Eli ignores it. It's like he can't even hear it. He keeps his steady gaze on me. "That's because my brother's friends suck. That's not going to happen to us, Jessa."

"And what happens when your mate is some super possessive wolf-girl who growls at me because she thinks I stand too close to you? Isn't that kind of what wolf-people with mates are known for? One time, I swear, I just glanced at your brother—"

"You're assuming I'll mate with a wolf."

I stop mid-sentence, my hand still up in a dismissive gesture, and my whole body freezes. "I...I didn't know that was in question."

Holding my gaze, Eli lifts his peppermint latte to his muzzle, sipping it slowly, the way I know he has to do so he doesn't make a mess. I bite back a smile.

"I've been talking to people online," he finally says once his thirst is quenched. "There are wolves everywhere that have mated with other species. It seems to come down to biology. As long as you're compatible..."

He trails off, and I pick up the thread. "You could mate with anyone."

This does something uncomfortable to my stomach. The idea that Eli could mate with a human has me trembling, inside and out. But it also somehow makes it worse. Because now that I know he's biologically able to mate with me, if he mates with a human woman that *isn't* me, I'll be sick.

And that's the thing about it. Eli doesn't get to choose. His body just does it for him.

"I hope everything works out the way you want it to, Eli," is all I can bring myself to say. Because if I say any more, I'll give myself away. I'll tell Eli that I've been in love with him since we were kids, and that I hope whatever weird mating hormone is taking over his body picks me, and that, even if he doesn't end up with some possessive wolf-woman, that this will probably be the last time I can bring myself to be around him because I can't spend the rest of my life watching him love someone else.

I lean forward quickly, while I have the courage, and kiss him on the cheek, reveling in the feel of his fur on my lips. When I lean back, his eyes are wide, so that I can see the entire black iris. "Bye, Eli."

I start to pull away, but he puts one of his big hairy hands over mine. I look down at it, at his sharp claws and the way his hand is almost twice the size of my own, fitting against his almost seven foot frame. "I'll see you tomorrow," he says, his voice low and firm.

I nod, even though I know it's not true. "See you tomorrow, Eli." I carefully slide my hand out from under his and walk away.

Chapter Three

On my way home, I stop to buy a container of cookies and a bottle of wine. My parents are out tonight, so it's just me at the house, alone with my abject misery. I don't even bother with a glass. I just uncork the wine and drink straight from the bottle.

I've been dreading this night since that day in Health class when we learned about the mating. It feels exactly like I thought it would. It feels like my heart is being ripped from my chest. I lay down in my bed and eat half the container of cookies while I watch old sitcoms.

Maybe this is the push I finally needed to move out. It's not like I plan on living with my parents forever, but I went straight from high school into starting my own business, and finding a place for myself just took a back seat. Next thing I know, I'm twenty-two and still living in my childhood home. But I've wanted to leave Amber Hills forever. This stuffy little town is the bane of my existence. The only reason I stay is because of Eli.

Eli, who's probably gearing up to go have sex with a stranger right now, a stranger he's going to be having sex with for the rest of his life. The thought makes me sick. Eli and I have engaged in harmless flirting over the ten years of our friendship, but other than the occasional glance at my cleavage or my ass, he's never made a move. And neither have I. I've always been too scared to fuck up the best thing in my life.

I turn over in my bed, still fully dressed, and start to cry. I want Eli so bad. I can't imagine ever loving anyone other than him. He's my best friend, the person who's been beside me through everything, and the thought that I'm about to lose him makes me want to die.

Now I know I have to move. There's no way I can stay in this town and run into Eli at the coffee shop with his new mate. Or see them out at the park. Or at our favorite Chinese restaurant. Oh, God. I think I'm going to throw up.

When I'm halfway through the bottle of wine and most of the way through the cookies, I crawl under my covers and pull them up over my head. I'm still in the stupid outfit I put on to get Eli's attention, and now I feel like a complete idiot. He's never going to look at me with that heat in his eyes again. My Eli is gone.

Chapter Four

I don't know how long I've been asleep before the noise wakes me up. In the midst of my half-awake grogginess, the noise seems far off, like something happening a mile away. But when I realize that the light *tap-tap-tap*-ing is coming from outside my window, I spring up in my bed, my heart already racing before I'm even fully awake.

The world is dark outside my window. It's a middle-of-the-night darkness, shadows blanketing everything. It takes a moment for my mind to make sense of the shapes in the dark.

And when the *tap-tap-tap* comes again, I see the bright red eyes that peer in through my window, looking right at me. It's all I can see, those red eyes and nothing else, and it's all I *need* to see. I don't even think; I just run.

Scrambling out of my bed, I don't even bother putting on my shoes. I race through the house and out the back door. I don't have a car, so it's not like making a run for the road is going to do me any good. No, I know where I have to go. Eli's apartment is just on the other side of the woods from my house, and if I can make it to him, he'll protect me. I know he will.

I'm breathing hard as I run, the sound of it loud in my ears. The only thing keeping me up as I dodge trees and scrape my bare feet on branches is the knowledge that I don't want to find out what will happen when whoever was at my window catches up to me.

I reach for my phone in my pocket before I realize that not only does this skirt not have pockets, but my phone is still sitting on my bed where I left it. I can't call the police or Eli. I just have to run. Run hard and not stop.

I know these woods like the back of my hand. I've crossed through them so many times, but they seem bigger now, longer, like it'll take days for me to get through them. And all the while, I don't know where that person is. Was it just someone playing a prank on me? Was it someone trying to get my attention? Or was it a vampire? An orc? A bat-person? I don't know every species or creature on the planet, but I know that some of them would gladly hurt me without question.

I see the light from Eli's apartment building through the trees. I'm almost there. Out of the woods and away from whatever was at my window.

And then I hear the sound of heavy footsteps behind me. They crunch through the leaves and branches. Not just two feet, but four. On four legs, whoever it is is bound to catch up to me without effort. I can feel the terror rising in my throat. Why is this happening to me? Why would anyone want to hurt me?

I run harder, keeping my eyes focused on the lights getting closer and closer and not the person behind me getting closer and closer. But before I can reach the tree line, something huge slams into my back, knocking me to the ground and crushing me beneath its weight. The leaves and dirt press in all around me as I scramble, trying to get out from under this creature, but it's so heavy, and with it on my back, pushing me into the ground, I can't even tell what it is.

"Get off me!" I scream, clawing at the dirt. And then something wet touches my ear. Hot breath puffs out against my face as the creature says, "Did you really think you could outrun me?"

I stop fighting. I hold very, very still, trying to process what's happening. I know that voice. Of course I do. I would know the voice of my best friend in any situation, even when I have a hulking creature on my back and I can't breathe and my heart is squeezing so hard, it feels like it'll burst. But this isn't Eli's normal voice. It's deeper, gruffer, more growl than anything else.

"Eli?" I squeak, trying to turn to see him.

But he holds me down, pushing my wrists into the ground with his furred hands. Oh, God. His claws. His claws are twice the size they normally are. What's happening?

"I know why you wear this outfit," he growls into my ear, sending goosebumps along my arms and legs. "You think I don't know you wear it because it turns me on? I can hardly keep myself from looking at every inch of your skin when you wear it, wondering what you would taste like."

I gasp and feel my pussy squeeze tight at his words. Is Eli... flirting with me? Is Eli talking *dirty* to me? I'm dead. That's the only explanation. I've died and gone to Heaven. In Heaven, Eli is mine.

"Eli, what are you doing?" I pant, as one of his long claws travels gently down my arm before tucking under me. He grabs a handful of my blouse and rips it open, the fabric dragging through the dirt. "Eli!"

"What is it, little mate?" he says, his tongue coming out to stroke my ear. "You going to pretend you don't want this?"

Mate. It's not that I'm too stupid to figure out that that's what's happening here. It's that I never, not in a million years, thought it would be happening to me. I readied myself. I was prepared for Eli to mate with someone I'd never met. Is it really me? Am I really his mate?

The thought turns my body into molten lava. I push my hips back into his, feeling his hard cock, bigger than any I've ever been closely acquainted with, pressing into my skirt. Eli growls at the friction, and I smile up at the moon, so happy I could scream from it.

My hands dig into the dirt beneath me as Eli paws at my breasts. He pulls at my nipple, and I'm shocked by how much his claws hurt, even more shocked by how welcome the pain is.

"Eli," I groan. "Make me yours." It's all I've ever wanted. And now that it's happening, I almost feel like I want it to happen faster, so that there's no chance he could be taken away from me before the deed is done. I need the mating to be complete so that nothing can tear us apart.

With a growl, he flips me over, and I'm face-to-face with that massive part of him that was pressed against me. He's completely naked. I was just guessing at his size before, based on the feel of it, but now that I'm looking at it, I'm starting to have doubts. There's no way he's going to fit inside me. And his knot...

I learned about wolf-people's knots on the internet, when I got curious what Eli's dick would look like. It was far less intimidating on Google. Back then, the knot was merely hypothetical. But now it's here in front of me, and I'm fairly certain Eli is going to want to put it inside me.

Like he can read my mind, Eli's mouth curves up in a devilish smile. "My mate will take every inch of me," he snarls. I'm amazed at how he looks like Eli but somehow doesn't at the same time. This is my best friend, but his eyes are glowing red, and he's looking at me like he's going to swallow me whole. This is not the wolfman I've always known, who would blush and avert his eyes if someone flirted with him.

Eli shoves my skirt up with his furry hands and rips away

my underwear. Apparently this whole outfit is destined to be ruined tonight. I can't think of a better way for it to go.

And then Eli bends his hulking body between my legs and swipes his tongue across my pussy. I cry out. Eli licks at me, lapping again and again up my slit until I'm writhing around in the dirt, ready for him to put me out of my misery. Instead, he shifts until his tongue is buried inside me. I bow up off the ground, grabbing his ears and holding onto them so I can buck against his face. His mouth parts slightly, and when he presses one of his sharp teeth against my clit, the whole world goes white, and I know I'm screaming loud enough for the whole neighborhood to hear. Like I give a shit.

When my orgasm finally starts to ebb, my body beginning to go soft, Eli pulls away, licking at his mouth as he wraps his hands around me and flips me over onto my stomach. Yanking my hips into the air, he notches the head of that monster cock against my entrance. I try not to tense. I know that if I don't relax, it will just hurt more. But when he starts to push in, even with my skin slick from his spit and my own juices, the stretch is painful.

I'm moaning, partially in pleasure and partially in pain when Eli lowers himself over me, until he's pressing me into the ground with the weight of his entire body. I watch his claws sink into the dirt on either side of my body, and then he shoves his cock deeper.

"Eli!" I scream, trying to anchor myself to something. But all I can do is scrabble at the dirt until Eli wraps one strong, solid arm around my middle.

"Take it all, little mate," he growls, and I just nod. I can't say anything in response. It's like I can feel his cock all the way in my throat. He's still going, still pushing, but then he stops. His knot is right up against my entrance, and it feels impossible. My body wasn't made for this.

I take a deep breath and hold onto the arm that's banded

around me, leaning back into his scruff and feeling his growl as it rumbles through him. His hold on me tightens, and then he pushes past my resistance, his knot shoving its way inside me.

I shout, and after a moment, I realize I'm shivering, from being so full, from being *too* full, from being completely and undeniably connected to Eli, from love and lust and everything in the universe.

"Eli," I whine, as he sinks the rest of the way in. And then he starts to rock, pulling only slightly out of me and then shoving himself back in, the knot never leaving my body.

The pleasure is intense. I'm stretched so tight, and now that my body has adjusted, all I can feel is the pleasure, pleasure that rockets so high that all I can do is press my face to the cool ground and close my eyes, letting Eli invade my body, claiming it for his own.

He roars, so loud it feels like the trees tremble, and when he starts to come inside me, the sensation of it and of his claws gently digging into my skin and his cock filling me puts me right on the edge. But when he bends down and sinks his teeth into my shoulder, I come. It's like a blazing explosion. My vision goes dark, and when I can finally see again, Eli is panting into my hair. I look down at the hand next to my face on the ground. His claws have begun to retract, going back to their normal length.

"Are you okay?" he says, and his voice is the voice of the Eli I've always known. Still deep, but far less ragged. "I was rough with you."

I stretch in his arms and wince at the feel of his knot still inside me. "I liked it," I sigh, tipping my face back so I can see him. His eyes aren't red anymore, just their normal black, those eyes I've always loved, and he's looking at me with an apologetic expression. I feel his knot getting smaller inside me, and then he starts to slip out. A part of me mourns the moment when he won't be inside me anymore, connected to me in a way we never have been.

"You didn't hurt me." To get that sad look off his face, I wrap a hand around the back of his neck and pull him down to me for a kiss. He's being so gentle with me now, his mouth just barely grazing mine. He pulls out of me and lifts me into his arms, holding me close to his body. He smells like pine needles and wet soil. I bury my face against his furry chest.

"Where are we going?" I ask, stifling a yawn. It's the middle of the night, and while I enjoyed it immensely, Eli *did* wake me from a deep sleep for all these mating shenanigans.

"My apartment."

I hum against him. "You're not wearing any clothes. And mine are all ripped up."

When he speaks again, the words rumble against where my cheek is pressed against him. "Everyone is asleep. We'll be fine."

I take his word for it, and as he carries me out of the cover of the woods and up the grassy slope I know so well, I fall asleep in his arms.

Chapter Five

I wake up in Eli's bed, the sun fighting its way into the room through the closed blinds. I sit up and grin when I look down at myself. Eli took off my ruined clothes but left me in my underwear. There are pink claw marks on my breasts and stray leaves scattered in his gunmetal gray sheets.

The bed is empty beside me. I take a moment to marvel at the situation. I'm Eli's *mate*. And now I'm in his bed, the bed I've been in so many times, platonically for the most part, but I'm practically naked and my best friend fucked the life out of me last night.

I crawl out of bed and dig through Eli's closet for a shirt to throw on. I can hear him in the kitchen, humming quietly to himself. It makes me smile. Eli is the sweetest, cheeriest, most wonderful person I know. And I'm his *mate*.

I head out to the kitchen, and find him there, scooping eggs onto a plate with bacon and strawberries. I know Eli. He doesn't do much cooking for himself because he's always at work. There's no way he just happened to have fresh strawberries. No, he bought those strawberries for today. He planned this breakfast. For his mate. Without knowing it would be me.

My stomach turns at the idea that some other woman could be standing here right now, human or wolf, enjoying this beautiful morning with the person I love.

"How are you today? Sore?" Eli asks. He might have been humming moments ago, but he's not his usual chipper self. There's a strange sadness in his eyes when he looks over at me that I don't understand.

"I'm amazing," I breathe. I push closer to him, trying to insert myself between his body and the counter. "Last night was incredible."

His eyebrows bunch together. "There's something I should tell you about the mating." He takes a step back from me and clears his throat. Somehow the action makes his voice go deeper. "I'm the only one who's biologically bound to this mating. Since you're not wolf, your body doesn't hold to it like mine will." He can't seem to look at me, staring down at the floor.

"I don't understand." I feel dread creep over me. What is he trying to say?

"If you don't want to be my mate, you don't have to be. I'll be forever loyal to you, but you don't have to—"

"You don't want me to be your mate?" The words come out of me choked. How did this turn on me so quickly?

Eli's eyes snap up to mine. He shakes his head. "Of course I want you to be my mate. Jessa, I love you. I've loved you since I was twelve. The fact that you're my mate..." He trails off and breathes in deep gusts for a moment before continuing. "Knowing you're my mate makes me happier than I ever thought I could be."

I feel like he's saying all the right things, all the words I've dreamed of him saying for years. But it doesn't erase what came before them. "Then why—"

"I want you to have a choice," he says, cutting me off. "For years I've hated knowing that I didn't have a choice. That my body would choose whoever was right for me. I hated that because I knew if it was anyone but you, the mating would be wrong. You're the only one for me, Jessa. But I don't want you to feel like you don't have a choice."

I almost want to laugh. The absurdity of what he's saying...

I reach up to grab his face, loving the feel of his soft fur under my hands. "I don't care about the mating, Eli. I would choose you every single day of my life. I already did years ago. I love you so much, I can barely breathe from it."

He yanks me against him, burying his face in my neck. It takes me a moment to realize that he's licking me, right in the spot where he bit me last night. I completely forgot about it, about the way he sank his teeth into me when he came. Marking me. Just the thought makes me shiver.

"I didn't want to tell you how I felt," he says against my skin, "because I knew I would have to take a mate someday, and I didn't want to break both our hearts."

With him curled around me like this, so big and furry, it's like he can block out the whole world, so it can just be the two of us. I press my face against him and breathe in the smell of him, the warm scent of whatever he used to wash this morning.

"No broken hearts here," I whisper.

He finally pushes me away, leading me to one of the stools around his bar. Eli's apartment is so nice and neat and adult, the exact kind of apartment you would expect from someone who works as an administrative assistant.

"Let me feed you," he says, going to where he abandoned the breakfast and coming back with two plates. He sets one in front of me, and my stomach immediately growls at the smell of it all. It turns out being railed by a wolfman in the middle of the night can really work up an appetite.

He takes a seat next to me and watches me with a smile in

his eyes as I devour my food. Eli did always think it was amusing how fast I could put away a meal big enough for two. As I finish off my breakfast, Eli reaches over and rubs at my shoulders, lightly running his claws down my neck. His hand slides down to my thigh, and he scratches at it lightly.

I whimper, and he smiles over at me, his expression absolutely predatory.

"I love that I'm allowed to touch you anytime I want now."

My eyes are closed, my head tilted back. I can't breathe. "You were allowed to touch me before."

He makes a growly noise in his throat, and his hand moves up my thigh, until his fingers are delving under the hem of his shirt and down into my panties. He rubs my pussy with his big, strong fingers, and I moan. "Was I allowed to touch you like this?"

I grab onto his wrist, holding him still while I rock against his hand. "I was always yours," I say, finally opening my eyes to look at him. His eyes have gone red, his breath bursting out of him in heavy puffs.

He pulls his hand away and reaches for me, lifting me by my hips and dropping me down onto his lap. His delicious cock is like a steel pole between us, and Eli has completely lost all of his patience. He rips at his pants until his cock springs free, red and straining and lifts me onto the bar long enough to slip my underwear down my legs before tossing them aside.

And then he's lifting me back into his lap, straight down onto his cock. I hold onto him tight as he works his way into me. I love that he's completely lost to his lust when he's like this, using me like his little plaything. I could get completely addicted to feral Eli.

He sinks in a lot easier than he did last night, now that I know how big he is, now that I'm relaxed above him. I rock my hips against him, rubbing my clit against the hardness of his pelvis as he works the rest of his cock into me. His claws sink into my ass, lifting and lowering me in gentle swells until I'm right up against that knot of his. I look down between us. In the light of day, I can see the shape it, bulbous on both sides of his shaft. How the hell did that fit inside me last night?

Eli doesn't seem terribly concerned with fitting it inside me now. He seems to be enjoying sliding himself all the way out of me and then shoving me back down onto his dick. I lift up on my knees and then let him lower me back down, my head thrown back. It feels so fucking good. I've never been with anyone even close to the size of Eli.

He growls, low and terrifying, and then rips through my shirt to bare my breasts. While he plunges into me, his long tongue laps at my nipples until the peaks are hard and standing up for him, and then he nibbles at them, riding the line between pain and pleasure.

"Eli," I scream. It's all too much. His claws and his teeth and that knot that's now pushing up against my entrance, begging me to take it.

"*Mine*," he snarls and then shoves me down until the knot finds its way inside me.

When I'm completely seated on him, he wraps me tight in his arms and rocks me, knowing that the friction is going to set me off. I'm so full, and my clit is rubbing against him over and over, and the orgasm crashes into me like a freight train.

I'm screaming, shouting right into his perky ears, when he comes. I feel it spill out of me, and just like before, he sinks his teeth into my shoulder, in the exact same spot. I dig my nails into his fur, screaming louder. I'm sure his neighbors are going to love us.

When I finally come down, I'm trembling all the way to my toes. I breathe against him, feeling the way all the tension starts to seep from his body as well. I lean back on his lap, his cock still firmly inside me.

"Are you going to do that every time?" I ask him, inspecting the bite mark he left behind.

His black eyes go to my shoulder, and he reaches out to gently touch the spot. It's swollen and bleeding. "No. I'm sorry. Does it hurt?"

I laugh. "Well, yeah. But it's also kinda hot."

He smiles, but his eyes show his worry. "Once the mating calms down a little, I'll most likely only mark you occasionally. But you'll have the mark forever."

"Oh, I see," I say, snuggling against him. "Claiming your territory?"

"Claiming my *mate*. If anyone else so much as looks at you, I'll rip their throats out."

I laugh and kiss him on his muzzle. "Easy, there. Men will look at me. It's just the way it is. But there will never be any doubt who I belong to."

There's a smile in his eyes, and then they flash red.

EPILOGUE

"I can't decide if I want a mocha latte or a caramel latte."

Eli makes a sound in the back of his throat. "Every time you get the caramel, you complain because it's not as good as the mocha." His tone is playful, but there's an uneasiness in the line of his body as we stand at the counter of our favorite coffee shop. His eyes flicker to the side, and I glance to see what has him on edge.

At a table by the window, two women that look to be about my parents' ages eyeball us and then whisper to each other.

It's always been like this. Before, people were always whispering about Eli. Even after all this time, the opinion about the non-human population of Amber Hills hasn't changed. When we were kids, uncomfortable stares and whispers followed everywhere we went. But it's worse now because we're holding hands in the middle of our town's only coffee shop, and it is not being well-received. As the women continue to stare, I clutch Eli's hand tighter. No stuck-up asshole is going to keep me from doing whatever I want whenever I want with my mate.

His eyes are still on the women, his head bowed slightly and his shoulders hunched, like he's trying to disappear. I tug on his arm to get him to bend toward me. I stand up on my tiptoes and press my mouth to his. I feel the way he whines just a little against my mouth, a sound he makes when he's feeling emotionally overwhelmed.

When I let him back up, he straightens to his full height and lifts his chin before glancing over at the women again. They're busy gathering their things.

"Absolutely disgusting," I hear one of them hiss to the other as they throw away their paper coffee cups on their way out the door.

"It'll only get worse from here," Eli says after we order our coffee. We find an empty table, ignoring the eyes of other people on us. They might be less hostile but they're still staring. "When we first moved here, that first year, it was all the time. Not just the staring and the whispering. Egging our house, keying my parents' cars, the incessant bullying."

I shake my head, feeling pain in the pit of my stomach for this person I love so much. I knew about all of these things, but Eli has always been so good at pretending they didn't hurt. He's not pretending now.

"Why did you guys stay?"

Eli shrugs. "Not many places wanted to hire my dad. He had to go where the jobs were. But that was ten years ago. Things are different now."

I roll my eyes and shoot a dirty look at a table of teenagers that won't stop staring. "Not that different, it would seem."

"Not in Amber Hills," he mutters. "But my brother and my parents say the city is so much more progressive."

"Then let's move."

His black eyes find mine across the table. "You'd...you'd come with me?"

I stare at him for a second, my mouth agape. "Do you not

get it, Eli?" I ask, loud enough for heads to turn toward us again. "I go where you go. I don't want to be away from you. Ever."

Eli leans across the table, his hands surrounding my head to hold me still so he can kiss me. Up at the counter, the barista calls his name. He ignores her and goes on kissing me.

The Vamp and I

The Vamp and I

A list of things I expected to do today:

- Crash my ex-boyfriend's party to get my box of stuff back

A list of things I didn't expect to do today:

- Get injured at my ex-boyfriend's party

- Let my ex-boyfriend's neighbor give me stitches

- Become very, very attracted to my ex-boyfriend's neighbor

- Find out that my ex-boyfriend's neighbor is a vampire

Chapter One

I don't know what the hell I'm doing here.

I'm standing on my ex's front porch, the bass from the party inside thumping so loud that the wooden steps are vibrating under me. I don't want to go inside, but Zac has been holding my box of stuff hostage for too long. Every time I text, he doesn't answer. Every time I come by to get it, he's not home. But he posted all over Facebook about this stupid party, and I'm not leaving until I get my shit back.

Except I can't seem to convince myself to walk up his rickety steps and go inside.

A car engine hums behind me, and I glance over at the neighbor's house. In the dark, I see a man getting out of the car at the curb, a sleek silver BMW. He steps around to the passenger side and reaches in for something.

Zac's neighbor.

We've never spoken, but I've noticed him. It's impossible not to. He's painfully beautiful, with blond hair and broad shoulders, and a V-shaped body to die for. When I was dating Zac, he would always get angry if he caught me looking over at the neighbor when he was taking his trash out or getting his mail.

Tonight, I can stare all I want to. Zac and I are done.

I watch him move, the nameless neighbor, watch the stretch of his muscles under his rolled-up sleeves, the way his shirt pulls across his back so that I can see the shape of him.

When he straightens and turns toward his house, a duffel bag in his hand, his eyes flicker over to mine. In an almost bashful move, he lowers his chin and offers me a kind smile, just barely lifting one side of his mouth in a *hello there* gesture.

I look away quickly and take a deep breath before plunging into Zac's house. There are so many people, bodies everywhere, pressed into every corner of his living room. I try to scan faces as I push my way through, but they all blend together.

"Chug! Chug! Chug!" Chanting seeps into the room, and I turn in time to see Zac being lifted over a keg through the open sliding glass door out to his back patio.

Jesus. He's twenty-five years old. Do people still do keg stands at twenty-five? I'm only twenty-one, and I stopped doing keg stands once I hit my sophomore year of college.

I force my way out of the house, past sweaty bodies and plumes of marijuana smoke, to the back patio. Somehow it feels like the party is louder out here, everyone speaking at a decibel only appropriate at pro sports games.

"Zac!" I shout over the cheers of everyone in the backyard as Zac is placed back on his feet. Some of the foaming beer splatters on my shoes. "Fuck!" I shout.

And that's when Zac realizes I'm here.

"Poppy? Hey, what are you doing here? Did I invite you?" He steps too close to me, his breath smelling like hops and pot, and I step away before he can put his arm around me like he always used to.

"I'm here for my shit," I tell him, loud enough that a few people still gathered around the keg turn and look at me.

"What shit?" Zac asks. His eyes are half-lidded. God, he's so high, and probably drunk as well.

"The stuff I've been trying to get from you for a month. My box of stuff. I want it."

Zac shrugs, already losing interest in the conversation. His eyes are glued to what appears to be a completely invented game over by the fence. Three guys are all standing in a line, throwing their empty beer bottles at a target that looks like it's been drawn on the wooden fence with sidewalk chalk. The beer bottles shatter into brown chunks of glass.

"It's upstairs somewhere," Zac says to me. "Go up and look."

I smack him on the arm. "Are you kidding? I'm not going up there so that I can listen to your roommates screw their girlfriends while I try to find the box you swore to me you would give back. Go get it."

Zac rolls his eyes. "Fine." His shoulders slump, and he slinks off like an eight-year-old who was just told they have to skip dessert.

"Incoming!"

I turn my head in time to see a beer bottle coming right at me. I put up my hands to protect my face as the bottle shatters on the brick wall beside me. Chunks of glass fly, and I feel one land in my arm. I yelp and look down to see the entire neck of the bottle, jagged at the bottom, sticking out of the flesh of my upper arm.

"Fuck!" I shout, reaching over on instinct to pull the broken glass out of my skin and watching the blood well up.

"Shit, I'm sorry, Poppy!" someone shouts, and I don't even have time to see who it was who threw the stupid bottle when a form appears between me and the rest of the party.

He appears so quickly that I flinch, suddenly looking at a

broad chest and the line of buttons all the way up to a firm, shapely throat. He reaches out to grab my arm, and I grimace before finally looking up at his face.

It's the neighbor, the one I just watched carry his stuff in. Where the hell did he even come from?

"Are you okay?" he asks, his voice low as he examines the cut on my arm. It's bleeding at a worrying rate, but I'm finding it hard to care when this man I don't know is standing so close to me, close enough for me to smell the laundry detergent he uses.

When I don't answer his question, his eyes shift to mine, and I feel a jolt go through me at the blue of his eyes, so bright, even in the dark.

I blink, pulling myself out of whatever trance I'm in. "I'm fine. Who are you?" I might be a little distracted. His fingers' hold on me is slowly loosening.

"Gabriel. And you're not fine. I think you need stitches." He's so soft-spoken, somehow speaking barely above a whisper and still perfectly easy to hear over the party behind us, the party that's somehow faded into the distance.

Gabriel.

I'm still looking at him, examining the lines of his mouth and the jut of his cheekbones, when he starts to tug at my arm. He begins to pull me toward the gate in the fence that leads around to the front of the house, and I look over my shoulder to find that everyone else at the party is watching us go.

What the fuck just happened?

"Where are we going?" I ask, but I don't fight him. Honestly, wandering off with a gorgeous stranger is much more interesting than watching Zac and his idiotic friends do keg stands.

He leads me to his house, letting me go to unlock the door. He must have come through the back. Was he at the party? That wouldn't make sense. What would a guy who's twice the age of anyone at that party be interested in wasting his Friday night there?

"I've got some medical supplies inside. I can stitch you up. Save you a trip to the ER."

I scoff. "I don't think I need stitches."

He pushes the door open and raises an eyebrow at me. His eyes fall to the wound on my arm, and when I look down, I realize there's blood on my clothes, smeared across my top and dripping onto the porch under us.

"Shit," I hiss, reaching for the hem of my shirt and lifting it to press it to the cut. There's no way that glass went that deep. Why is it bleeding so much? I look back up at Gabriel in time to see him look away from the strip of stomach I just exposed.

"It'll only take a moment." He steps into the house, dark inside with the exception of a light glowing from somewhere far off down a hallway. He holds the door open and waits to see what I'll do.

I glance back at the party. I really want my box. But he's right. I clearly need stitches.

This is definitely how people die, walking into a stranger's house just because they're hot and they told you to.

I follow him inside and look around while he shuts the door behind us. Compared to Zac's place, this place looks like a museum. Everything is neat, expensive-looking, stylish.

"Over here." Gabriel flips on a light in the dining room and begins pulling things out of some kind of medical bag. I walk over carefully and look at everything. It all looks pretty standard: one of those curved needles, black thread, gloves and antiseptic.

I'm about to ask him why he has all of these things when he glances at me and pats the tabletop. I realize that I went into this man's house without asking any questions, but I didn't quite process that I would have to let him touch me. My heart pounds in my ears as I push myself up onto the table. My legs dangle over the edge, and to my surprise, Gabriel steps between them, his hips between my knees. I feel like the only sound in the world is the sound of my heavy breath. I look up at him as he puts on gloves and readies his needle, seemingly unbothered by our proximity.

When he has his needle ready, he sets it aside and reaches for an antiseptic wipe. He takes my wrist and lifts my arm. With his eyes on me, he says, "You can grab onto my shirt." To illustrate, he brings my hand to his side and fists it manually in the fabric, silky under my fingertips. "Your arm will get tired, and I need you to be still."

I feel like I should say something. Ask questions. Thank him. Anything. Instead, I watch silently as he bends close to me and starts to clean the wound.

I gasp when the cold antiseptic hits my skin.

"Sorry," he says. Why does it seem like everything he says is a whisper?

"That's okay." It's not so much that it hurts. It was just startling. "I've never gotten stitches before."

Gabriel makes a sound in the back of his throat but doesn't comment. He's concentrated on my arm, carefully wiping away the blood. Now that I can see the wound, on the soft part of my inner arm, I see that there's more than one cut and that there's still some glass embedded in my flesh.

When he's done cleaning it, Gabriel takes a big pair of tweezers and starts to pull out the remaining glass. I try not to flinch as he does it. I focus on him instead of what he's doing, on the gentle slope of his neck and the pieces of his blond hair that are falling into his eyes.

"Were you at the party?"

His hands stop moving for a second, a brief hesitation, and then he keeps going. "No."

"Then how did you—"

"I thought the two of you broke up."

It takes me a second to catch up to him. "Who, me and Zac? We did." He carefully keeps his eyes averted, so he doesn't see when I bite back a smile. "Have you been spying on us? Do you have a pair of binoculars around here somewhere?"

One corner of his mouth tilts up. "It's polite to know your neighbors."

I purse my lips, thinking about all of the doors that line the hallway of my apartment building. I've never seen any of them open. "I could be living next to a talking spider and wouldn't know it."

His eyes flicker to mine, and I have to look away. Heat is starting to rise in my stomach. I'm very aware of where I'm still holding onto his shirt, aware of the brush of his body against my fingertips when he moves.

I tell myself it's just because I haven't had sex since Zac and I broke up. It's been weeks, and this man smells very good. And looks very good. And is taking care of me even though he doesn't know me. Those are the kinds of things that make you go slick between your thighs for a complete stranger. I just need to be distracted.

The curved needle that Gabriel holds up between us does the trick. "You can look away if you need to," he says as he threads it.

"I'm fine." Needles don't scare me. "Are you a doctor?"

"A paramedic. It's my night off actually."

"Oh." I remember him getting out of his car earlier, that duffel bag in his hand. Where was he coming home from then? The gym? "Sorry you have to do this on your night off."

He chuckles, a gentle breath of a sound. "You can hardly apologize for having a bottle thrown at you."

I roll my eyes and then bite my lip as he sticks the needle into my skin. Needles might not bother me, but I don't appreciate being stuck by big ones. "In their defense, I don't think whoever threw the bottle was aiming for me. Not that that makes them any less of a moron." I think about Zac and the way he used to tell me that I was boring because I didn't like the parties and the drinking and the general merriment. I'm much more of a peace and quiet kind of person.

"That's why we broke up," I tell Gabriel, even though I'm not sure why I'm imparting my relationship drama on him. "Zac is a child. Probably always will be. He's twenty-five, four years older than me, and he acts like a teenager."

Gabriel makes a quiet sound in the back of his throat but doesn't look away from what he's doing.

"How old are you?" My question comes out a whisper. It feels a little salacious to ask, even though I'm dying to know. He looks like he could be my dad's age, definitely in his forties. And that's...hot.

And it's even hotter when Gabriel bends just a little closer to me and says, "How old would you like me to be?"

A shiver goes through me, and I realize I'm staring at his mouth, at the shape of it, wondering what it would feel like on my skin. "I don't know. Is there some kind of age requirement for—" My words slam to a stop.

The corner of one sharp fang has worked its way out from beneath Gabriel's top lip. He seems to know exactly what has happened because he says, "I'm far older than I look."

While I watch, the fang seems to lengthen, finally coming to a satisfying point. I'm still staring at it.

"What are you?"

"Would you believe me if I told you I was a vampire?"

My eyes move up to him. They were a clear, ice blue before, but a golden circle has appeared around his pupil, making his eyes almost...angelic.

"I think I would need proof."

He chuckles. "The fangs aren't proof enough?"

I shake my head. I've read about all kinds of fang-toothed

monsters that hide under your bed. They're not all vampires. And none of them are real.

Holding my gaze, he bends toward my open wound. My eyes are glued to him as he runs his tongue up my arm, licking away the blood that has dripped from my cuts. The blood smears, and he laps at it again, until all that's left is what's dotting the skin where the needle and string are holding it together.

I've stopped breathing. There is absolutely nothing left in my lungs. I watch as he licks the last drop from his lips and then uses his teeth to bite the end of the string. He ties off my wound, straightens, and takes a step back from me.

And I'm left there, speechless and quivering on the edge of the table, with my legs still spread, wishing he would come back. Wishing he would push my legs wider and lick me the way he just licked my arm.

Holy shit, I'm so wet.

"You're all set," he says, wiping at his mouth, and I feel like he just ravished me, even though he barely touched me. I've never wanted anyone more in my life.

When I don't move, he smiles, and it's absolutely predatory. "You better get off my dining room table, or I might mistake you for dinner."

My limbs move without my permission. I slip off the table and stand in front of him, not sure what to do now that we've done what I came over here to do. I don't want to leave, but I guess it's time.

"Thank you," I say, my voice a little wooden.

He just gives a gentle nod and motions toward the door, somehow kicking me out while also being polite.

So, I go. And as soon as I'm out in the night, the door shut firmly behind me, I wish I could beg him to let me back in.

Chapter Two

I can't stop thinking about him. The next morning when I wake up, all I can think about is Gabriel. I think about his eyes and the way they changed color. I think about his fangs and the way they grew while I watched them. I think about his tongue and the way it swiped along my skin.

That last bit has me reaching for my vibrator before the sun is even up. I've been hot and bothered all night, thinking about the way he was so careful with me, until he was licking my blood from my arm.

I come, thinking about it. I scream loud enough for my neighbors to hear, thinking about it. I lay in a sweaty puddle in the middle of my bed, thinking about it.

And then I have to do something about it.

I have a shift at the grocery store where I work in a few hours, but I figure that's enough time to go see him and figure out what's going on between us. Maybe it's nothing. Maybe I made it all up in my head, but it doesn't feel that way.

I feel almost *desperate* to see him.

I drive over, making just one stop on the way, and then pull up behind his car. He said he was off last night, and he's also a vampire, so I can only assume he'll be home during the day.

It feels strange to be parked here, on the curb between Gabriel's house and Zac's. For months, I parked here and walked up to Zac's door. And now I'm preparing to walk up to the house next door. Nerves make me glance at Zac's house while I get the bouquet of flowers out of my passenger seat that I stopped for. There are still cars in front of his house, so I assume quite a few people got drunk last night and crashed. Hopefully nobody is looking out the window right now.

I rush up to the door and knock, feeling excited and turned on and nervous all at the same time as I wait for him to answer. I hear his footsteps on the hardwood and then the door opens a crack. I can't see inside. It's all darkness and shadows, like the inside of a black hole.

"Gabriel?"

"Poppy," he responds from somewhere inside. I can't recall telling him my name, but I feel a thrill deep down that he somehow knows it anyway. "What are you doing here?" He doesn't sound particularly excited about me being here, but it doesn't dampen my own happiness. I'm here, and he's here, and I'm with him again.

"I came to see you."

There's silence for a moment, and then the door widens just enough to let me pass through. The door closes behind me, and I'm suddenly completely in the dark. Gabriel must have covered all of the windows with blackout curtains, and all the lights are out.

I hear him move behind me, and then the light in the dining room comes on. Just like that, I'm transported back to last night. The stitches in my arm still hurt.

Gabriel stands in the dining room, his hands in his pockets, watching me. Even though he clearly has no intention of leaving the house, he's still dressed like he's on his way out, in dark jeans and a button-up, his blonde hair slicked back.

"I brought you these," I tell him, stepping forward and offering him the flowers. I'm not even really sure why I brought them. I just had this *compulsion*. They're the cheapest ones I could get, and looking at them now, the colors aren't particularly inviting.

He doesn't take them. He looks at them and sighs, his hands still firmly in his pockets. "Poppy, you shouldn't be here."

I pull the flowers back, pressing them to my chest. "I wanted to see you."

He nods. "I know. I wanted to see you, too, but not like this."

I don't know what he means by that. But I don't care. I want him, and I'm not taking no for an answer. I let the flowers fall down to my side. "I thought about you all night, and I thought about you while I got myself off this morning." The words just burst out of me. I've never said anything like that to anyone before.

His eyes meet mine, and even across the space between us, I can see that his pupils get wider, his eyes going black. His chest rises and falls, rises and falls. I can see him deciding, if he'll come to me or if he'll push me away.

Finally, he shakes his head. "You need to leave."

I rush toward him. "Gabriel, please." That desperation is there in my stomach again, this bone-deep need to be near him. "Please, I just need—" I hold out the flowers to him, and he snatches them from my hand. Immediately, the blooms begin to die, the whole thing withering away in his fist, and then his hand wraps around my throat.

I gasp, and his hand tightens, until I can't breathe anymore. His hand is cold, hard, the opposite of what I thought it would feel like the first time he touched me.

"*Get out of my house,*" he growls.

He releases me, and I cough, bent over at the waist. Gabriel drops the wilted flowers at my feet, and a part of me dies at seeing them lying there. I back away from him, even though every instinct in my body is telling me to get closer.

And when I step back out into the sun, I start to cry.

Chapter Three

The next day, I feel hungover. It's like I'm getting over the flu or something. My brain is cloudy the whole time I'm at work, and everything that happened yesterday feels like a fever dream.

I'm a zombie at work, until my boss finally pulls me off the registers and sends me to restock the breakfast cereals because what else is there to do when it's almost ten o'clock at night, and the store closes in fifteen minutes? I honestly just want to go home and climb back into bed.

I'm halfway through the Kellogs varieties when I feel someone walk up behind me. I glance over my shoulder, ready to move out of the way of a customer trying to get to a box of Frosted Flakes, but when I see Gabriel, I spin around and slam myself back against the shelves so hard that a bunch of boxes clatter to the floor.

Everything comes back in a weirdly colorful, hazy way. The wilted flowers. The darkness of his house. The grip of his hand around my throat. I press myself back harder.

"Wait," he says, holding up both of his hands. In the harsh

fluorescent light, his skin looks so washed out, like he's made of ash. "Please. I came to apologize."

My heart pounds in my ears. He scared me yesterday. Yes, of course he did. He had his hand around my throat, and I couldn't breathe. But I didn't *feel* scared in the moment. It was almost like he could have done anything to me and I would have accepted it.

But not now. Now, I'm so scared that I'm looking down to the end of the aisle, waiting to see if someone will pass by, but nobody does.

"I didn't intend to hurt you," Gabriel says, taking a step closer to me, and when I look back at him, I get lost in the color of his eyes. They're so blue in the light, like icebergs waiting for me to crash right into them. Something in me pulls in his direction, but when I blink, it snaps.

I gasp. "Did you...did you put some sort of vampire spell on me?"

Gabriel's hands fall to his sides, and he sighs. "Yes. Yes, I did."

Everything makes sense now. I didn't feel like myself yesterday. I would *never* go to some guy's house and beg him to spend time with me. I would never bring a guy I didn't even know flowers, for fuck's sake!

"Why?" I demand. "Are you some kind of serial killer or something? You lure women to your house and then brainwash them so you can have them for supper later?"

"If that was my plan, why would I have kicked you out yesterday?"

My brain grinds to a halt. I don't have an answer to that. He makes a good point. I was under his spell and in his house yesterday. So, why didn't he bite me? Why didn't he drain me dry?

I glance at the rainbow-colored cereal boxes at our feet.

This seems like a completely ridiculous time to be having a conversation like this.

"Then, why?" I whisper.

He sighs again, and it's such an adult sound that I bite back a smile. Even knowing what he did to me, he's still really adorable. He glances down the aisle and then back at me. "Because I wanted you."

"Then why didn't you—"

"I didn't want your *blood*. I wanted *you*."

My breath stutters out of me. I wait for him to elaborate, caught like a fish at the end of a hook.

"It's been a long time since I've been with a woman. This is not exactly a life that's easy to share with someone." He takes a big step toward me, and I'm suddenly pinned between him and the shelf behind me, his body pressed all along mine. "But then you were spread out on my dining table, and you smelled like dessert, and all I could think about was pushing you onto your back, lifting that skirt of yours, and fucking you."

I gasp, and he leans forward like he's trying to suck the sound into his mouth.

"It was almost involuntary, what I did. A reaction to the way I wanted you. And then you were all starry-eyed, so I made you leave. To save us both. I figured it would wear off in a day or two, and it would be like nothing ever happened. But then you were at my house with those flowers and that look in your eyes like you would have done anything I asked you to. I wanted to take advantage of the opportunity, but I just... couldn't do it." He steps back, putting space between us.

"Why not?" I breathe, feeling like he just flattened me on the ground.

His eyebrows curve in gracefully. "Because it wouldn't have been right."

Right. Yes. It is definitely not okay for a vampire to put a spell on someone and then seduce them while they were under said spell.

Except...

"You didn't have to put me under any spell."

His eyes travel up to mine slowly. He calmly watches me for a moment. "What are you saying?"

I'm not sure how to say it, how to make the words come out of my throat, with him watching me the way he is.

He moves so fast, his body up against mine, shoving me back against the shelf. When he opens his mouth, his fangs are entirely extended. His hand finds the hem of my skirt, and I gasp when his fingers travel to the inside of my thigh.

"Are you saying you want to be mine?"

I can't breathe, can't think, but I still feel completely in control. This isn't some vampy spell. I just really want this man.

"Yes," I breathe, and his mouth crashes down onto mine. Just as his tongue touches mine, his hand finds the edge of my underwear, and I moan into his mouth.

"Ladies and gentlemen, the store will be closing in five minutes. Please bring your selections to the nearest register. Thank you."

I pull away from him with a gasp. Oh my God. I'm at work! If anyone sees me getting felt up in the middle of the cereal aisle while I'm on the clock, I'll get fired.

Gabriel seems to see all of this play out on my face. He removes his hand and takes a big step back. "Come to my house after your shift."

And just like that, he's gone.

Chapter Four

Everything is different the next time I'm standing on Gabriel's front porch. I don't feel the desperate, unexplainable tug that I felt when I came yesterday. Instead, I just feel hot, my whole body on fire, my skin tingling.

I don't have to knock. It's like Gabriel can hear the sound of my heart beating through the door. While I'm still standing there, the door swings in. Gabriel stands at the threshold, his predatory eyes on me. And then his gaze shifts to something just beyond me.

I turn, looking over my shoulder, and see Zac. He's standing at his mailbox in his pajamas, his mouth hanging open as he stares at me.

Without a second thought, I ignore him and turn back to Gabriel. I follow him into his house and let him close the door behind me.

"I want you to know," Gabriel says behind me, "that I'm nothing like *him*."

I spin around to face him. "I don't want you to be anything like him."

Like he's blinked out of existence and then back into it, he moves from the door to me so fast. And just as fast, his hand grips my hair, pulling my head back enough to expose my throat.

"You want a man, Poppy? Is that it?"

"Yes." The word stutters out on a shaky breath.

He bares his fangs at me, his tongue peeking out to touch his bottom lip. "Are you going to be a good girl for me, Poppy?"

A thrill runs through me like an electric current, and a whine escapes my mouth. "Yes, Daddy."

He growls in the back of his throat and then devours my mouth. I feel his fangs growing as we kiss, and I slip my tongue into his mouth, running it along the sharp edge of one of his fangs.

When I reach the tip, I'm surprised, even though I really shouldn't be, when the point of it cuts into the flesh of my tongue. I jolt, immediately tasting blood in my mouth. I pull back, but with a growl, Gabriel grabs the back of my head, pulling my mouth back to his. His mouth opens, begging me to open mine in turn, and when I surrender, he coaxes my wounded tongue into his mouth, wrapping his lips around it and sucking.

My eyes roll back into my head. Gabriel's tongue sweeps into my mouth, licking for traces of my blood. I've started to tremble, my body feeling weak under the pressure of my own desire, and when my knees give out, Gabriel scoops me up into his arms.

But instead of taking me into his bedroom, where I'm absolutely dying to go—what does his bed look like? What do his sheets smell like? Oh, fuck, does he sleep in a coffin?—he carries me over to the dining table and spreads me out on the empty surface. It's cold against my back, and my nipples immediately pucker under my shirt.

Once I'm settled, Gabriel steps back and looks at me like

he just put the finishing touches on an oil painting. His jaw tightens, and the longer he looks at me, the more I squirm. I'm starting to get wet between my thighs, and I want him closer, not staring at me from a distance.

"Gabriel—" I start, but he speaks over me.

"Take it all off. Show me everything."

I don't hesitate. Keeping my eyes locked on his, I push the straps of my dress off my shoulders and arch my back off the table to peel it down my body. I'm not wearing a bra, so as soon as I push the dress down my hips and kick it onto the floor, all that's left is my underwear, the red lace panties that I wear when I want to feel good. When I put them on this morning, it didn't occur to me that Gabriel would see them.

When I don't make a move to take them off, Gabriel growls, "All of it."

I hook my thumbs in my underwear and push them down to my knees. Before I can kick them off too, Gabriel is there, pulling them down my legs, running his fingers along my calves as he goes. I shiver, and Gabriel tosses the underwear aside.

"Be a good girl and spread those gorgeous legs for me."

I have to fight every instinct to shy away from being so blatantly on display. I'm used to doing this with the lights off, with boys who are in a hurry to get inside and race to the finish line. I'm not used to being...admired.

With a deep breath, I let my legs fall open, baring myself to him completely. I stopped shaving between my legs when Zac and I broke up, but Gabriel doesn't seem to mind. His eyes zero in on my pussy, and his nostrils flare, like he's smelling me.

Slowly, he walks around the side of the table, running his hand up my leg and along my hip. He stops when his fingers find the juncture of my thigh, towering over me.

He bends, and when I think he'll kiss me again, instead,

his mouth finds one of my nipples. He licks it first, making me bow up off the table. His tongue swirls and flicks and laves, trailing along my chest to find the other nipple, all while his fingers part me down below. One gentle fingertip finds my clit, and this time when I arch with a cry, Gabriel sinks his fangs into my breast.

I come immediately. It's all so unexpected, the pleasure and the pain and the way he knows exactly how to deliver it all with expert precision. For a long moment, the world is just light, static flooding my ears, and when I come back down to Earth, it's to find Gabriel licking away the last traces of blood from the teeth marks on the curve of my breast.

His eyes meet mine, and I know he's checking to see how all of this has made me feel, how I'll respond to the fact that he just drank my blood while giving me an orgasm.

I pull my bottom lip between my teeth. "Do I taste good, Daddy?"

A growl emanates from the back of his throat, and so quick I don't see it happen until it's too late, Gabriel moves lower and sinks his teeth into my thigh, inches from my still-throbbing pussy.

It hurts, but not like I thought it would. It's this absolutely decadent pull from somewhere deep in my body, and that, mixed with seeing his face so close to my pussy, has me bucking my hips. Gabriel finally comes up for air, and when he does, I bury my hand in his hair, trying to shove him toward where I want him.

He just chuckles and straightens. He's still completely dressed, but I can see the full shape of him behind his pants, the hard, heavy length. I reach for him, but he takes my wrist in his hand, lifting it to his mouth for a soft kiss before settling into one of the dining chairs beside me.

It's bizarre, the way we sit for a moment, him in a chair

like he's sitting down to an indulgent dinner, and me spread out on the table in front of him like a five-course meal.

I'm still quivering when he looks me in the eye and says, "Get over here."

I sit up on the table, and like he's impatient even for me to move myself, Gabriel spins me on the surface and pulls me into his lap, straddling his hips. He pulls my mouth down to his, and I immediately become frantic for him again. What he just did to me on the table was just the beginning, I can tell. His mouth tastes like blood, my blood, and I lick into it as my hips begin to rock.

Gabriel clamps his hands down on my hips and pulls me harder against him, so that his cock is rubbing against my clit with every movement, nothing between us but the material of his pants.

"Get me all wet, baby," he says against my mouth. "Come again before I've even gotten my dick inside you."

So I rock harder. Now that I know he wants me to come again, it's all I can think about, rutting my swollen pussy against that thick length of him until I'm bouncing myself right into an orgasm, my tits jumping with each movement of my hips.

"That's it, baby girl," he says as I come back down, my bouncing turning to rocking again, and my hips eventually going still.

While I try to catch my breath, I take his face in my hands. My thumb finds his fang again, much more carefully this time. "Do they come out when you're turned on?" I ask, remembering how his fangs slid free in the bright aisle of the supermarket.

He shakes his head slowly. "They come out when there's something around that I want to bite."

I can't help but smile at that, even as he lowers his mouth and licks at the blood that still dribbles from the bite mark on my breast. His tongue travels from my breast up to my neck, and I feel him pulse between my legs just as the tip of one of his fangs grazes the skin at my throat.

"I need inside you," he says, and the two of us are ripping at his belt buckle in seconds. As I unzip his pants and free his cock, he grabs onto my hips to arch me forward, giving me the space to find the opening of my pussy with the tip of him. As soon as we're lined up, he pushes me back down, lowering me all the way down the length of his dick.

I moan, my eyes falling closed. I'm exhausted—from his vampire spell wearing off, from a long shift at work, from two intense orgasms—and all I can manage to do as he fills me is wrap my arms around his shoulders and let him use me to get himself off.

He holds me still and pumps up into me, and I get lost in the way he throws his head back, exposing the entire beautiful column of his throat, the way his mouth falls open, the way he whispers, "Holy fuck, your pussy is so good," almost like he doesn't intend for me to hear it. I want to hear it. I want to hear every thought in his head while he fucks me.

I grab onto the back of his chair, shifting back so I can watch him, and then I push up onto my knees and slam myself back down onto him. My eyes cross, but I focus on him. Every time I lift myself and drop back down, his mouth opens a little wider, his fangs gleaming in the light.

"Does that feel good, Daddy?" I ask him. I've broken out in a sweat, but I feel like I could do this all day, watching him take his own pleasure.

Like he's just remembered that I'm here, he lifts his head and those blue eyes find mine. He bares his teeth at me, and I have the presence of mind to feel a little frightened. He doesn't look like himself anymore. His fangs are out, and his eyes are hard, like he's lost himself to something deep and primal.

"I want to own this little cunt," he says, fucking up into

me faster, until I'm holding onto the chair so that he doesn't buck me off of him. "It's mine to fuck," he growls. "Mine to use as I please. Isn't that right?"

"*Yes*," I whine. "Yes, it's yours."

"So fucking wet," he says, his eyes glued to where he's sliding in and out of me fast and hard. "I want to live between your thighs, pretty girl."

I didn't think there was any way I could come again, but seeing him lose control, watching the way he turns into an animal before me, it has my clit throbbing again. I reach down and rub it, no teasing, hard enough to make me go off quick, and when Gabriel sees me, his eyes flash bright.

"Bite me," I tell him, just as my orgasm crests again.

He doesn't hesitate. Wrapping his hand in my hair, he yanks my head to the side and sinks his fangs into my neck.

I swear I almost pass out. My pleasure rockets high, my vision going white, and by the time I've come back down, Gabriel's fangs are gone. So is the feral expression on his face. All that's left is the gentle face of the man I've always seen from afar, eyes kind as he looks me over, probably assessing the damage.

I'm going to be sore as hell tomorrow.

He stands, lifting me into his arms. I'm still wrapped around him as he walks me further into the house, until he's setting me down on a bed in a cool, dark room. He turns on the bedside lamp, soft and yellow. His sheets are silk, soft against my bare skin as he cleans all the bite marks he left behind and then applies ointment to them. He cleans between my legs too, and by the time he's pulling the blanket up around me and turning the lamp back off, I'm half-asleep.

"I have to go to work," he says into the dark, and my groggy eyes open. It takes me a second to process his words, but when I do, I sit up, the blanket falling down to my waist.

"Do you have to?"

He sends me a gentle smile. I can make out the shape of it in the dark. "Yes. I'm sorry. I know the timing is terrible. But please, stay. I'll be back in the morning."

I don't want him to go. I want to beg him to stay so that we can figure out what the hell is even going on between us, but I don't have it in me to argue, even if my chest is tight with sadness.

"Goodnight, Poppy," he says, and then I hear the sound of his footsteps moving out of the room and down the hall. And just before I fall asleep, I realize he did all of those delicious things to my body without ever even taking off his shoes.

Chapter Five

When I wake again, I have no idea what time it is. Not only because I'm not in my own bed and therefore my phone isn't on the nightstand, but also because Gabriel's industrial black curtains are blocking out any light that would naturally tell me what time of day it is.

I crawl out of his bed and take one of his button-ups from his closet, which smells distinctly like cedar.

Out in the kitchen, I finally get a look at the clock on his oven. It's almost seven, about the time I would normally get up in the morning, so I decide a little breakfast is in order.

But of course, Gabriel's cabinets are empty. And his fridge is stocked only with white paper sacks that I absolutely refuse to open. And as I'm trying to decide where I can get food delivered from this early, the front door opens and Gabriel sweeps in. Over his shoulder, I get a glimpse of the sky that's beginning to brighten with the rising sun just before the door slams closed. Gabriel leans against it and sighs before dropping his medical bag at his feet.

"That was a close one," he says to himself, and I realize that he hasn't noticed me here yet. When he straightens away from the door and sees me, he stops, holding very still until I come around the kitchen island.

He gets a look at my thighs, just barely covered by the hem of his shirt, and sighs. "Dammit. I intended to buy you breakfast, but then we had a man go into cardiac arrest moments before I was due to clock out, and it was either buy you breakfast or get inside before the sun turned me to dust. I hope you don't mind." One corner of his mouth turns up, and I can't help the flutter of emotion in my stomach.

"I'll be fine. I was just about to order delivery."

He nods, but I can see the discomfort on his face, the tension in the set of his shoulders. "You'll find that it's not very easy to be in a relationship with a vampire. It's the reason it's been so long since I've been with a woman. Humans have a tendency to dislike staying inside all day and sharing their refrigerators with pig's blood."

I shrug. "I don't think I'd mind."

Gabriel's eyes finally find me again. For a long moment, he just stares at me. And then he comes closer, crossing the living room until he's standing right in front of me. "Is this what you want, Poppy? Darkness and blood and bite marks?" He reaches one hand out like he might touch the bite mark he left on my neck, but then he pulls his hand back. "I had a nice time last night, but perhaps it's time for you to get on with your life."

I scowl. "I don't want to get on with my life. I'd...I'd like to stay here...with you...if you'll let me." I feel like a child asking for permission, but I don't care. I don't want to be here unless he wants me here.

He scoffs, the air rushing out of him in a gust. "If I'll let you? Poppy, if it were up to me, you would never leave. You asked me when we first met if I was watching you and Zac, and the truth is, yes. I watched you the entire time the two of you were dating. I watched you walk up his front steps and sit in the lawn chairs in his backyard. I watched you fight with him through the windows. I watched you stand on the sidewalk and turn your face up to the sun, and I wanted you like I haven't wanted anyone in a very long time."

He comes closer and finally reaches out to touch me, running his index finger along my bottom lip, until I shiver. "I think I've loved you for a while now, Poppy. But this life is a difficult one, and I just want you to be happy."

Opening my mouth as his thumb makes another swipe, I nip at it, trying to find brevity in the fact that he just told me he loved me, that he *has* loved me for a long time. "Then let me stay."

I don't really know Gabriel yet. I know him in a distant way. I know the sound of his car as it pulls up at the curb. I know what kind of music he likes from all the nights he listened with his windows open. I know what his cologne smells like and the gentleness of his hands. And in a weird way, looking back at all those nights I spent at Zac's, it's like I could feel him there, right on the periphery of my life, always watching, always close by. So, even though I don't know if I'm ready to say I love him yet, I know I feel safe with him. I know I want to be here with him, to get to know him and to share in his complicated life.

He nods now, both his hands caressing my face, and I grin a devious grin.

"How long was it before me?"

His eyebrows dip in confusion. "How long was what?"

I push up on my tiptoes and put my mouth against his ear. "How long did you go without having a woman?"

One of his hands slips under the hem of my shirt, finding me bare underneath. "Sixty years or so, give or take."

I settle back on my feet and pout my bottom lip out. "That's a long time to go without, Daddy."

He sucks in a breath between his clenched teeth when I drop to my knees in front of him. "Poppy..."

He sounds like he's going to try to stop me, to try be noble or some such shit, so I ignore him and unbutton his pants instead. By the time I've yanked them down, his cock is hard, ready for my mouth. When I lick a stripe up the underside of him, Gabriel fists his hands in my hair.

"Oh, Jesus," he breathes. "Your mouth is so wet and so warm."

I suck him down as far as I can, and when I start to gag, Gabriel's fists tighten in my hair, holding me down for just one more second before letting me up with a gasp of air. While I catch my breath, I smile up at him. I love this. I love being on my knees for him, pleasing him.

"Can I fuck this pretty mouth, baby?" he asks.

I nod eagerly, and he pulls me forward. I open my mouth and let him use me, pumping his cock deeper and deeper, until all I can do is close my eyes and focus on breathing. I hum in pleasure, reaching down to play with my clit while he uses my mouth to get off.

"You like my cock down your throat?" he asks on a growl. I lift my eyes and smile around his cock when I see that his fangs are all the way extended. His eyes are burning through me, flitting down to where my hand is buried between my legs. "Are you going to get yourself off while I come down your throat?"

I pull my mouth away from him, slipping out of his grasp, and nod. "Yes, Daddy," I say, before dipping lower and slipping his balls into my mouth.

"Oh, fuck," he barks, his hand jerking fast over his dick while I lick at him.

I rub at myself harder, and just as my pussy begins to spasm helplessly, Gabriel tugs my head back and slips his cock back into my mouth. I come, screaming around him, and then the first spurt of his semen hits my tongue.

I melt, my body going soft in post-orgasmic bliss as I swallow down every last drop of his release. When he's finished, he tugs on my hair again, bending my head back so I can look up at him, still on my knees.

"You're fucking perfect," he says to me, and right there on his floor, I feel more loved than I ever have before.

EPILOGUE

It can be hard to explain to a moving company why you absolutely have to keep their moving truck so you can move out of your house late at night, but in the end, they were understanding enough. Now, the giant truck sits on the curb, waiting for Gabriel and me.

"You sure you want to do this?" Gabriel asks, arms folded as we walk down the steps of our porch one last time. While I will definitely miss the beautiful house that Gabriel and I have shared for the last three months, I'm ready to move on.

But not without my box.

"He's had it long enough," I say over my shoulder as Gabriel moves toward the truck and I move away from it, toward the house next door. Zac's house.

"Be gentle with him," Gabriel calls out after me.

I flip him the bird over my shoulder, and I hear his chuckle, following me all the way down the sidewalk. I take the path up to Zac's door and knock. The *bang bang bang* resonates much louder than I intended. It's the new vampire strength. I still haven't quite gotten used to it. It's only been two weeks since Gabriel turned me, after all.

I hear the sound of shuffling inside and then Zac opens the door. The warm light from inside his house floods out onto the shadowed porch, along with the ever-appetizing aroma of pot.

"Poppy," he says, his voice full of surprise. His eyes immediately go over my shoulder to the moving truck that's blocking the street. "Are you going somewhere?"

Inside, I can see Zac's roommates in the living room, contorting themselves to try and see around Zac.

I cross my arms, even though Gabriel told me to be nice. I don't really feel like being nice. "Yes. Gabriel and I got a place downtown."

"Downtown..." He lets the word trail off, his eyes scanning over my face. I know he can see the differences. I still see them when I look in the mirror, the way my skin is smoother, paler. The way I can go still as a statue now, no breathing, no ticking pulse. He seems to snap back to reality. "So, you and that guy. That's still going on?"

Zac and I have never discussed the fact that I moved in with his neighbor, but every once in a while, we catch each other's eye through an open window or pull up at the curb at the same time. I know he knows Gabriel and I are together, but it's not like he's coming over to ask for a cup of sugar.

"Yes," I snap. "Listen, I just came over here to—"

"To what? To rub it in my face?" His voice immediately does that thing it does when he's decided to play the victim. "Because I have to be honest, Poppy. I think it's pretty fucked up that you're dating someone who's clearly old enough to be your dad. How long do you really think that's going to last?"

"Zac," I growl. I fight down my anger because I know if I get angry, my fangs will come out. I haven't quite mastered the art of keeping them hidden, and after I almost bit someone at a gas station, Gabriel told me I needed to stay away from people as much as possible until I can control myself.

So, I dig for control. I want Gabriel to be proud of me.

"I came for my box," I say to the shocked expression on his face. "You still have it."

"Oh." He's still searching my face, like he's checking me for signs of injury or something. I roll my eyes.

"Now," I demand, and he nods before scampering off.

While I wait for him, I turn and catch Gabriel's eye. He's in the driver's seat of the moving truck, that half-smile on his face that I love so much. I wonder how he feels about road head.

"Here ya go."

I turn back to Zac and take the cardboard box from his hands. Very quickly, I look inside to make sure everything I wanted is in there: a copy of my favorite book, the concert pass I left hanging from his rearview mirror, my dad's old t-shirt.

"Thank you," I tell him, turning to head back down the path. "See you around, Zac."

"Poppy," he calls after me. I turn and look at him over my shoulder. "Just be careful, okay?"

I want to tell him what a fool he is, standing on his porch in his Trojan pajama pants, telling me to be careful around the one person on this planet that cares about me more than anyone else. I resist the urge to roll my eyes again.

"Yeah, thanks, Zac." I open the passenger door of the moving truck and set the box on the seat next to Gabriel. Climbing up and shutting the door, I sigh. "God, get me the hell away from here."

Gabriel chuckles and starts the engine. "Let me guess, your ex doesn't approve of your new boyfriend."

"I suppose I can't blame him," I say as we roll down the street. "You are a terrifying man."

Gabriel raises an eyebrow at me. "Hey, I'm not the one who almost ripped the throat out of a biker in front of a crowd of people."

"He deserved it."

Gabriel smiles. "I fucking love you."

Reaching over, I run my fingers through his hair. "I love you, too," I tell him.

On the inside of my arm, there's a smooth patch of skin where there was once an ugly scar from the broken neck of a beer bottle. Gabriel turns and presses his lips to it, and even though I don't bleed anymore, he still opens his mouth and bites.

THE RAVEN IN MY WINDOW

The Raven in my Window

The raven followed me home from the park one day.

I didn't think twice when it sat in the window during my live show.

But then someone tried to break into my apartment, and suddenly the raven in my window was turning into a man.

A man who had spied on me.

A man who had protected me.

A man who I had invited inside.

<h1 style="text-align:center">Chapter One</h1>

"Oh! Hello, there!" I stare down into the big, shiny black eyes of the raven at my feet, reflecting the sun back at me. The raven twists its little head, pointing its beak up at me, and then tiptoes a little closer.

I look down at the blackberries in my hand that are turning my fingers purple and sigh. "Fine," I say, bending at the waist and setting a few of the blackberries on the concrete in front of my park bench.

The raven happily trots closer and begins pecking at the blackberries. When one of the blackberries is gone, the raven tilts his head back to look at me, and I feel a tug in the middle of my chest. I drop the rest of the blackberries on the ground and wipe my hand on the napkin the blackberries were wrapped in.

I watch people walk by on the path in front of me, some of them walking in pairs, some of them jogging by in the setting sun, and I just...wish I wasn't alone. I take my phone out of my purse but then I put it right back. I need to find a hobby outside of work. Maybe I could take a yoga class or something. I could meet other women. I could make new friends.

I can't believe you would do that, Layla. That's absolutely disgusting.

I cringe, replaying my ex-best friend's words in my head for the nine millionth time since she said them to me a year ago.

What's the point of making friends if they're just going to judge you and what you choose to do for a living?

I start to gather my things but when I stand, I realize the giant black raven is still at my feet, its feathers glistening in the fading sunlight. It's staring up at me, like it's completely forgotten about the blackberries.

"I don't have anything else," I tell it, ignoring the strange looks I get from a jogger as he runs by in his tracksuit and earbuds. I think I read somewhere that ravens mostly eat dead things and baby birds. I grimace down at it. "I'm a vegetarian," I hiss.

God, I'm talking to a fucking bird.

I sling my bag up over my shoulder and head toward home. I'm almost all the way out of the park when I hear an agitated squawk behind me. I stop and turn.

The raven. It's *following* me.

"What do you want?" I whisper to it, glancing around to make sure that nobody is watching me make a complete fool of myself. "I gave you my berries and you left them." I motion back toward the park bench, and as if it understands me, the raven twists its little head to look at the abandoned berries.

And then it turns back to me, still looking like it's waiting for something. I groan. "Fine. You can follow me, but it's not going to do you any good. I don't have anything else." I keep walking, not looking back until I'm out of the park and back on the road that leads home.

I subtly glance back, not surprised when I see the raven hopping along after me. Jeez, as if I wasn't weird enough already. Now, I'm Snow White and animals are following me around?

When it's time for me to cross the street to my apartment building, I hesitate. I don't want the raven to not cross fast enough and get hit by a car or something. The raven stands beside me on the curb, and we look at each other.

"You better be fucking careful," I tell it, and then look both ways before plunging into the intersection. When I reach the other side, I turn and find that the raven is gone. I glance around, making sure it hasn't been turned into roadkill, but the street is empty.

I sigh in relief. Good. It's gone. That was weird.

I let myself into the building and take the stairs up to my apartment. It's just a studio, nothing fancy, but when I close the door behind me and drop my stuff on the floor, I feel a wave of contentment. There's just no place I feel as comfortable as my own home. Everywhere else feels like someplace I have to put on a show.

At home, I can just be me.

And tonight, I have work to do. I boot up my computer where it sits in its special set up at the end of my bed and then go to the closet to pick out what I'm going to wear tonight. I'm not feeling like I want to role play. No kittens or schoolgirls or nurses. I just want to be me.

So, I choose a particularly sexy set of lingerie and change into it. I run my hands over my legs and stomach, loving the feel of my own soft skin, before I turn on some music. I'm heading back to the bed when I spot it.

The raven. It's sitting in my window.

"What the hell?" I throw up my hands and walk over to the window. "What do you want from me? You want some nuts or something? I'm not stupid, okay? I know if I feed you, you'll just keep coming back."

The raven quietly stares back at me. My window faces the

brick wall of the building next door and a tree that somehow managed to grow sandwiched between the two apartment complexes. It's leafless, so I don't know that it's a particularly cozy environment for a raven.

I relent, rushing to the kitchen as I hear the sound of people entering my chatroom on my computer. Every time someone pays to enter, a noise rings out quietly, like a little doorbell. I grab a handful of the unsalted peanuts that I keep in a container on my counter and leave them on the windowsill by the raven's feet before crawling onto my bed. I smile up at the camera.

"Sorry about that," I say, reading through some of the greetings that have already been posted. "I seem to have picked up a little raven friend on my walk through the park today. He doesn't seem to want to leave."

BIGBOIII: I WOULDN'T WANT TO LEAVE EITHER

COWBOYBILLY: IS HE GOING TO WATCH THE SHOW?

USER34511: I'VE BEEN WAITING ALL DAY TO SEE YOU TOUCH YOURSELF

I glance over at the raven, still sitting on the windowsill, just watching me. Is it weird to do this when an animal is watching? I mean, how many people are doing their live shows while their dogs or cats or hamsters are watching?

"How is everyone tonight?" I ask, running my finger along the lace of my bra cup. "I bought myself a little present that I thought you all might enjoy. I saved it for you." Reaching onto the table beside my webcam, I pull out the tentacle dildo I just invested in. It was a request I found odd, not thinking that such a thing even existed, but when I looked it up, there were *several* different options. So I bought one.

"And look," I say, ignoring the very excited comments and the demands that I put it to good use right this second. I flip the dildo upside down. "I got one with a suction cup. I've always secretly wanted one with a suction cup. We'll have to figure out how to use this one together."

I laugh when I see all the comments flooding in, along with all of the tips.

Here's the thing about being a cam girl: I didn't make the decision because I was lonely. I actually was far less lonely when I began than I am now because, back then, I still had my best friend. I still had my family. But none of them could handle my new career path.

No, I do live sex shows because I enjoy it. I figure, if I'm going to get myself off every day anyway, might as well let some strangers watch and make enough to cover rent. I like the attention. I like to lay in my bed and watch the comments rolling in, praising me, telling me I'm beautiful, saying things that sometimes get me so wet, I come in minutes.

I look at the comments now, responding to a few of them, especially the helpful ones that tell me my new suction cup tentacle dildo will attach to the wall above my bed. This causes my brain to snowball a little bit, like it sometimes does, wondering if the men and women on the other side of those screen names are handymen, contractors, used to fixing things around their houses for their families.

I push the thoughts away and mount the dildo to the wall, making sure to give the camera an enticing view of my backside as I do. When I feel it's confidently attached, I turn back to the camera. And my attention is immediately pulled to the window. The raven is still there, still watching me. Its black eyes seem to examine me as it executes a little hop that brings it onto the edge of my desk, situated in front of the window. I want to bark at it not to come into my apartment, but I don't want to wreck the sexy vibe on my show, so I try to ignore it and hope it stays put. Or better yet, leaves. I don't need my desk covered in bird poop.

"Who wants to see me try this thing for the first time?" I give the end of the dildo a little flick of my index finger and watch in satisfaction as it bounces. I run my finger along the bottom of it, where there are little round silicone bumps meant to look like suction cups. On instinct, I lean down and run my tongue along them, mostly out of curiosity, but also because I know my viewers will like it.

Getting on my hands and knees, I face the screen and see all the tips that just came in. One guy who just tipped me the equivalent of ten dollars asks me to take off my lacy bra, so I hook my fingers in the cups and pull them down until they're pushing my breasts up at the camera. I think it's hotter that way. Sometimes when I'm in the middle of a show, I see my reflection staring back at me in the screen, and seeing my own breasts jiggling or my swollen pussy will get me even more turned on. Visual stimuli is amazing. I slide my panties down too, until they're stretched between my thighs. Leaving them on makes it all seem more urgent.

Reaching back, I check to make sure I'm wet enough for this. I'm definitely wet but probably not wet enough for the girth of this thing. So, I reach my hand between my legs and rub at my clit, reading through the comments as I do.

> USER34511: I'D LIKE TO STUFF THAT PRETTY PUSSY

> CHATADDY: I LOVE JERKING OFF TO YOU

> FEMMELOVE: YOUR PINK NIPPLES ARE SO PERFECT

I rub harder while I read them, and it doesn't take long for me to be wet enough for the toy.

"You all made me so wet," I say, sucking on my fingers. I go up on my knees and show them, opening myself wide and dipping my fingers in to show them I'm soaked. Then I position myself in front of the dildo and push back on it, feeling it stretch me. It's a tapered thing, small at the tip but wide at the base, and when I'm fully seated on it, it's almost shocking how full I am.

I moan loud, making a euphoric face that I know they'll love. The computer makes a cash register sound over and over as the tips come pouring in.

And then I sort of forget about them. My mind is on the dildo inside me and how good it feels to rock back onto it. When I close my eyes, I can pretend there's someone back there, someone holding onto my hips and forcing their cock deep.

"Yes, fuck me," I say to my imaginary partner as I reach down for my clit again. I make sure I'm loud, and as I start to get closer to coming, I push back harder on the toy, needing it deeper, craving more of it as my muscles start to clench.

"Come with me," I say into the camera. "Please, give me your cum."

I figured out really quickly that my viewers enjoy it more if I pull them into the scene with me. They want me to act like I'm being fucked by them. And I like it that way too. I like to pretend that I'm being touched by someone who wants me as much as these men do.

I've never been wanted this much by someone who actually put their hands on me, of that I'm sure.

My orgasm starts to wane as I think about all the men I've had sex with, all the selfish lovers I've had, who only wanted for themselves. They didn't care about clits or g-spots. They slammed into me hard and fast and didn't care if it wasn't enough for me. Because who cares if a woman gets off?

My eyes focus again on the chat at the side of my screen.

BIGJERK12 TIPPED 500 COINS FOR
[SCREAMING ORGASM]

These people. They care.

I rock back hard on my dildo and bury my face in my mattress as I come, screaming into my sheets loud enough to give Bigjerk12 exactly what he paid for.

When it's over and the dildo slips out of me, I set my face against the bed and smile up at the camera. "Sorry about that. I guess I went off pretty quick."

Sometimes I'll sit in front of my webcam for hours, usually when I'm in the mood to role play. I'll tease and take my clothes off a little bit at a time. And there's definitely something to be said for those chats, where the men stay and tip and talk to me all night.

But I like these kinds of shows, too. Where the orgasm comes in fast and fierce. They're always a little wild, and they make me just as much in tips.

> CALICROCK: I LIKE IT WHEN YOU COME FAST.
> WE GET TO COME TOGETHER
>
> USER34511: I MADE A MESS OF MYSELF
> SEEING YOU GO OFF LIKE THAT
>
> USER7376: SO FUCKING HOT. WANT TO SEE
> YOU SQUIRT NEXT TIME

"Alright, guys and gals and nonbinary pals. I think I need a shower. Thanks for hanging out with me tonight. It was my pleasure. Literally." I laugh, smiling up at the camera. "I'll see you tomorrow."

> BIGJERK12: GOODNIGHT, BEAUTIFUL
>
> USER34511: I MISS YOU ALREADY

With that, I turn off the camera and exit out of my chat, looking at my post-chat stats. I made over $200 in an hour-long chat. Why would I want to do anything else?

Picking up my discarded underwear, I roll off the bed, unsticking my new dildo from the wall so I can clean it.

I head for the bathroom, but as I pass the window, I jump.

The raven. I forgot all about it. It's still there, sitting on the windowsill. I feel ridiculous now, being completely naked in front of it. I use my mostly see-through underwear to cover my tits and walk over to the bird.

"What is it that you want from me?" I ask it quietly. I'm feeling much more generous towards it now that I've had an orgasm. I step closer to it, careful not to be seen by the people walking on the sidewalk down below.

When I realize it's not going to budge, I reach out, and I pet its tiny little head. It's probably the biggest bird I've ever seen. I run my fingers across its head and down its feathered back. It lets out a squawk and flaps its wings, which I think is a sign of appreciation, but I don't really know anything about birds, so I'm not sure that's what it is. It could be a warning that it's about to attack, but it doesn't feel nefarious, so I don't move.

It flutters and settles, and I find myself smiling down at it. "Well, I hope you enjoyed the show." With a laugh, I head for the bathroom. I take a shower and get into some comfortable clothes, and the next time I pass the window, the raven is gone.

Chapter Two

I smile as I take my grocery bag from the cashier and tuck it under my arm. "Thank you!" I tell her with a smile and head out into the night.

I'm running late. I totally slept in today, and then I tried out a kickboxing class and had a million errands to run, and by the time I got around to stopping for groceries, it was well past the time I would normally be doing a live show.

I know my audience generally doesn't care, but I like keeping a schedule. It lets those viewers who keep coming back know when they can expect me. I don't like to let them down.

I'm rushing down the sidewalk, trying not to jostle the eggs I just bought as I hurry. Luckily, the market is only a few blocks from my place.

But as I approach my apartment building, I hear a familiar squawk behind me. I spin around and find my little raven friend on the sidewalk. I crouch down in front of it, ignoring the fact that people on the sidewalk have to go around me, and reach out to pet the bird. It's surprisingly soft. Even though, logically, I always knew feathers were soft, I guess I thought that a bird in the wild would be dirty, grimy, covered in dirt and dust and all kinds of things.

But my raven friend is clean and warm as I pet down its back. It gives a little ruffle of its feathers, and I smile.

"Look, I'm in a hurry, but if you come upstairs, I'll give you a little snack." I stand and motion up to the window that I can see the corner of from where I stand, on the other side of that big tree. I don't know if the raven really understands me, but it was smart enough to follow me up to my apartment yesterday, so if it wants some more nuts, it's going to have to figure it out.

I leave it there on the sidewalk and head for my building. When I have the first door into the vestibule unlocked, I turn and find a man behind me. He's waiting for me to finish unlocking the inside door, so I do, holding it open for him with a smile.

He smiles back and motions for me to go up the stairs in front of him. I don't recognize the guy, but there are plenty of people in this building I don't recognize, and people are always moving in and out. This is New Jersey, after all. People come and go often.

I move up the stairs quickly, hearing him behind me the whole way. I don't live on the top floor, but I do live one floor down from the top, so when I step onto my landing and hear the man still behind me, I just assume he's going up one more level. I know most of the people on my floor. I see them most days, going by on their way to or from work, some of them accompanied by children or pets.

I stop at my door and listen for the guy's footsteps. I hear him come up the stairs to my floor just as I have my door open, but as I move to step inside, I feel the press of a body against mine. I'm shoved into my apartment by the weight of the guy, and when I turn, it's to see him stepping all the way in, one hand on the door like he's about to close it behind him. My pulse rages loud in my ears as I shout, "No!" I drop my groceries, hearing glass shatter in the paper bag.

I lunge forward and shove the guy as hard as I can, satisfied when he stumbles backward out into the hallway. I turn on my phone screen as I wrap my hand around the pepper spray attached to my keyring. But before I can dial 911, the man shuffles back to his feet and charges toward me.

I lift the pepper spray, but before I can use it, there's a squawk behind me and the distinct sound of flapping wings. Something flies past my head, and I have just enough time to register the fact that it's the raven, flying straight toward my intruder, before it's not a raven anymore.

The raven dives, but what hits the intruder is a man. The two of them slam to the ground as I watch, stunned, trying to figure out what the hell just happened. A tall, lanky man with long black hair hanging in his face cocks his fist back and punches the guy who tried to get into my apartment. He doesn't stop at one hit. He hits him twice and then three times before wrapping his hand around the guy's throat.

"Is this what you get off on?" the long-haired man snarls in the other guy's face. "You like following women into their apartments and attacking them? Does that make you feel like a real man?"

The guy on the floor is beginning to turn purple, and the other guy turns his head to look at me, his eyes the same all-consuming black as the raven's. "Are you okay?" he asks me, and without thinking, I lift the pepper spray and push down on the button.

Chapter Three

I don't miss the way the police officer in front of me is eyeing my computer set up. It's pretty obvious when someone is a cam girl, and the costumes in my open closet and the collection of dildos on my bookshelf don't exactly help.

The man who tried to attack me is handcuffed and sitting in the hallway, and the other guy...

"And you were in her apartment before she got here?" the police officer asks him. The man—raven?—stands beside me, his arms crossed. With the sleeves of his button-up rolled up to his elbows and his dark hair now pulled into a half-bun so that it's no longer in his eyes, he looks like he just came from a dinner party or something. I can see the blotchy red irritation of the pepper spray along the side of his face.

He definitely doesn't look like he was a bird an hour ago, who turned into a man to save me from a would-be attacker. He glances sideways at me, clearly trying to communicate something to me that I don't understand, and then he says, "Yes. I was just waiting for her to get back from running her errands so that we could have dinner together."

Dinner. Right. I was going to feed him nuts and berries. BECAUSE HE WAS A BIRD.

I think the panic reads on my face because the police officer turns to me. "And what happened when you got home?"

I sigh. I've already told him once, but I guess he wants confirmation. "That man," I say, pointing to the burly guy with his head leaned back against the hallway stair railing, "followed me into the building and up the stairs. I thought he might live here, but when I opened my door, he shoved me into my apartment and tried to get in behind me."

"Yeah, but she shoved him back out," the raven man says, his black eyes finding mine again. "She was about to call the police when I barreled into the guy."

Okay, so we're definitely not going to mention the fact that he can turn into a bird. Cool.

"And you hit him?" the police officer asked.

The guy shrugs. "Of course I did. He tried to hurt my girl."

I make a shocked little noise, and both the police officer and the raven guy look over at me. *My girl.* My stomach twists into knots at hearing him say that, but I can't tell if they're good knots or bad knots. I mean, he followed me home too. He let himself into my apartment too. Is it really so different just because he was a bird?

I think about saying this exact thing to the police officer, but I'm afraid he won't believe me if I tell him I saw this guy shift from a bird into a human, and if he doesn't believe me about that, he might not believe me about the guy in the hallway either. And then they might let him go.

Gotta pick my battles. One of these men tried to hurt me and the other didn't.

I don't know if the guy in the hallway saw the raven, but I'm sure if he mentions it, everyone will just shrug it off.

The police officer nods. "Well, I'm very glad you're both safe. I'm going to drive this guy down to the station. If you need anything, please don't hesitate to give me a call." He hands me a card, walks out of the apartment, and *leaves me with the raven guy.*

As soon as the door shuts, the silence is so loud, it's deafening.

I don't even realize I'm trembling from head to toe until the raven guy turns to me and says, "I'm so sorry I scared you, but I swear to God, I'm not going to hurt you."

"I...you were...I don't even...how could you have..." I back away from him, scrubbing a hand over my face.

"I'm sure you have questions," the guy says.

I bark out a disbelieving laugh. "Oh, ya think? I watched you turn from a *bird* into a *man.* You sat in my window. You–" I break off, horrified. "Oh my God. You watched my show last night!" I feel like someone has doused me in ice water. I cover my face with my hands. "I can't believe you!"

"That was wrong," the guy says. "I know that, and I have no excuse. You were just..." He trails off, and I pull my hands away from my face. He's standing before me, his shoulders hunched, his hands at his sides, and a devastated expression on his face. "Could I maybe just...start over?"

I should say no. I should definitely, *definitely* say no. But I can't bring myself to because I want to hear what he has to say. I want to know *what* he is. I'm so curious. I glance over my shoulder at my computer set up. I should be working.

But maybe it can wait just a little while longer...

"I want to know who you are," I tell him, and he lights up. He straightens up to his full height, smiling at me, and I'm startled for a moment at how tall he is. At least 6'4". My ceilings are low, a fact that I never really even noticed before, but now that this guy's almost tall enough for his head to brush the ceiling...

"I'm Mac." He holds out a hand to me, and I just look at it, remembering the way his wings fluttered every time I pet him. Oh, God. I *pet* him. My face burns with embarrassment. When I don't shake his hand, Mac drops it. "Long story short, I've been able to turn into a raven since I was a kid. It just came out of nowhere. I don't know how I can do it or why. I just know I can."

I pace away from him. "This is absolutely bananas."

"Yeah, just imagine turning into a bird in the middle of sixth grade Field Day."

His words make a horrified laugh bubble up in my throat, and when Mac smiles at me again, it's like a punch to the gut. God, he's really fucking cute. Tall, broad-shouldered, and the kind of face like he would help little old ladies cross the street. It's annoying how cute he is because I want to be mad at him. I want to make him suffer for deceiving me.

He takes a step toward me, and this time, I don't back up. I just let him come closer. "When I saw you at the park, and you gave me those berries, I don't know, I just wanted to be wherever you were. I was just...drawn to you."

He takes another step closer, and it's starting to get harder to breathe. I can smell his skin now, like leaves and summer air. "I didn't really intend to follow you home, but it's like my feet wouldn't let me stop. And then you..." His eyes shoot to the bed, where my computer is waiting. "I knew it was wrong to watch, but it was the sexiest thing I've ever seen in my life."

His eyes drop, and I can feel the heat of his dark gaze on the pulse in my neck. Oh, I definitely should not be on the verge of forgiving him for being a total creeper, but...what would I have done in that situation? If roles were reversed, and I was sitting on his windowsill, enjoying some dinner, when he started stripping in front of me, would I have been able to leave?

Nope. Definitely not.

I slide my eyes up to his. "You know, you probably owe me at least a tip for what you got to see."

He holds my eye for a moment and then reaches into his back pocket. He pulls out his wallet and flips it open. I see the unmistakable glint of a foil condom wrapper as he fishes out a bill and holds it up between his first two fingers. "What does a twenty get me?"

"Honestly? Access to the room and not much else." I turn away from him, feeling the weight of his eyes on me as I go. I walk into the kitchen and open the fridge. Grabbing the container of blackberries I keep there and the container of nuts on the counter, I walk back to him.

"Here," I say, handing him the berries and the nuts. "Enjoy your dinner. I have to get to work."

Unbelievably, his cheeks and neck turn red. Is he kidding right now? He saw me fuck myself on a tentacle dildo last night, and now he's bashful? His eyes trip to the bed again. "You're going to...?" He lifts his chin in the direction of my computer cage.

"Yep. Rent is due at the end of the week, so I can't really afford to take a night off. Eat up and flutter away." I start to turn for my closet and then spin back to him. "Where do you live?"

One side of his mouth turns up in a flirtatious smile. "In an apartment on Norfolk, but I have three roommates, so I don't spend a ton of time there."

"Why would you, when you could be flying anywhere you want?"

He shrugs, the two containers still in his hands. "Exactly."

"So, you've never...slept in that tree?" I gesture to the tree outside my window, and his smile drops.

"I swear, yesterday was the first time I've ever been to this building, and as soon as the show was over, I went home. I know I shouldn't have stayed. I'm sorry."

I turn away from him and walk the rest of the way to my closet. What do I want to be tonight? A nurse? A secretary? A teacher?

What would Mac like, I wonder?

"I'm Layla, by the way. And there's no need to keep apologizing," I say as I flip through my outfits. "It's not as if it was a private moment. There were plenty of other people watching me last night."

"It's different when they're in the room." He hesitates. "And they're a bird."

I look over my shoulder at him. He's not looking at me. He's looking down at the containers in his hands. Finally, he sets them both on my coffee table and sticks his hands in his pockets.

"I guess I should let you get back to your life."

I'm still watching when he turns into his raven form. Fluttering his wings, he goes to sit on the windowsill, but before he can take off, I say, "Wait!"

I don't know what the hell I'm doing. *Just let him go, Layla.*

But I can't, and I don't know why.

With a voice that's trembling, I say, "Do you want to stay?"

It feels bizarre to be talking to him like he's human when he's a bird, but it's not like he can't understand me. He hops through a little turn on the windowsill so that he's facing me, his little birdie head tilted to the side, like he's asking me a question.

I bite my lip and nod toward the reading chair in the corner of the room. "If you stay, you sit there and you don't move unless I tell you to. It's the least I can do for the guy who saved my life."

For a moment, he just blinks his big black eyes at me. And then he spreads his wings and flies toward the chair.

Just before he lands, he turns back into his cute, manly self, landing gracefully in the big leather chair and smirking at me.

I turn away from him, my heart racing. I don't know why I'm doing this. I just...don't want him to leave. Glancing subtly over my shoulder, I catch him watching me and turn back to my closet, biting back a smile.

Making an impulsive decision, I step into my closet and shut the door behind me. I quickly change into an outfit, and when I step back out, a bright laugh comes from the corner of the room.

I rush over to the bed and jump into the middle, feeling my fairy wings bounce on my back. I try to ignore Mac as I boot up my computer and my chat website. As soon as I log in, my own picture pops up on the screen, showing me in my glittery green lingerie and my sparkling fairy wings.

As soon as people start to log on, I smile into the camera and say, "Well, good evening, babes. Whose wishes am I going to make come true tonight?" I wave my little plastic wand at the camera.

DINODICK: SEXY LITTLE FAIRY

CHATADDY: OH YES. I'VE BEEN WAITING FOR
THIS TO COME BACK AROUND

COFFEEDADDY: FUCK, YOU LOOK HOT

I run my fingers through my hair and sit up on my knees, maneuvering into a position that makes my tits look great and gives everyone a perfect view of my outfit. "I'm here to make wishes come true, but it comes at a price."

Between my computer screen and my ring light, it's almost blinding enough to make Mac, in the corner of the room, disappear completely. But the shadow of him is there, just at the edge of my vision, and he was right. It's different when someone is actually in the room. It's different when there isn't a screen between us. The whole apartment is buzzing with... possibility.

My eyes flit over to him and away again. Wait. Is he *eating the blackberries*?

My brain short circuits for a moment, but I put my smile back on for all of my viewers.

COFFEEDADDY TIPPED 300 COINS FOR [TIT REVEAL]

"Oh, I see what you want, Daddy." My hands tremble as they come up to my breasts. I definitely shouldn't be this nervous to bare myself in front of a man. I literally do this every single night. It's just...what if I *like* Mac? It's really hard not to develop a bit of a crush on a guy who pummeled an intruder for you and then didn't complain that you pepper sprayed him.

I palm myself for a minute, and then I slide the straps of my bra down my arms. In the corner of my eye, I see Mac shift. I glance over in time to see him lift another blackberry to his lips as he sits up straighter in the chair. He puts the blackberry in his mouth and sucks his finger clean. Every muscle inside me tightens.

Oh, yeah. I definitely have a crush.

Looking back at the camera, I reach behind me and unclasp the hook on my bra, feeling a little deflated at how little time I actually spent with it on. Sometimes the guys want me to spend a lot of time teasing, but then sometimes someone pays to hurry things along.

But maybe I don't mind because when the bra lands on my mattress and I'm bare from the waist up, nothing left but the fairy wings, I can hear Mac's heavy breathing. I fight not to look at him, even though all I want is to ask him if he likes it. So, instead, I ask the men on the chat.

"How's that, Daddy? Is that what you wanted?" I pinch my nipples, turning them from a light pink to a deep flush.

COFFEEDADDY: YES, THAT'S GOOD. I LOVE YOUR TITS.

"Aw, thank you, Daddy."

I continue to talk to the viewers. They seem perfectly content to talk to me while I'm topless, the show not really moving forward, and I love it because I can feel the tension coming off of Mac in waves. He's watching me patiently, his body still as stone.

HRNYBUDDY: ARE YOU WEARING A PLUG?

I shake my head. "No, not tonight. Would you like that?"

HRNYBUDDY TIPPED 700 COINS FOR [BUTT PLUG]

"Your wish is my command." I wave my wand enthusiastically and then hop off the bed, absolutely shaking. All of my toys are on the shelf beside Mac. I'll have to go over there with my tits bouncing around to get a plug. Not to mention actually inserting the plug *while he watches*.

I've never been this nervous in my life, and I don't even know why. I want to please him. I want him to like this. I want him to like *me*.

Moving quickly, I pretend not to see him as I go over to the shelf and open my box of plugs. I only have a few, since I don't really use them that often. But a lot of viewers like them. I have one with a big pink heart-shaped jewel on the end, and I grab it without thinking. I guess it goes with the outfit.

But when I turn, I'm suddenly looking right at Mac. He hasn't moved from the chair, just like I told him, but his eyes are on me, raking over my body, my bare chest, my face, and I can't ignore him. Not when he's so close.

My eyes fall to his lap, and I almost moan at the obvious bulge in his pants. He's definitely hard, and all I want to do is get on my knees in front of him.

But I have to work. There's a whole room of people waiting for me.

I stay for another second though, and with his eyes on me, Mac's hand falls to his belt buckle. His Adam's apple bobs, and he lifts one eyebrow at me in question. I remember how he tilted his head as a raven. This expression has the same effect. Breathless, I nod, and all the air rushes out of him in a gust. I hesitate one more second, watching as he undoes his belt buckle and then lowers his zipper.

But before he can take his dick out, I turn and rush back to the bed. Because if I get one look at him standing that close, I might be tempted to just hop right on.

Back on the bed, I look right into the camera and stick the butt plug into my mouth. It won't be enough lubricant, but people really like to think that spit is enough, so I let them. I wiggle out of my thong and reach past where the camera can see for the bottle of lube I leave beside the camera. I lube the pug up really quick and then go back to where I was, this time facing away from the camera.

I bend over, giving everyone a perfect view of my bare pussy and ass. With my face pressed to the mattress and my head tilted at an awkward angle, I find myself looking right at Mac.

Mac, who has his cock in his hand and is looking right back at me as he strokes it.

Oh, fuck.

I reach between my legs and rub my clit while I watch him. For a long moment, it's just him and me, both of us getting ourselves off. I don't know about him, but I'm racketing higher and higher, and by the time I remember that I'm supposed to be inserting a plug for my viewers, I'm already right on the edge of orgasm.

With one hand still on my clit, I lift the other and finger my back hole, stretching myself out. The dual pressure is almost too much. I almost slip right over the edge. I manage to keep my cool long enough to get myself prepped for the plug. And then I position it where I need it, slowly but confidently pressing in.

I squeeze my eyes shut and let myself feel the pressure of it. Once it's all the way in, I take a deep breath and flip onto my back, spreading my legs wide, giving everyone a perfect view of my wet and throbbing pussy and the heart-shaped jewel sitting snug against my ass.

From the corner of the room, Mac emits a groan, and without thinking, I say, "Oh my fucking God." I reach between my legs again, rubbing furiously at my clit. I want to get off so bad. Turning my head, I watch Mac, his hand moving up and down. Pushing my hand lower, I put two fingers inside myself and move at the same rhythm, pretending it's him inside me.

The viewers. Fuck. I keep forgetting about them. Pushing up on one elbow, I look at the screen.

BIGTEX: IS SOMEONE ELSE THERE WITH YOU?

HRNYBUDDY: WHAT DO YOU KEEP
LOOKING AT?

USER34511: YOU'RE EVEN WETTER THAN
USUAL.

I smile, feeling suddenly very devious. "You want to see what I'm looking at?" I pick up my wand, and like I'm magically summoning him with it, I wave it in Mac's direction, beckoning him to the bed.

He hesitates, and then he stands, hiking his pants up

around his hips but leaving his hard cock out, standing straight up around his open belt buckle.

"I think," I say to the camera, "that I want to make one more wish come true. Is it anyone's wish to see my friend come all over me?"

Mac's breath rushes out of him in an audible huff, and I smile up at him. Scooting to the edge of the bed, I get on my knees in front of him, checking in the screen to make sure we can both be seen. I'm still all lit up by the lights, and Mac's cock can be seen in the burgeoning shadow. I watch in the screen as he wraps his hand around his cock and starts to jerk it.

YOURFRIEND: WHO IS THAT?? YOUR BOYFRIEND??

COFFEEDADDY: FUCK YES. CUMSLUT.

ITSMYBIRTHDAY: DAMN I WISH THAT WAS ME.

"Are you sure about this?" Mac's voice is gruff, hoarse like he just woke up.

I look up at him, slipping my hand between my legs. I'm so fucking close. "Do you want to?" He nods enthusiastically, and I smile. "Well, I want you to. So bad. Don't make me beg for it."

That's all it takes. The first spurt hits my chin, but the rest of it lands in streaks across my breasts. I look down at it and then up at the expression of ecstasy on Mac's face. I orgasm hard. I scream, feeling my muscles spasm around the plug, pushing my climax even higher.

By the time I come back down, I can barely catch my breath. I've collapsed on the bed, and just out of view of the camera, Mac is looking at me like I'm an actual fairy, like he's forgotten that he's the one who's magic.

I give the camera a sleepy smile. "Thank you for hanging

out with me tonight, everyone. I can't wait to see you again tomorrow."

I log out of the chat. I can feel Mac watching me, and when I finally have the courage to look over at him, he gives me an exhausted smile. He's already tucking himself back into his pants, but he still somehow manages to look a mess.

"Can I stay?"

I look down at his cum all over my chest. "That depends. Are you just using me so you don't have to go home to your three roommates?"

He smiles. "My favorite tree in the park doesn't need saving from potential serial killers. If I was looking for a place to sleep, that would have been a lot easier."

Chapter Four

When I wake up the next morning, I'm alone in my bed. After I showered last night, Mac and I got in bed, and while we didn't exactly cuddle, I did fall asleep while he ran his fingers through my hair, which is more than I've gotten from any of the men I've slept with in the last year.

But now, the bed is empty, and the sun is getting high in the sky. It's almost afternoon.

I guess I didn't really expect him to hang around, but I would also be lying if I said I didn't think Mac and I are sort of connected to each other now. I don't know if the whole raven thing is a secret, but whether it is or not, I know him on a level that most people probably don't. And I feel like he knows me on a level that no one else does, too.

And not just because I let him come on me.

I'm making my bed, not quite ready to change out of my pajamas, when someone knocks on the door. Something prickles under my skin, picturing that man from yesterday sitting in the hallway. I don't know anything about the justice system. He's probably already walking the streets again. What are the chances that he came back for revenge?

I tiptoe over to the door and look out the peephole. Mac stands outside, a brown paper sack in his hand. I feel my heart creep up into my throat. Shit, I shouldn't be this excited to see him. We just met.

When I open the door, Mac smiles at me and lifts the sack in his hand. "Look at me, coming through the front door like a normal human being." There's a slight flush to his cheeks.

"These are the kinds of things normal human beings don't have to point out for approval." I open the door wider and step out of the way.

Mac smiles at me and comes inside. "I brought lunch. I thought you might be hungry, but I wasn't quite sure if it was breakfast time or lunch time, and I'm not really a brunch kind of guy. So, I got black bean burgers."

In response, my stomach growls. Mac grins.

"How did you know I don't eat meat?"

He scowls, his eyebrows furrowing in confusion. "You told me. That day in the park."

And he was listening.

We sit at my tiny kitchen table and unwrap black bean burgers and fries. After a few silent moments, Mac says, "So, tell me about yourself, Layla."

All I can do is laugh. "Seems ridiculous to be getting to know each other after the night we had."

Mac blows out a heavy breath and shakes his head. "Nope. Don't talk about it. I've been trying not to think about it all day so I don't end up with an incurable hard-on."

I get warm in the stomach just thinking about it. I sort of can't believe I let him, a complete stranger, do that to me. But I just feel so...comfortable with him.

"Okay, well, you know what I do for a living. I've been doing this for a little over a year. I grew up in Pennsylvania and moved out here after high school. I was a dancer. Ballet. But I tore my ACL and was never really able to get back to it after I recovered."

Mac grimaces. "That sounds rough. I'm sorry."

I shrug. "That all feels like it happened a million years ago. I waited tables for a little while, but I just didn't enjoy it."

"And you enjoy this?" He doesn't sound accusatory, just curious.

"Yes. I really do."

"Seems like a fun job," he says with a cheeky smile. Yeah, I bet he had a lot of fun last night.

We eat quietly for a little while, and when my burger is gone, I lean back in my seat and regard him. "What do you do for a living?"

He rolls his eyes. "It's going to sound like such a cliche, but I'm a bartender."

"Oh, really? Where?"

He points one thumb over his shoulder, and it's only now that I realize he's not wearing what he was wearing yesterday. He must have gone home to change when he left this morning. "*Saints*, on Franklin and 7th. You ever been there?"

"Can't say I have."

He leans back in his seat, and something about his posture reminds me of last night, the way he sat and watched me, eating those blackberries. "I'd love to take you some time. I think you'd really enjoy it."

I bite back a smile. "Are you asking me out on a date?"

He shrugs and smiles out the window. "Feels like the least I could do after you showed me such a good time." He sets both elbows on the table wind leans across it, those black eyes looking right back into mine. "I'd love to see you there on the other side of the bar while I'm working. I'd slip you free drinks all night and growl at any man who came within a mile of you. And on my break, I'd take you into the bathroom..."

When he trails off, my heart thumps loud in my ears. "What would you do to me in the bathroom?"

One side of his mouth lifts in a smug smile. "What do you want me to do to you in the bathroom?"

I shove up out of my chair, lean across the table, and kiss him. He takes my face in his big hands, cradling it, like he's trying to be sweet, but I don't want him to be sweet. I want him to fuck me. I move around the table, slide onto his lap, and slick my tongue along his bottom lip. He groans, grabbing onto my thighs and pulling me closer, until I'm pressed to him from shoulder to hip. I rock against him, and he groans into my open mouth. That incurable hard-on he mentioned earlier has definitely made an appearance.

"Fuck," he says, ripping his mouth from mine. "What is it about you? I can't get enough."

I smile. "Maybe I'm just not the kind of girl you get enough of." And with that, I climb off his lap and get on my knees in front of him.

His hand immediately fists in my hair, and I haven't even gotten his pants open yet. "Layla, you're going to kill me. I don't know if I can take it."

I tug his pants down, his underwear going with it, until that delicious part of him that I remember from last night springs free. It makes my mouth water. "Oh, I think you can take it." I lick a stripe up the underside of him, reveling at the feel of him on my tongue and the way he shudders sweetly before watching me with a wrinkle in his brow as I take the length of him into my mouth.

He jerks, like I shocked him, and then groans loud enough to wake the dead. "You look so pretty with your mouth full," he says with awe in his voice, and I want to laugh. He hasn't seen anything yet.

Taking a deep breath in through my nose, I push all the way down on him, until I have to fight down a gag. Mac groans, and his head falls back. I start a rhythm, keeping him as deep as I can the whole time, sliding my hand up his chest, until his hand comes up to clutch mine. While I've got him so deep that oxygen is a thing of the past, he takes my hand from his chest and presses a kiss to the center of my palm.

I come off of him with a gasp.

"What did I do to deserve this?" he asks, his hand cupping my chin, while the other holds on tight to my hand.

With the tip of him sliding along my wet mouth, I say, "You can take this as an apology for pepper spraying you."

He chuckles. "I don't want a blowjob. I don't want to finish in your mouth."

I trail kisses down the length of his cock. "Are you sure?"

His hand slides into my hair, and he pulls my mouth away from his dick. "I want to be inside you. I want you to use me the way you use your toys. Use me to pleasure yourself."

A shiver runs through me. He certainly doesn't have to ask me twice.

He helps me to my feet, and with our mouths attached, we cross the few steps to the bed, falling into it together. He kisses his way down my throat, finding the collar of my ratty old t-shirt and pulling it aside to dip his tongue into the hollow of my throat. I wear lingerie every night during my shows, the sexiest things I can afford, but Mac is making me feel ten times sexier in a New York Giants shirt that I bought at a thrift store. He cups my breasts through the material, palming my hard nipples.

"How do you want me?" he whispers in my ear.

I wiggle beneath him. He wants me to take control of the situation. Well, I can certainly do that. I push on his shoulder until he lets me up and then I shove him onto his back in the middle of the bed. Standing at the edge of the bed, I reach under my shirt and strip off my underwear. Giving him head made me so wet that when I crawl on top of him, my pussy immediately leaves a wet spot on his pants.

I think about what he said: *use me the way you use your toys.* If this was a show, what would I do? To make myself feel good but also to excite my viewers?

Reaching over to my nightstand, I pull out the little vibrator I keep there. This isn't really for the shows. This is the vibrator I use on myself when I wake up horny or when I need to get off in the middle of the day, long before the show starts.

Turning it on to one of the lower settings, I press it between us. It's hitting my clit really good, but when Mac makes a noise in the back of his throat and throws his head back against the mattress, I know it feels good to him too. I grind against it a few times and then lean forward and run my tongue up the line of his neck, loving the feel of his Adam's apple.

"I want you naked," I tell him before climbing off of him, taking the vibrator with me.

Mac scrambles to do my bidding. He rips at the buttons of his shirt and then yanks comically at his belt, unable to get it off as smoothly as he did last night.

I sit on the edge of the bed and watch him. Inching the hem of my shirt up my thighs, I wait until I'm completely exposed to him before putting the vibrator against my clit. Ratcheting it up a few more settings, the buzz of it fills the air, and I moan.

Max watches, entranced, as I jiggle the vibrator against my clit. His eyes race between my face and the spot between my legs. "Does that feel good?" he asks, breathless.

"Uh huh."

He shoves his pants down his legs, and my pleasure ratchets even higher when I see his gorgeous dick. Even though I was up close and personal with it last night, I didn't really get a good look at it. It was dark, and Mac was jerking off furiously. And earlier, I was too concerned with getting it into my mouth. But now, I see the way it curves ever so slightly up toward the ceiling and that delicious spot under the head where the skin meets up at a point. That's where I set the vibrator.

Mac's hips jerk, and he lets out a surprised yelp. And then his hips start to rock, effectively fucking the vibrator in my fist.

I smile up at him. "Does that feel good?" I mimic what he asked me a moment ago.

Instead of answering, he leans down and presses his mouth to mine. God, he's a good kisser. But he doesn't linger for long. Instead, he gets on his knees in front of me, pushing the hem of my shirt up to my stomach. I whimper, waiting to feel his mouth against my clit.

But he doesn't put his mouth on me. At least, not yet. Instead, he grabs my wrist and forces it between my legs, until the vibrator is right up against my clit. I buck, but Mac holds me down against the mattress, and when I finally feel his tongue on my pussy, it's going straight into my opening.

"Oh fuck," I breathe, as Mac slips his tongue in and out of my pussy while holding the vibrator against my clit. It feels good, so so good, but then Mac's tongue is gone.

And when I feel the pressure of it lower, static against my asshole, I explode. My legs tremble as I come, feeling Mac lapping at my hole over and over until I start to come back down.

Once I've settled, Mac stands. "Please, Layla, I'm begging you. I need to be inside you or I'm going to fucking die."

I grab onto his shoulders and turn to shove him down onto the bed. I straddle his hips, but before I can sink down on him, he stops me. "Condom?"

Right. Even though I'm on birth control, this man is a virtual stranger to me, and I should probably at least attempt to be smart about this. I reach over to the nightstand and grab a condom from the box I keep there. Tossing it to him, I watch him rip it open, all the while rubbing at my clit. Everything about what he's doing is making me need to come again, and I don't even really know why.

Maybe it's because I'm covered, my old t-shirt still firmly in place, while he's naked. Maybe it's because he didn't even think twice before letting me take the lead. Maybe because I know that he's so turned on by me, turned on enough that his cock is bobbing furiously as he attempts to put on the condom.

I laugh. And that's another thing. When was the last time I just felt this...happy to be having sex with someone? "Do you need some help?" I ask him.

He grips his cock in his fist and holds it still as he rolls the condom down. "I think you've helped enough," he says on an exhale. "If you put your hands on me, I might die. I can't quite figure out how I'm going to get inside you without going off in three seconds flat." All of this comes out in a rush as he's distracted by the condom. When he has it in place, his eyes meet mine, and he sighs, laying his head back against the bed. "I'm at your mercy, baby. You can do whatever you want to me."

His words are the gun at the starting line of a race. Gripping his cock in my hand, I go up on my knees, position him where I need him, and sink down on him. I shudder when I'm fully seated on him, his cock as deep as it could possibly go. For a moment, we stay just like that, him gripping my thighs and me throwing my head back just to feel and feel and feel.

And then I lift off of him and slam back down. We both groan in unison, and I don't give either one of us a chance to catch our breaths. I just start to ride, watching the way his eyes are glued to my tits as they bounce under my loose t-shirt. God, he's sexy, his eyes so dark, the only part of him that still remembers the raven, even when he's in human form.

I plant my hands on his chest, leaning forward to let my clit push against his pelvis each time I bounce back down onto him, but with his eyes on mine, Mac reaches for something in the bed. His hand finds the abandoned vibrator and without a word, he flips it on and presses it between us, right over my clit.

I whimper, holding his eye while I rock on him, the vibrator pushing my pleasure higher and higher. There's nowhere left to go. I'm at the very peak over the most intense pleasure I've ever felt, pleasure that feels unrestrained and honest. This man has seen a part of me that everyone else has rejected, and he's wanted me for it. This man has put himself between me and danger, using his fists to protect me. This man has sat back and let me take control of my pleasure, letting his touch bring me higher and higher when I needed it.

I don't know much about him, but I've seen his true self like he's seen mine, and it feels like I could fall in love with him with very little provocation.

And it's that thought that shoves me over the edge into orgasm. I shriek, digging my nails into his chest and watching him watch me fall apart. He waits, waits until I'm done and pushing the vibrator away from that spot between my legs, before he flips me onto my back, shoves my knees up and apart and fucks the life out of me.

He's focused on his own pleasure now, watching where he disappears inside me over and over until he begins to shake, his hips stuttering as he spills inside me. I immediately regret the condom, making a mental note to have that conversation as soon as possible so that maybe we don't have to use one ever again.

Mac sighs when his orgasm is done and turns to plant a kiss to the inside of my ankle. How does he do that, find gentleness in the middle of such an animal act?

He pulls out of me and collapses onto the bed beside me.

Wrapping an arm around my middle, his eyes find my computer set up, the webcam that sits beside the computer screen.

"You have to accept it," I say, feeling worry start to brew in the pit of my stomach. He may have liked what he saw, but he could still ask me to stop doing it.

A worry line forms between his eyebrows. "Accept what?"

I nod toward the camera. "I would really like it if we could spend time together, but I'm not going to give up my job. I like doing it, and I need to be with someone who can accept that."

With the tip of his index finger, Mac turns my face toward his. "Why the hell would I want you to give it up? I don't mind those men seeing what's mine and not theirs. As long as I'm the only one who gets to fuck you."

I grin. "Deal."

EPILOGUE

SIX MONTHS LATER

> NOLABOY1985: FUCK HER HARD.
>
> PUNISHER2222: GOD I'M SO FUCKING
> JEALOUS OF THIS GUY.
>
> PARKINGNON: SHE LOOKS LIKE SHE CAN'T
> GET ENOUGH OF HIS DICK.

I laugh when I read that last comment, my head bent at an awkward angle against the mattress as Mac rails me from behind. He has my hair wrapped in his fist, and I watch him on the screen as he reads the comments. He likes it too, seeing what people are saying about us as they watch him fuck me.

After our first full show together, he told me that it gets him hot to know that people pay to watch him fuck his girl-friend. We still fuck off screen like bunnies, but Mac is different in front of the camera. Where he always keeps that gentleness under the surface when we fuck alone, there's a wildness to him when we go at it for our viewers, and I like this side of him, the side of him that's merciless, that uses me like his little toy for everyone to see.

NOLABOY1985 TIPPED 600 COINS FOR [FINGER
IN HER ASS]

I feel Mac's hips stutter as his concentration shifts to the screen. We both have to read the tips to make sure that the viewer gets what they want, as long as it's within the realm of what we're willing to do.

And we're definitely both willing to do this.

"That sounds like a great idea," Mac says between his teeth. I watch on the screen as he sticks his thumb in his mouth, getting it all wet, and just that act alone is enough to have me moaning in the back of my throat before he sets his thumb against my asshole and starts to press in. I let my eyes fall closed and my mouth open on a whimper.

"My pretty little slut loves having both her holes filled."

I whimper louder. I love it when he talks to me like that, and I know I'm not going to last long with his thumb up my ass. He knows it sets me off and so do the viewers.

"You should feel how tight she's getting around me," he says to the camera. "She's about to come. I can feel it."

I can hear the excitement in his voice and that pushes my own excitement higher. I've never met anyone who loves to make someone come as much as Mac loves to make me come. Sometimes it feels like the sex itself is just for me and that he could spend his life just getting off to my orgasm.

I press my face into the blanket and shout through my orgasm. It rips through me in waves, the whole world disappearing except for Mac fucking me. For me, this *is* the whole world, Mac and the home we share together and this job that he does with me when he's not at the bar. Why would I ever need anything else?

Mac pulls out of me, shoving me onto my back and straddling my chest. He jerks his cock quickly, and I open my mouth, waiting for the taste of him.

"Tongue out," he grunts, and I obey just as he comes,

some of it making it onto my tongue, but the majority of it landing on the rest of my face.

I giggle, wiping it off my chin, and Mac smiles down at me.

His eyes move to the camera, and I wonder, like I always do, what our viewers think of his dark black eyes, so much bigger and darker than is natural. Maybe they think he wears contacts. Maybe they don't even notice.

He snatches up the camera and points it down toward me. "See that? It makes her so fucking happy to have my cum all over her face."

I laugh because it's true, and then I blow all the viewers a kiss before Mac stops the live video. As soon as the screen goes black, Mac reaches for a tissue and helps me wipe my face clean.

"I have to get to work," he says, climbing off the bed.

I stay where I am, in the center of the bed, and watch him get dressed, feeling lazy all the way down to my bones.

He smiles over at me as he buttons his shirt, and then, just like that, he's my raven, flapping his wings and coming to perch at the end of the bed.

"I can't wait for you to be back home," I tell him, feeling that tug in my stomach I get every time he leaves. "I love you."

He squawks back at me, and I can't help the laugh that bursts out of me.

"I suppose I'll accept that as reciprocation." I reach out to run my hand down his back, loving the way his feathers flutter. He told me it feels good when I do that, like I'm running my hands down his bare chest.

He flaps his wings, flying out the window, and I watch him disappear on the horizon, waiting for the moment when he'll come back to me.

Five Nights With The Fire Monster

Five Nights with the Fire Monster

There's a monster standing in the shadows of my bedroom.

He has fire for eyes and horns made of steel.

He says he came through a portal from another realm.

He says he came here to make me his bride.

There's no way I'm going to agree to marry him...right?

Chapter One

Night 1

This break up is never going to end. Trent sits across from me at my little kitchen table, explaining why, exactly, I'm the worst person he's ever had the misfortune of meeting.

"I mean, do you even see yourself?" he growls out now.

I'm only halfway paying attention. I'm mostly thinking about how my body hurts from sitting in this chair for the half hour that I've been trying to detach myself from Trent, my boyfriend of two years. My limbs are heavy, and all of my joints ache.

"You can't spend the rest of your life like this," Trent says. A bubble of spit lands on my table, and I think about how I'll use bleach to clean it later, scrubbing away every last remnant of proof of this encounter, of Trent himself. "Your grandmother died six months ago. How long are you going to be depressed over it? How long are you going to stop living your life? You think you'll be satisfied when you have no love life, no friends, and no job?"

I stare down at the table, completely blank. Trent has no

idea how depression works. Or grief, for that matter. But who cares? All I have to do is survive this breakup and then Trent will leave, and I can go back to bed. My soft bed instead of this unbearably hard chair.

"This is pathetic," Trent sighs, and he finally stands. Oh, thank God, he's going to leave. He turns toward the front door, but before he's even made it out of the kitchen, he turns back to me. "Someday, you're going to snap out of this haze you're in, and you're going to realize you threw away the best relationship of your life."

And then he finally, *finally* leaves.

As soon as the door shuts behind him, I go back to bed. I don't even bother turning on the light in my room. The light from the kitchen gives the room a gentle glow, and that's enough for me.

It's not quite bedtime, and I know that if I get in bed now, just after sunset, that I'll wake up in the middle of the night, but I don't care. I feel so heavy, and I just want to sleep.

I crawl into bed fully clothed and pull the blanket up over my head. But just as I'm about to drift off, my eyelids drooping, the shadows in the corner of my room shift, and my eyes spring back open. I hold still, feeling certain that whatever I saw was just a trick of the light. Grandma always told me that if you stared hard enough into the dark that it would start to feel like the dark was staring back.

And right now, I feel like the dark is staring back.

I squint into the shadows, and as my eyes adjust, I see a form taking shape, big shoulders and a dark face.

"It's not real," I whisper to myself. I creep one hand out from under my blanket and switch on my bedside lamp.

And then I scream.

There's a monster in my bedroom. An actual, literal monster, with horns and skin the color of coal, so big that the tip of its giant horns almost scrape my low ceiling. As I shriek loud enough to wake the dead, the monster steps out of the shadows with its hands up.

"Please," it says, and its voice echoes like it's three voices in one, all of them surrounding me. A male voice. "I swear that I'm not here to hurt you."

I don't know when I stopped screaming and started crying instead, but I can feel the warm tears slipping down my cheeks.

"I'm so sorry," the monster says, stepping closer to my bed. "I didn't mean to frighten you." When he moves into the light, I get a better look at him. His horns look as if they're made of metal, jutting out of his head and then up into the air at a ninety degree angle. His face is dark, like the rest of him, with a nose and a mouth but no eyes. Instead of eyes, there are only two dark holes the size of softballs, both of them housing a small flame, like candles burning.

I'm trying not to let him see me tremble. "Are you a demon?"

His face changes, like a grimace. "No. Nothing like that." He comes closer, one big step, and then he bends over me, so close to my face that I can feel the heat of those flames in his eyes on my skin. While I hold very still, he reaches up with his black hand, his fingers tipped with dark claws, and brushes away the tears first on one cheek and then the other, so gently that my trembling stops.

Even without eyes, I can see the way the creature looks at me, his features tilting in just slightly with quiet sympathy. The fear starts to melt away.

"I don't want you to cry anymore, Annaleigh," he says, and I'm too distracted trying to learn every inch of the creature's face to wonder how the hell he knows my name.

"What *are* you?" I whisper.

"I'm a captain."

I have no idea why this makes me giggle, but it does. He

says it in this completely innocent way, like when you ask a child how old they are, and they're so excited to tell you that they do it with their mouths *and* their fingers.

"I just mean," I say, still examining his dark face, the holes where eyes should be, the human-shaped mouth, the extremely prominent cheekbones. "You're not human."

He scoffs, almost like he's offended. "No. I'm not human. My name is Kale, and I'm Captain of the Guard of my realm, Isiriel. I watch over the portal."

I stare at him, trying to make sense of his words. "Realm? Portal?"

All my fear is gone now. My grandmother once told me that I was good at reading people, that I could tell whether they had good or bad intentions just by being in the same room with them. And while I was never really sure I believed her, I think I do now. I don't feel like this...person...is here to hurt me. I mean, if he was going to hurt me, he would have done it by now, right?

He nods his chin toward my window, causing his giant horns to tilt and then right themselves like a ship on an ocean wave. Outside, my backyard is mostly dark. "There's a portal to Isiriel just outside your window."

I blink at him. And then I blink at the open field outside my window. There's nothing out there but grass and lightning bugs. "I don't see any portal."

Tilting his face toward mine, Kale raises one hand and crooks his long, clawed finger at me. "Come here, and I'll show you."

I definitely shouldn't trust a monster who tells me to come closer. Didn't I learn anything from Little Red Riding Hood? But I do it anyway. I get out of bed and shuffle over to him. I don't miss the way his face moves, like his non-existent eyes are sweeping down my body, taking in my denim shorts and my Star Wars t-shirt and my fuzzy socks. Am I the first human he's ever met? Am I currently representing the entire human race?

My gaze quickly sweeps his body. He's shirtless, showing off the ridges of his dark torso, and the only thing he's wearing is a pair of loose-fitting cloth pants. He's not even wearing shoes, and I can see that, while he has five fingers on each hand, he only has three toes on each foot.

When I'm close enough, Kale reaches out and gently pulls me in front of him, so that I'm facing the window with my back to him. In the glare on the glass, I can see him behind me, bending so that his face is beside mine. He reaches around me and points to a spot outside my window, between two trees.

"Do you see it?" His breath puffs against my neck, hot like the steam coming off a pot of boiling water, and it causes me to shiver.

I focus, trying to see what he's showing me, but all I see are the trees, the black sky, the grass that desperately needs to be mowed.

And then. There. A long, vertical line between the two trees that shimmers like a snail's slime trail in the sun.

There's a moment when you realize that your life is never going to be the same. The way it once was is no longer the way it can be. That's what I feel now, looking at that portal and knowing that there's another realm out there, other creatures besides humans.

"I see it," is all I can say to Kale. I turn my face to look at him. He's so close to me, and I'm amazed by how comfortable I already feel with him. Safe.

Safe enough to look into his eyeholes and watch the fire there flicker and crackle. "So," I say, not taking my eyes off those twin flames. "If you're supposed to be on the other side of that portal, protecting your realm, why are you here?"

"I came here to make you my bride."

I jerk away from him, pressing my back to the wall, as far from him as I can get. "Excuse me?"

He puts his hands up again, and I get this strange feeling that he's used to this, having to show his harmlessness to humans. "I have watched you through the portal for many years now, but I have been far too busy protecting Isiriel to come and meet you. Today, my king finally gave me leave to visit you."

I'm still pressed to the wall, palms flat against the floral wallpaper, like I can just disappear right into the drywall. "Because you want to marry me?" My voice comes out a squeak. "You can't just show up in my bedroom and think I'm going to marry you after five minutes! That's not how things work here!"

"Of course not," he says, his clawed hands dropping to his sides. "I came here to get to know you. I came here to tell you about my realm and learn all about you."

I realize I'm breathing hard, and when neither of us is speaking, the sound of my huffing is loud in my silent room. I know there are more important things than the question I'm about to ask, but all I can think about are all the things Trent just said to me. And so, the question just comes out.

"Why would you want to get to know *me*?"

Somehow, it's like he gets bigger. His shoulders seem to get broader, his body taller, his horns sharper. It's like he's stretching like a shadow along the wall. And then his empty eyeholes are burning bright. Whatever small flame there was when I looked into them before has flared up into twin infernos, burning all the way up to the base of his horns.

"I heard what that man said to you. He told you lies. I have watched you, and I know the truth. I saw the way you cared for your grandmother. I saw the kindness you show your friends. I saw the toll that caring for others has taken on you. I have wanted to come to you for so long. I've watched your sadness and yearned to hold you. I've seen your fear and longed to comfort you. I have seen many females in all of my days, but my heart has belonged to only you since the moment I first saw you."

I just stare at him. I can't find words. I can't find breath. All I can manage is to peel myself off the wall to stand in front of him.

Little by little, the inferno in his eyes dies down, until they're small flickering flames again. "I want to take you away from this place that hasn't been kind to you," he says, his voice like a whisper inside my head.

I step away from him and perch on the end of my bed. I try to imagine what the last few years of my life must have looked like from his perspective. If all he could see was this room, this side of the house, my window, then he must have seen when I moved into this house five years ago to take care of my grandmother when she got sick. He must have seen how I worked all day to pay bills and then spent all night trying to keep my grandmother comfortable and happy. He must have seen the hills and valleys of my mental health, the anxiety and depression that have ruled my life. He must have seen me start dating Trent. He must have seen my grandmother die and how I haven't been able to put myself back together since.

"I can't imagine why you would want me, Kale, but going to your realm with you isn't going to fix me. What's wrong with me, it's biological. My brain is broken. I'm broken."

Even without looking, I feel him shift, coming toward me and then kneeling in front of me. His face appears in my field of vision, and even though he doesn't have actual eyes or eyebrows, there's still a strange shape to his face that shows me I've made him sad.

"There's nothing wrong with you, Annaleigh," he says. "We all have our circumstances that we can't change. This... thing that you feel is broken inside you is something you must live with, just like I must live with the fact that I cannot touch you when I become flame. It is simply who you are, and it doesn't make you any less perfect."

I feel a lump rise in my throat, and without giving myself a chance to consider whether or not it might be a bad idea, I reach out and press my fingertips to his jaw. He doesn't flinch away from me, just holds my gaze as I run my fingers along his skin. He's hot, like touching the outside of an oven while it's on, and when I pull my hand away, there's ash on my fingertips.

"I know that coming to Isiriel will not solve all of your problems, but I believe I could make you happy, Annaleigh. There are other humans in Isiriel, a whole village of them. It is my belief, really and truly, that you belong by my side there."

I don't know what to say. Because...maybe he's right. I can't believe I'm even thinking this, but maybe a change of scenery is exactly what I need. Being here in my grandmother's house every day is just a daily reminder that I'm alone, but I have nowhere else to go, not now that this house is mine, free and clear.

"You really want to marry me?" It's completely preposterous. He's a monster. He's made of ashes. He has horns and no eyes and he's from another realm, and this is all completely crazy. But maybe that's okay. Maybe that's why it's so exciting.

Kale nods slowly. "But I know you'll need time to make a decision like that. My king has seen the way I want you, and he's given me leave to visit you every night, to spend time with you, to show you who I am."

I gasp when his hand brushes against mine where it sits in my lap, his fingers running down my palm. "Why only at night?" I manage to ask.

Kale sighs, and the steam that bursts from his lips is almost comical. "I cannot tolerate your sun. It is very different from the sun in Isiriel, and even there, my people live under the mountain. Your sun is very harmful to my skin, so when I come to see you, I can only come at night."

I try to imagine living in a cave all the time, no sunlight. That sounds...rough. My eyes travel along Kale's body. His skin might be made of coal and ash, but something that almost looks like veins travel along his torso, glowing the color of burning embers. That fire in his eyes, it seems to burn beneath his skin too. It's like he's *made* of fire.

"May I see you again tomorrow?"

My eyes lift to his. Or at least, to where his eyes should be. "You want to come back?"

His mouth curves up in a smile, the first one he's shown me since he stepped out of the shadows. "I would never leave, if I didn't have to."

This is insanity. But what's even more insane is the way I immediately nod, no hesitation. Because I think...I want to see Kale again. I think I want to learn about him and where he comes from. I want to learn about Isiriel.

"I should return." Kale stands, unfolding himself one bit at a time, until he's towering over me, a dark sentry. It makes my heart pound to look up at him, to see him looking back down at me.

"Right," I whisper. I stand too and go over to the window, opening it and standing aside, like I just walked him to the front door after a dinner party. "Then, I'll see you tomorrow, I suppose."

"May I..." He trails off, bowing his head and shaking it. "No. I'm sorry. I shouldn't ask for such things." Like someone with a nervous tick, he reaches up and wraps his hand around the base of one of his horns before letting it drop back down to his side.

"What is it?" I ask, feeling charmed. Is Kale...cute?

His face tilts up. "May I kiss you?"

I suck in a breath. I shouldn't let him. I definitely

shouldn't let him, right? He'll get the wrong idea. He probably wants to kiss the woman he now sees as his future bride. I can't lead him on like that. Even if I went to Isiriel, it wouldn't be as Kale's wife. That's absolutely impossible.

"I've never felt the touch of a human woman's lips before."

Oh, God. I'm so weak.

I press close to him and put one hand on his muscled forearm. Going up on my tiptoes, I lift my chin, knowing that he'll have to come more than halfway to meet me. He bends at the waist, and then his shockingly soft mouth is on mine. He's so gentle, barely touching me at all, but then his lips part, and his breath is so warm, like a furnace.

Before I've even realized what I'm doing, I wrap a hand around the back of Kale's neck and dip my tongue into that hot mouth.

Kale groans, and the sound is so overwhelming, so all-encompassing, like it's completely surrounding me, making all the walls tremble. All I can do is whimper against his mouth. And then his tongue finds mine, so many degrees hotter than my own body.

Holy shit, what am I doing?

I rip my mouth away from his and settle my feet flat on the floor again. I can barely catch my breath, but Kale doesn't seem to be having any trouble. One side of his mouth is turned up in a smile, clearly proud of himself.

"Good night, Annaleigh." He bends and carefully crawls through my window, swaying his head gently so that his horns don't smash the glass.

When he's out on the grass, tracking through the shadows of my backyard toward the portal that's now so clear to me, I say, "Good night, Kale." When I reach up to touch my lips, they're smeared with ash.

Chapter Two

Night 2

Alice sets a steaming mug of tea in front of me and takes the seat across the table, in the same spot Trent sat twenty-four hours ago as he told me I was a useless human being.

"What a bag of dicks," Alice sneers. If she had fangs, she would be flashing them right now like an offended guard dog. "Good riddance. You don't need that asshat around fucking with your energy." Her eyes sweep along my face. "Actually, you look okay. Did you get some sleep?"

I wrap my hands around my mug, the warmth of it bringing back memories of the warmth of Kale's skin, the way he seemed to burn under the surface. I actually did get some sleep last night. After Kale left, I had this strange sense of comfort at knowing that he was just on the other side of the portal, watching over me. I went to sleep, and when I woke up, I felt almost rested, something I haven't felt since my grandmother died.

"Yeah, I went to bed as soon as he left," I tell Alice, not technically a lie. "So I slept like twelve hours."

Alice grimaces. "That's not good for you. You have to be careful not to let the sleep suck you under. You know how hard it is to crawl back out. Have you been taking your meds?"

I nod. I appreciate that Alice wants to take care of me, but a part of me always feels like I'm failing her when the depression takes over. I want her to be proud of me. After all, she's the only one who truly cares about me.

At least, I used to think she was. I'm not so sure anymore.

"Want me to stay the night? We could watch Netflix and eat ice cream."

A little bubble of dread forms in my stomach. I want Alice to stay, but if she stays, I won't get to see Kale. And I think I really want to see Kale. Now that I know something exists out there that I didn't know about, I want to learn more about it.

"I'm okay. I think I'm going to take a bath. Maybe check out job listings."

Alice reaches across the table and covers my hand with hers. "If you need help with applications or anything, just let me know, okay?"

"I will."

A loud crash sounds in my bedroom, and both of us jump.

"Oh my God, what was that?" Alice whispers, already halfway out of her chair.

But I already know what it was. Kale.

Alice is moving toward the hall, but I jump out of my seat and grab onto her wrist. I can't let her go back there. I can't let her see Kale. There's no telling what she'll do if she finds a giant fire monster in my bedroom.

"It was probably the wind," I say, subtly tugging her back from the hallway. "I left my window open, and sometimes the wind knocks stuff around in my room."

Alice turns worried eyes on me. "That was way too loud to be the wind."

"It probably knocked over the vase on my nightstand. I

keep forgetting to move it." I try to keep my voice casual, even though my heart is pounding in my ears. I need to get Alice out of here. "Anyway, I'm going to go hop in the bath. Do you want me to walk you to your car?"

Alice's eyes are still on the dark hallway, but she just shakes her head. "No, I'll be fine." Her eyes finally find mine. "You'll call me if you need me, right?"

"Of course." Alice has been trying so hard to be there for me these last few months, but even I can see the toll it's taking on her to always be responsible for me. I'm a hard person to care about.

I walk Alice to the front door, and as soon as I have it closed and locked, I rush to my bedroom.

Sure enough, there's Kale, his massive hulking figure bent over on the edge of my bed. He's got his face in his hands, but when I close my bedroom door, his head comes up. The devastated look on his face makes me freeze.

"I'm so sorry," he says, and I almost gasp. In the last twenty-four hours, I've forgotten the way his voice seems to echo like it's coming from the air all around me. Yesterday, it was terrifying. But today, it's a comfort. He picks up something off the bed beside him and shows it to me.

It's the picture frame that has always sat on top of my dresser, right by the window. A picture of my grandmother and me at my high school graduation sits behind broken glass.

"I managed to get into the window but forgot to account for my horns once I was in. I was just excited to see you–"

"Kale," I cut him off, setting the picture frame on my bed and tentatively reaching out to touch his shoulder. Under my fingertips, his skin is warm and ashen, just like I remembered. "It's okay. It's just a picture frame. I can replace it."

When he finally tilts his face up to mine, there's sadness written in the downward curve of his mouth and the inward pucker of the skin at his brow bone. "I don't want to bring any harm to your life," he says. "You've already lost enough." He reaches one hand up, stretched out toward me, and I take it.

He gently tugs me closer, until he's settling me on his lap. My skin immediately goes hot, feverish. Having him pressed to me in so many places is like sinking into a hot tub. I press a hand against his chest because I'm not sure what else to do with it, and that feels...right.

Kale runs a single finger down my cheek, his claw just barely grazing my skin. "How have you been since we last spoke?"

I scoff and nod toward the open window. "Don't you know? Weren't you watching?"

He smiles, his teeth alarmingly white against the darkness of his skin. He has fangs. How did I not notice that yesterday?

"I am the highest ranking protector in all of Isiriel. I have many responsibilities. There are several paths into Isiriel that must be guarded, and yours is the least likely to produce a formidable enemy."

"Wow, thanks."

His hand, still cradling my jaw, slides down, until it's pressed to my throat. The size of it is startling. He wraps his entire hand around my throat, his fingers touching on the other side with room to spare. "Humans are fragile things," he says. "There are creatures in other lands ten times the size of the biggest warrior in Isiriel."

"Isn't that you?" It's hard to think that there's anyone bigger than Kale. How massive and terrifying that person must be.

"No. I am the highest ranking officer and the best fighter. But I'm not the biggest. However, even the smallest person of the Isiriel race is significantly bigger than a human."

I love listening to him talk like this, about a world he knows that I don't, like listening to someone talk about a country on the other side of the world. It almost doesn't feel real until you've seen it with your own eyes.

"So, you don't watch me all the time?" I ask, bringing the conversation back to where it should be. This has been on my mind since last night, along with that kiss he gave me just before he left. If Kale has been watching me since I moved in with my grandmother, what has he seen? He made it very clear that he saw the dark days, the ones where depression held my head underwater. But what about all the times Trent fucked me in this very bed? Was he watching that? What about all the times Alice and I pulled all-nighters, binge-watching Netflix and listening to the sound of my grandmother cough from the other room? Did he watch while I lost my job because Grandma needed me? Does he know I haven't been able to find a new one because every time I come close, the depression swallows me again? Do I want him to know any of those parts of me?

"No," he says, slowly removing his hand from my neck and trailing it down the inside of my arm so softly that I shiver. God, that feels good. I can't remember the last time I was touched in any affectionate way.

"My friend, Alice, came over today. It was hard not to tell her about you. I wanted to."

"I never said you couldn't."

I smile, the action coming so easily. "I don't think she would handle the knowledge of your existence very well."

"You did."

Did I? Yes, I suppose I did. Maybe it was because I've always hoped there was something else beyond this world, more than just this life that makes people miserable and tears them down. I always wanted there to be a greater purpose, and here it is. Other realms, other species of intelligent beings. Finally, something worth being alive for.

I shift in Kale's lap, surprised when he makes a little bark of a noise in the back of his throat and his eyes spark high. And then I feel something hard pressed against my hip. My eyes dip down of their own accord. Kale doesn't seem to have any interest in wearing a shirt, but his pants look surprisingly like a pair of camo cargo pants, and I remember him saying that there were humans in Isiriel. Did they show the Isiriel how to make clothes that look like ours?

"I'm sorry," Kale says, shifting me away from where his massive erection is pushing against me. "Your nearness, the scent of you, it affects me." All I did was wiggle in his lap for two seconds and touch his chest. Is that all it takes to get an Isiriel male hard?

"Don't apologize," I whisper.

I must have lost my mind because next thing I know, I'm standing and throwing my legs over Kale's wide hips, straddling him. As soon as I sit down, all of me pressed to all of him, he groans so loud, I swear the window vibrates. Yes, I must have lost my mind because am I really thinking about dry humping a fire monster from another realm right now?

I haven't stopped thinking about that kiss all night—how it was strange at first but how right it felt before it was over, how I should probably be afraid of Kale but I'm not. Not even a little bit.

And so, I press my lips to his. He makes a surprised noise against my mouth and then kisses me back, taking my hips in his big, clawed hands as I push closer. I gasp into his mouth when the entire length of him is pressed to my stomach. It didn't really equate before, when he told me he wanted to marry me, that if I agreed (which I'm *not*; I'm not that insane), we would have sex. And if we had sex, he would have to put this enormous cock inside me, this cock that's straining so hard against the fabric of his pants that the material might as well not be there at all. Between that and the very flimsy fabric of my athletic shorts and underwear, I can *feel* him.

And I can feel...ridges?

As Kale slips his tongue into my mouth, I rock against his cock, trying to get a better feel for what's going behind his pants. Whatever those things are that are protruding along the length, they graze my clit as I shift, and it feels so good that I howl.

And suddenly, I'm being pushed away. Kale lifts me as if I weigh as much as a teddy bear and sets me on the bed beside him. "We should not do that," he says, his voice booming loud enough to hurt my ears and his eyes matching flames that blaze out at me. The vein-like lines under his skin grow so bright, he's almost blinding.

"I'm sorry." I scramble off the bed and rush to the other side of the room, pressing my back against the door. "I'm sorry. I thought you would like it. I won't do it again."

Kale slumps. The fires in his eyeholes disappear, smoking like a candle put out. "I did like it," he says, defeat in his voice. "You cannot possibly know, Annaleigh, how badly I want you. But in Isiriel, we mate for life. And if you take me inside you, you will be mine for eternity." He looks up at me. "I do not wish to force you into a decision you're unprepared to make. And so, I must keep my distance to keep from losing control."

I process his words, rolling them around in my head. I take one tentative step toward him. "So, are you saying that...you're a virgin?"

He scowls. "The humans on Isiriel have taught me many English words, but I don't know this one."

I can't help but smile as I move back toward him, almost close enough to touch. "It means you've never been inside a female." It feels strange to use that term, but I guess female Isiriel aren't really technically *women*.

He shakes his head. "That is a sacred bond that only the married may share with each other."

Something deflates inside me. "Well, then." I can't even

believe I'm going to entertain this train of thought, but I'm curious. And it certainly doesn't hurt to ask, right? "I'm not a virgin. I've been with men. Does that mean that we can't marry?"

"Of course not," he says, standing. "The custom of mating for life is an Isiriel custom. We understand that humans have different customs."

Oh, God. Why do I feel relieved?

"And from what I'm told," Kale goes on, "humans of your age have often already had several sexual partners."

My eyes go wide. "I don't know about *several*, but there have been a few. Four, to be exact. I don't exactly know the average number of sexual partners for a twenty-four-year-old."

Kale nods. "Your sexual past is, of course, your own business. I only ask that, if we were to wed, that you be mine from that moment on. Mine alone."

"Of course I would be faithful," I say, my voice rising, and then I cut myself off. What am I even saying? We're not getting married, so we're not mating for life, and I don't have to be faithful to him. I need to get a grip.

"I have no doubt," Kale says, evidently not noticing my very mild panic. He looks unsure for a moment and then says, "It is true that I cannot put myself inside you. But I've heard the humans talk of another intimate practice, one that I admit I find a little strange. It's said to bring human women great pleasure. I would be happy to perform this practice on you, if you would like."

"Um," I stutter. "I don't really—I mean, I don't know if—"

"I have heard that human women," Kale says over me, "like it when a male licks between their legs. Is that true?"

I don't know how to react. I almost laugh at the idea of Kale learning from some random human woman about oral sex. At the same time, an image floods my mind of Kale putting his mouth on me, and the thought makes heat rush through my body.

"Yes, most women like that. If their partner is good at it, that is."

Kale's eyeholes widen slightly. "I would like to be good at it. I would like to learn. I would like to bring you pleasure. Please, let me try."

I'm frozen in place. This is bonkers. Absolute madness. I can't let a monster eat me out. Except maybe I could. It's just sex, right? I've never exactly been good at the whole casual sex thing, but then, I've never tried having casual sex with a fire monster from a different realm.

"Um. Okay?"

His mouth spreads into a grin, and before I can change my mind, Kale has taken hold of me, spun me around, and laid me out on the bed. I tend to be self-conscious in bed, preferring the room to be dark and for my partner's eyes to stay glued to mine so they don't see all of my little imperfections.

But Kale doesn't give me a chance to hide. He climbs onto the bed, his hulking form bent over mine, and begins taking off my clothes. For someone who only wears pants and claims he's a virgin, he doesn't seem to have any trouble disrobing me. At least, not until he gets to my bra.

He studies me for a moment, laying here in my underwear, and the concentrated scowl on his face is almost adorable. He runs his finger along one of the shoulder straps, making me shiver, and then anchors his fingers beneath the underwire, like he's going to try to lift it off over my head.

"Wait, wait, wait." I laugh and push his hands away. He watches as I reach behind me and unhook the bra. I consider taking a moment to educate him on how to use the hooks but decide against it when I see that he's already distracted. I'm mostly naked in front of him, and he's taking me in.

It takes all my willpower not to cover myself up. I want to

put my hands over my breasts that aren't perky. In this position, they sag outwards, my nipples facing opposite directions.
I want to cover the scars on my legs from my younger years,
when the only escape I had from my parents was a straight
razor. I want to cover the places where my stomach is soft and
my flesh puckers.

But Kale is running his hands along my skin, leaving
behind black streaks of ash. And I wonder, how would I feel if
Kale hated himself the way I've always hated myself? What
would I do if he said he didn't want me to look at him because
he doesn't have eyes like mine or didn't want me to touch him
because I might get that black ash on my hands? What if he
tried to turn off the lights so I couldn't see the glorious shape
of his horns?

Kale is beautiful, and if he can be beautiful exactly as he is
then maybe I can too.

I lose track of my thought process when Kale's fingertips
find the elastic band of my underwear. With a questioning
look up at me–one that I answer with a nod–Kale pulls my
underwear down my legs and sets them gently on the bed.
Kale does everything gently, like he's capable of breaking
everything and has to move carefully at all times.

When I'm finally completely naked, he takes me in
completely. And when he gets to the spot between my legs, I
part my knees and let him look. He reaches out one hand and
runs the pads of his fingers through my folds.

A desperate cry makes its way out of my mouth, and I'm
almost embarrassed by it. Even on his best day, Trent never
looked at me like this. He never touched me with reverence
and knelt before me like he was kneeling before an altar.
That's what Kale does now, kneeling on the floor at the end of
the bed and tugging me to the edge.

"You will show me how to please you?" he asks, his voice

uncertain. "Human females are quite different from Isiriel females."

The fiercest warrior in Isiriel, asking for guidance. I smile up at the ceiling. "I thought you said you'd never been with anyone."

"We are all taught both male and female anatomy when we're quite young. Isiriel females have something like, well, like this." He leans back on his heels and sticks his fingers into the side pocket of his pants. "It protrudes from the skin and has ribbed walls on the inside for the ridges of an Isiriel male to stimulate. This brings females much pleasure. You, however..."

With my legs still wide open, he reaches down and parts my folds so that he can see better, the stimulation on my swollen pussy making my toes curl.

"You have...a tunnel," Kale says, amazement in his voice, and I laugh. This isn't exactly how I imagined this going, but I don't mind. This is fun. I can't remember a time I've ever felt comfortable enough in bed to have this kind of fun.

"Yeah, something like that. You put your, um..." I trail off and gesture toward where his cock is still hard. It's a wonder it hasn't popped out of the top of his pants yet. "What do *you* call it?"

"Oh," he says, looking down at himself like he forgot he even had a penis. "My sword?"

Throwing my head back, I howl with laughter. Tears spring to my eyes, and while I'm still trying to catch my breath, Kale crawls up onto the bed beside me. "You're laughing at me," he says, his voice full of mirth.

"It's just such a *guy* thing to call it," I tell him when I can breathe again. His face is just inches from mine, so I hook a hand around the back of his neck and pull his mouth down to mine.

Kissing is different when you're naked. It's not like it was before, when what would happen next was still a bit of a mystery. Now, as he kisses me, Kale's hands find my breasts, lazily touching my nipples before moving on to find the space between my legs. When one of his fingers accidentally grazes my clit, my hips buck, and I moan into his mouth.

Kale pulls away, looking down at me in fascination. "Was that good?"

I nod. "That's my clitoris. To put it bluntly, if you rub it right, I'll come."

"Come where?"

I giggle, covering my face with my hands. "No, Kale. I mean, I'll orgasm."

"Ah." He grins, bringing his hand up to look at the moisture on the tips of his fingers. He examines it the way someone might examine something through a microscope. "This sounds most interesting. And if I lick it?"

In response, that particular bundle of nerves begins to pulse. "I might come a little harder."

Like I've just fired the gun to start a race, Kale scrambles down my body, places a hand on either one of my knees, and licks me all the way from my opening to my clit.

I gasp. Holy shit, it didn't even occur to me how good that hot tongue would feel on me. Somehow it makes the sensation even better as he licks me again and again, like he's tasting an ice cream cone for the first time.

"Show me this *clitoris*," he says, pulling away. His breath puffs out in steamy gusts against me, until I've begun to sweat.

Reaching down with two fingers, I scissor my lips apart. With the other hand, I tentatively rub my clit, holding in a mewl at the sensation. Carefully, Kale pulls my fingers away and replaces them with his warm tongue.

"Ah!" Oh, God. It feels so good. The heat of him and the way he's swirling his tongue around my clit has my hips jerking up off the bed. It doesn't even faze Kale. He settles his hands under my hips and holds my pussy against his mouth, rubbing and licking and eating me up.

And when he starts to rotate his tongue back and forth and back and forth, my eyes roll back in my head. My hands shoot out, grabbing onto the base of his horns. Keeping his head still, I fuck his face, completely unable to stop from writhing on his tongue as my orgasm slams into me.

When the spasms stop, my entire body goes limp, and Kale slowly lowers me to the mattress. My entire body gelatinous, I look up in time to see him put his fingers in his mouth and suck them clean.

Standing, he walks around to the side of the bed and pulls my blanket up over me. "I will let you rest," he says, nothing but a black shadow hanging over me in the light of my bedside lamp.

Exhaustion settles into my bones, but I find it in me to reach for him, my hand just barely grazing his wrist as he turns from me to go to the window. He stops and looks back.

"You can't stay?" I ask, my words heavy.

"I'm afraid not, my love. My king awaits. But I'll be back tomorrow."

I just nod, even though it feels like he's pulling something from the very center of my chest when he finally steps out of my reach.

And it isn't until he's ducked back out of the window and disappeared from sight that I realize he called me "my love."

Chapter Three

Night 3

I've already eaten dinner, taken a shower, and cleaned my room in preparation for Kale coming back tonight, and the sun isn't even close to setting. I'm not really sure what else to do with myself until he gets here, so I get in bed with my head at the foot, so that Kale can see me from the portal, and read.

I've started to grow tired and begin to wonder if I should take a nap before Kale gets here so that I have the energy to spend time with him. But just as I'm putting away my book and settling into the covers, someone knocks on my front door.

I freeze. I really should have listened to Alice and gotten one of those doorbells with the camera so I could see who was outside without having to actually get out of bed. It's most likely someone selling something because the only person who would come to see me would be Alice, and she's still at work. No one else even knows where I live.

I hold my breath and wait for whoever it is to leave, but then they knock again, louder and longer this time. I slowly creep out of bed, trying not to make a sound as I move toward the front door. I stand on my tiptoes to see out the peephole and sigh when I recognize the face on the other side.

Trent.

Unlocking the door, I rip it open. "What is it, Trent?" I'm way too impatient for this. The last thing I want is for Trent to be here when Kale shows up. If Trent is the reason I don't see Kale tonight, I might murder him. "Did you forget something? Because I told you if I find any of your stuff, I'll bring it by."

And then I get a good look at him. His skin is pale and sallow, his hair messy and greasy, like he hasn't washed it in days. He has bags under his eyes, and I briefly wonder if this is what I look like on my bad days, when taking care of myself feels like an impossible task.

"Trent, what are you–"

"I want to get back together."

I immediately feel sick, like I might throw up on his shoes. "Are you kidding? After the stuff you said to me?" Even if he hadn't said anything awful, this would still be a pretty firm *no* from me. I broke up with Trent for a reason.

He runs a hand over his face. "I was just upset. It's hard to live with the fact that the woman you love is breaking your heart because she has a mental illness. I know how you are. I know you get in these funks, and I also know that you'll find your way out of it. When you do, I want to be there for you."

He wants to be there for me *after* the funk? And during, I guess I'm just on my own. I fight not to roll my eyes. This is exactly the reason I broke up with him. When the depressive episodes came for me, Trent was always halfway out the door. He couldn't handle it. And when I managed to re-surface, he was always there for the good stuff, the jokes and the spontaneous dates and the sex.

I've watched your sadness and yearned to hold you. I've seen your fear and longed to comfort you.

Next to Kale, Trent looks like a washed up plastic bag.

"Trent, I appreciate you thinking of me." The nicest thing I could think of under these circumstances. "But I've moved on. And I think you should too."

I start to close the door, but Trent sticks his foot in the opening. The door bounces off the rubber sole of his shoe and springs back open. Trent steps into the house, forcing me back until I'm standing in the middle of the living room. He slams the door shut behind him, and my stomach creeps up into my throat.

"What do you mean, you've moved on?"

Oh, God. Why did I say that? I wasn't thinking.

Trent stalks toward me, and I back away. He's always had a temper, a head just hot enough to throw things across the room in his anger but never hot enough to throw them directly at me. He's never left bruises on my skin, but he's yelled at me like I was a child and raised his hand before thinking better of it.

But there's fire in his eyes now, and I don't think he's going to stop himself this time.

"Trent, you need to leave," I say, trying to stand my ground. "We're done, and you have no right to just let yourself into my home."

His jaw grinds shut, and then he reaches out and latches his hands to my upper arms. I don't have any hope of stopping him as he pushes me back against the living room wall. Trent is bigger than me, stronger.

"Stop it!" I shout, trying to struggle away.

"You stop it," he growls back. "This sickness in your head, it's controlling you. You don't get to treat me like shit just because your brain is all fucked up." One of his hands comes up to wrap around my jaw, and I feel the tears starting behind my eyes. "You don't just get to move on like we were nothing."

I take a deep breath to keep my eyes from going blurry and then I lift my leg hard, kneeing him in the crotch. He grunts and doubles over, letting me go.

Trent is between me and the door, so I run in the only direction I can. I race down the hall, not really sure what I'll do when I get to my room. Lock myself in and call the police, at the very least. Maybe I should just go through the portal. It's there, and Kale is on the other side of it.

I don't get the chance. I'm halfway through my bedroom when Trent smashes into me from behind, knocking us both to the ground. I scramble against the wood, trying to get out from under him and to the window, but he grabs my wrists and holds them to the ground.

"I know you, Annaleigh," he says in my ear, the smell of his hot breath causing me to gag. How did I ever let this man kiss me? "You'll snap out of this."

"Get off of me!" I shout, trying to elbow him in the stomach. But he's got my arm in a tight grip, only letting me move by inches.

"Do you remember what I used to do when you couldn't get out of bed?" he asks, and I stop moving, bile rising up in my throat.

Yes, I remember what he used to do. I squeeze my eyes shut. I let him do it so many times. I didn't have the strength or the will to care when he would crawl into bed with me. I'd spend all day sleeping and feel lethargic by the time he would silently take my clothes off and fuck me from behind, like I was a sex toy. And I would let him because he was my boyfriend, and I felt like I owed it to him. And because when I was numb like that, it felt like love, something I let him do so he wouldn't stop loving me. It never occurred to me that he was just taking advantage of my emptiness.

I'm never going to let him touch me like that again.

He releases my wrist, but his hand snakes down, pushing down my sweatpants.

I take in a deep breath and, as loud as I can, scream, "Kale!" His name bursts out of me, cracking under the force of my lungs.

Trent stops tugging at my clothes. "What the fuck? Who are you screaming for?" His hand comes up to the back of my neck, and he shoves my face into the wooden floor. "I'm the only one who gives a fuck about you, Annaleigh."

I don't know when I started crying, but my warm tears are a puddle under me as Trent growls those words into my ear. But I know they aren't true. Kale cares. Alice cares. They care, and he can't take that from me.

Finding the last bit of breath I have as Trent crushes me between the hard floor and his body, I scream for Kale one more time. One of Trent's hands has found its way under the waistband of my underwear, but when I try to scream for Kale again, he slaps his other hand over my mouth. I'm trying to open my mouth to bite him when something flashes over my head and slams into Trent. I gulp in air now that he's not holding me to the ground and struggle to get my clothes back into place as I shove up onto my knees.

As soon as I do, my eyes meet Kale's. They're on fire, the flames burning so high that they're practically touching the ceiling. He has his arms around Trent, his body latched onto him from behind.

Trent starts to scream, a terrible howling, and that's when I realize that Kale's eyes aren't the only thing on fire. His whole body is on fire, getting brighter and brighter, as the flames cover him–and Trent.

"Kale!" I shout, but it's too late. The two of them are nothing but a blazing inferno as I watch. And then, slowly, the fire starts to die, and all that's left is Kale, smoke rising from his skin and a pile of ashes at his feet.

Stepping over the pile, Kale comes to me. "Are you okay, my love? Did he hurt you?"

I think I'm in shock as he settles his hands on my shoulders, so hot that I have to fight not to wince. I can't believe that just happened. I can't believe Trent did that. I can't believe Kale did that. I can't believe Kale is here.

Kale.

My hands settle on his chest, and I finally notice the patches of broken skin on his bare torso, big pink welts.

"You're hurt," I whisper, confused, my fingertips finding the rough edge of one of the spots. It can't be from the fire. Kale is *made* of fire, so that's impossible.

"It's nothing," he says, tilting my face up to his. When I see the setting sun shining off the wall behind him, I remember what he said about our sun being harmful to his kind. Is that what left these marks?

His fingertips travel down the length of my arm, lightly caressing, and I look down to see that I have finger-shaped marks there, marks that will surely be bruises when I wake up tomorrow. Kale bends and presses his lips to one side.

"I'm sorry," is all he says, but before he can move to the matching finger marks on my other arm, he screams. Falling to his knees, he covers his ears and cries out in pain.

"Kale!" I take his face in my hands, hot in my hold. His eyes flare up again, the flames close to my fingers. "Kale, what is it?"

Without a word, Kale bursts up off the floor and toward the open window. He throws himself out of it and races across my backyard. In seconds, the portal swallows him up.

And I'm left standing there, with a pile of ashes that was once my ex-boyfriend and a broken heart.

CHAPTER FOUR

NIGHT 4

I can't stop crying. I cried all night and all day, and now the sun is starting to set again, and I'm still in bed, crying. It's like there's a never-ending well inside of me that's been opened. And the worst part is that I don't even know *why* I'm crying.

Maybe because my ex tried to rape me. Maybe because Kale killed him. Maybe because Kale just vanished as soon as it was over, seemingly in pain.

What if he's never coming back? What if whatever we could have been is over now?

I cry so hard that I can't breathe.

"Kale," I whisper as the sky outside my bedroom window grows dark. He heard me yesterday. Maybe he'll hear me today. Only, today, I don't have the strength to scream.

When nothing happens, I fall asleep.

My eyes are crusty when I wake, and the house is dark, the full moon spilling in through the window acting as the only light. I lie there for a long time, waiting for my eyes to adjust, and when they do, I gasp. Kale's tall, dark shape stands out against the shadows in the corner, glowing slightly from the fire that burns under the surface of his skin.

I throw myself out of my bed and run to him. When I'm close enough, he lifts me into his arms, and I wrap myself around him. I press my face into his neck and try not to sob.

"I thought I was never going to see you again," I say. "Why did you go?"

Holding me tighter to him, he walks over to the bed and sits down on the edge of it, but I don't let him go. I need the reassurance that he's really here. He seems to understand because he just starts talking, not moving to push me away.

"I did not have permission to come to you when I did. I was supposed to be guarding the king. But when I heard you scream, I couldn't stop myself. I would have torn everyone in Isiriel apart to get to you."

I pull back, meeting his eye as best I can, considering there are no actual eyes, just the small flames that always flicker there. "So, you got in trouble?" It sounds like a childish explanation for what he must have gone through, but he nods nevertheless.

"I broke the law. When I left you, it was because the king forced me back to the portal. I couldn't refuse. He could have had me executed for my actions, but he was merciful."

My blood runs cold. "*Executed*?"

Kale takes my face in his hands. "The king is my closest friend. When I explained to him that you were in danger, he forgave my transgression. There is no need to worry."

"I'm sorry."

Kale's hands press a little harder into my skin, until I can feel the warmth radiating under his palms, pulsing like a heartbeat. "I never want to hear you apologize for the actions of that man, do you hear me?"

"Yes." The word comes out breathless. My body is beginning to respond to the proximity of his. He's pressed against me from hip to shoulder, my hands on his chest, feeling the flex of his muscles.

"I'm sorry to have left you with a mess." His head turns slightly, toward the spot where I had to sweep up Trent's ashes yesterday. I cried as I dumped him in the fireplace, but not for Trent. Trent dug his own grave. No, I cried because Trent had taken Kale away from me.

But now he's back.

"It's okay," I tell him, using a finger to turn his chin back toward me. "You were protecting me."

A small flame flashes in his eyeholes. "I was protecting what's mine. You are mine, Annaleigh, and anyone who hurts you will burn."

All I can do is stare at him. I don't know how to explain the way it feels like the whole universe has shifted. Because I'm suddenly very aware that I *want* to be Kale's. I want to belong to him. I want to be his to protect.

I want to be his wife.

I lean forward and kiss him, reveling in the way he groans into my mouth. I wonder how old he is and how long he's wanted to have sex. He said he waited this long because he wanted me more than anyone else, but surely he's fantasized about being with other females. When I feel his cock getting hard between us, I can't keep from imagining him stroking it, bringing himself to climax while he waited for his mate to show up.

Is it me? *Can* it be me?

Barrelling forward, I rock my hips against the length of him and smile when he hisses like he's in pain. This monster, this perfect male specimen, has never been with anyone. And I fully intend on being his first. His only.

"My love," he says against my mouth, hands latching onto my waist to stop me from moving against him. "If you keep that up, you'll be the death of me."

I smile and press my forehead to his. I'm halfway on top of him now, his hands shifting to cup me from below. He has a handful of each of my mostly bare ass cheeks under my oversized t-shirt. Depression has never done me any favors, but just this once, it did me a solid by convincing me not to put on pants today.

"Tell me about the ceremony," I say.

Kale pulls back, chin tucked so that he can see all of my face. "What ceremony?"

I bite my lip, ready for what I know will come as soon as I speak. "The wedding ceremony. How does it happen?"

The flames in Kale's eyes get brighter, his entire body getting a few degrees hotter, until there's a layer of sweat on my skin. "You wish to know how the Isiriel wed?"

I nod, and if I'm not mistaken, he gets even harder.

"We do not have a wedding ceremony. Because the Isiriel only mate with their spouses, the act of mating is all it takes to claim a husband or a wife."

I blink at him. "Are you saying that all I have to do to be your wife is deflower you?"

His brow wrinkles. "I don't know what the term *deflower* means."

Reaching down, I wrap my hand around him through his pants and give one slow stroke that sends a quiver through his body. "It means that I put this inside me."

His breath trembles from his lips. "Yes. If we mate right now, you would be my bride. For all eternity."

Taking his face in my hands, I press my mouth to his. And then I reach for the hem of my t-shirt and take it off over my head, leaving me bare except for my underwear. I watch the way his chin tilts, the way I can feel his gaze sweeping down my body, taking me in.

"Annaleigh," he finally breathes, "are you certain? If you're not ready—"

"You knew I would be, didn't you?" I didn't even know this thought was in my head until this moment, until it's slipping out all on its own. "You knew that I would fall in love with you."

Looking into my eyes, he shakes his head. "I merely loved you with everything I am and hoped that somehow I could convince you to feel the same."

This time, when I reach for him, I unbutton his pants first, sliding my hand under the fabric and finding that part of him that I've been so curious about. In my hand, he's burning up, like holding something that just came out of an oven. And the ridges...the ridges that I was so sure were there. I feel them now, from the base of him all the way to the smooth tip. I can't help but stare as I push his pants down and the full length of him springs out.

I press my fingertips to each individual ridge, traveling down from the tip in an ever-increasing slope, flaring out at the base. I've never thought a penis was beautiful, but with the orange veins, pulsing bright with the heat of him, traveling around the shaft and in between each ridge, his dick is a work of art.

I'm finally able to tear my eyes from his cock, and when I look up at his face, desire bursts to life in my chest. He has his head thrown back, his mouth open and gasping for air. I marvel at the sharp angle of his horns, dipping so low they almost touch the bed.

And all from just having my hand wrapped around him. Watching closely for his reaction, I keep my hand in place and slide off his lap. Kneeling at the edge of the bed in front of him, I lean forward and put my mouth on him.

He roars so loud that I swear the walls shake. I smile around him and then focus on what I'm doing. I don't know if fire monster dicks work like human dicks, but when I take him as far as I can down my throat and suck on my way back up, he starts panting like he just ran ten miles at a sprint.

"Yes," he says, his hands coming up to cup my face. He seems to come back from the depths of paradise long enough to look down at me. He cradles my face in his hands and smiles. "You're so good at this."

I take my mouth off of him and grin. "Well, unlike some of the people in this room, I'm no blushing virgin."

With gentle hands, he guides my mouth back to the tip of him. He has this strange look on his face, like there's something he can't quite figure out. I watch him, sticking my tongue out and letting the tip of his cock rest on it. He grimaces, almost like he's in pain. Clutching my chin, he pulls my face away from the tip. And then he slips his thumb into my mouth. He slides his thumb back and forth across my tongue, like he's testing the texture of it. He pushes a little further, just a little too far, and I gag.

He immediately slips his finger back out. "I'm sorry," he says, his voice laced with worry.

Something about his softness, about the way he clearly wants to be rough with me but isn't sure if it's going too far, makes me want to be playful. It makes me want to beg him to do whatever he wants with me. With my lips against the underside of his wet cock, I say, "You don't have to worry about hurting me, Kale. You won't break me."

His mouth turns down in the corners. "I could easily break you, my love. I want to know every part of you. I want to learn every bit of your body. But I need your pleasure like I need my own."

I slide my tongue up along the hot ridges of his cock. "This brings me pleasure."

One of his big hands slides up into my hair, lightly fisting. With the smallest movement, he guides me down, until my mouth is resting against his balls. They're so much hotter than the rest of him, almost enough to be uncomfortable, but when he nudges me against them, I happily open my mouth, licking and sucking until he lets out a sigh of relief.

I giggle, a sound that seems to snap him out of his pleasure haze.

"Are you laughing at me?" There's a hint of amusement in his voice that makes me smile.

I push back on my heels and look at him, my huge fire monster, with his thick cock so hard it looks like it's made of steel to match his ferocious horns. "I've never wanted to please anyone this much," I tell him. "But I'm as inexperienced as you are when it comes to pleasing another species. I want to know how to make you feel good."

He bends, running his fingers down my cheek. "You couldn't do anything that didn't please me. Everything you do feels so good I must fight not to lose control. When I've imagined this, I never once thought to imagine you on your knees, with your mouth on my sword. If I tried to lead you, I fear what I would miss out on."

I press my forehead to his knee and sigh. "You make me dizzy with desire, Kale."

He tips my head back, so that I'm looking all the way up at him, hovering so tall, even when he's sitting down. "Then show me how to give you relief, my love."

Surging onto my feet, I crawl back into his lap and attach my mouth to his. His hands cover me in seconds, starting at my shoulders and sliding down to my breasts. One of his claws slides across my nipple, and I moan into his mouth. Kale jerks his mouth from mine, watching closely as he does it again, lightly scratching my other nipple. My mouth falls open on a gasp, and the flames in Kale's eyes burn hotter.

I tug his face down to my chest and watch with satisfaction as Kale's tongue slides along my skin. I want to go slow, but I want him so bad. I want to feel those ridges inside me. So

I dig my knees into the mattress on either side of his hips and push on his shoulders until he's lying on his back. When I straddle him, I have a momentary sense of just how crazy this is. I'm on top of a fire monster who's leaving ash all over my sheets, and I'm about to take his virginity. And then we'll be *married*.

Life certainly is strange.

I shimmy out of my underwear quickly, and then we're naked together, all of his skin against all of mine, and I'm shocked by how right it feels. Everything inside me is calm, like my body has been waiting for this my whole life.

Putting my hands on either side of his head, I bend down until our noses are touching. "Can I have you?" I ask, and his eyes flare again. I wonder, briefly, how long it'll be before I accidentally get burned.

Kale jerks his hips between my legs. The ridges of his cock slide along my clit, and I hold in a scream. That feels better than anything I've ever felt in my life. I'm half-delirious by the time Kale says, "I'm yours to claim, my love."

I don't hesitate. Lifting my hips, I tuck Kale's cock against the entrance of my pussy and slide down onto him. I go in so easily; I'm so wet for him. And when I finally come back out of orbit, delirious from how far he's stretching me, I realize he's trembling. His head is thrown back against the mattress, his horns digging into the sheets.

"Are you okay?" I whisper. My pussy clenches around him, and we both groan.

"This is what I've waited two hundred years for," he says, seeming a bit dazed. And boy, do I relate. He's gripping my hips tight, like he's holding on for dear life.

I want to see him lose control. I want to be the *reason* he loses control. So with my hands on his massive chest, I lift up off of him and slam back down. Flame bursts from Kale's eyes like he's trying to set my whole house on fire. He does something with his hips, a little swirl of a movement, and that's when my focus shoots between my legs. I've been so focused on him, on what he's experiencing, that I didn't notice the way his dick is getting hotter inside me, the way it makes my insides tingle in the most pleasant way. And then one of his ridges pushes right up against my G-spot, and I shriek up at the ceiling. Holy mother of God, that feels good.

"Did I hurt you?" Kale asks, sounding panicked.

I shake my head again and again until I can regain the use of my tongue for actual language. "You aren't going to hurt me," I tell him. The tilt of his mouth tells me he doesn't believe me. I lean forward, pressing my chest into his, so our mouths are inches apart. "If you did hurt me, I think I would like it."

His eyes blaze again, and even though I move out of the way of the conflagration quickly, I hear a sizzle as one of the flames burns the tip of a lock of my hair. Kale hurriedly pulls my hair into a knot at the nape of my neck and holds it there with his fist. I can't decide whether to laugh at the fact that the room now smells like burnt hair or marvel at the fact that having Kale's hand gripping my hair like this is making my pussy throb.

"I can feel it when I do something you like," he says. "I feel you tighten around me." As if to prove his point, he reaches up and pinches one of my nipples. My muscles clench around him, and he huffs proudly.

Two can play at that game. Clenching as hard as I can, I lift up and slam down on him again. His mouth falls open, and his hand tightens in my hair. So I do it again and again, until we're moving in an intoxicating rhythm. My head is bent back, pulled by the strength of Kale's hand. Even though I can't see him, my blurred gaze fixed on the ceiling as I ride him, I can hear every sound he makes, grunts and groans and growls. I can even hear it every time the fire in his eyes burns brighter because of a particularly good circle of my hips or squeeze of my muscles. All of his sounds are liquor to my blood as I slam my eyes closed and let myself feel and hear it all.

After a moment, I feel the press of one of Kale's fingers down low, against my pussy. Without letting go of my hair, he strokes me, all the way from where he's stretching me to my pelvis. When he sweeps back down, his finger brushes against my clit.

I moan up at the ceiling and hear Kale quietly mutter, "There it is."

I smile and suddenly realize that I can't remember ever being so happy during sex. It feels good, Kale so deep that it feels like he's taking up all of the room inside my body, but it's more than that. It's...fun. And then I realize, this is how I'm going to spend the rest of my life. Kale and I are *married* now.

Like he knows exactly what I'm thinking, Kale pushes up into me and strokes my clit hard, and I fall apart. Everything comes crashing down. The only thing left in the universe of my awareness is Kale's hands and the pressure of them.

And then the world tips. Kale has let go of my hair and lifted me off of him. He settles me gently onto the bed beside him and then, while I'm waiting for him to crawl on top of me and push back inside, he fists his cock instead.

I have my mouth open in protest, one hand reaching out toward him so he doesn't have to finish himself off, when he lets out a roar and liquid the color of lava squirts out of his cock. I watch in shock as it spills along his stomach. He's panting, the hand around his dick trembling, but I'm focused on his lava semen. It spills over the side of his stomach and lands on my sheets. While I watch, it melts through the sheet and the top layer of my mattress, leaving behind a steaming black spot.

In terms of afterglow, this isn't the most comforting.

"I should have warned you," Kale says, still breathing heavily.

"You mean, that the state of my organs relies on your ability to pull out in time?"

He rolls his head toward me, one horn coming to rest on the mattress between us. "Yes. There's a lot I didn't quite get the chance to tell you. I thought we would have more time before the mating."

I raise an eyebrow at him. "Is that the nice way of saying it's my fault for peer pressuring you into sex so soon?"

He frowns. "I'm not sure what peer pressure is. I suppose, given the context—"

I put up a hand to stop him. "Does this mean we can't have kids?"

In response, Kale takes my hand and brings it to his stomach. When he presses my fingers against the fluid that's still there, I find that it's only just warm. I guess as long as it has time to cool, it's mostly safe. Well, safe for everyone except my mattress, which now looks like it's had cigarettes put out on it.

"It is a little more complicated," Kale says, "but not impossible."

I pluck a tissue out of the box on my nightstand and clean my hand and his stomach. The mattress will just have to do for now.

Cuddling up to him, I throw a leg over his waist and an arm over his chest. "Can you stay?" Usually by now, he's already halfway to the portal, but given the state of his very warm and very pliant body, I don't think he's going to be moving for a while.

"Yes," he breathes, his voice sleepy. "I will just need to leave before sunrise."

Before the flames in his eyes have gone out completely, I ask, "Did you enjoy your first mating?"

His face stretches into a smile. "There has never been nor will there ever be a night more perfect than this one."

Happiness blooms in my chest. Being close to him like this, I feel safe and content. I feel like I can set aside all the emptiness inside me, if only for a little while. I watch as Kale's breathing slows and then the flames in his eyes slowly burn out. I press myself to him, ready to embrace the new life I just took on.

CHAPTER FIVE

I stare down at my bed. I'm not entirely sure what to do with the sheets that are covered in ash and have holes burned into them. I guess I should just trash them. It's not like I'll be here much longer, right?

I sit on the edge of the bed and fight off the panic that rises in me. It's not that I don't want to go with Kale to Isiriel. He's my husband now, and I knew when I took his virginity last night that I was going to have to go to his realm with him. It was kind of one of the conditions of the whole thing.

But it's one thing to know you have to do something and another thing to actually do it. I'm about to leave my entire life behind, my entire *planet* behind, to move to a fire planet where human beings are minorities and everyone else has horns and fire skin.

I'm starting to spiral.

I rush to the window and look out. Kale should be here any moment, and I know that when he gets here, I'll feel better. He'll hold me and kiss me and tell me beautiful things, and the idea of going to a different realm with him will be easier.

Plus, maybe he's right about what it could do for my mental health. Maybe being away from the house where I took care of my grandmother and then watched her die will do me some good. And Kale assures me that I'll still be able to get my meds there, thanks to the human doctors that have crossed over. According to him, the human village on Isiriel is very much like Earth.

I focus on the glimmer in the yard that I know now is the portal. In the dark, it feels almost impossible to see, but sometimes I can spot it when the sun is up. While I wait for Kale, my mind floats back to last night, how gentle he was even when he clearly wanted to be rough, how he held me as he slept, how he woke me before the sun came up with a gentle kiss and a promise to return tonight.

I can't wait to see him. I've never felt like this before. I've had boyfriends, but I've never had someone who was so much *more*. I've never had someone who I thought I might actually want to spend the rest of my life with.

And now I have a husband.

My stomach does a cartwheel. I lean out the open window, my hands on the sill. I feel a kind of desperation in my blood. I guess, in a way, I keep expecting it to not be real. I keep waiting for the moment when I'll wake up from this dream, the moment when Kale will disappear forever, and I'll have to go back to my life here that I've never really felt like I fit into, the life I can't find my place in.

Maybe, all along, it was because my place is in Isiriel.

Like he can feel that I need him, Kale suddenly appears in the portal. He comes in horns first, bending low to duck through and then straightening to his full height. When his eyes fix on the window and see me, the flames in them burst like fireworks, and it sends a giggle up my throat.

I'm halfway out the window before I even know what I'm doing. I race across the yard and launch myself into Kale's arms. He lifts me high, his hands on my ass, and kisses me. His tongue finds mine as he walks us back to the window. He bends to set me on the sill and then gets on his knees in the grass, and I wonder if he's just going to fuck me right here. My house faces the woods, and even though I have neighbors, they aren't likely to be in their backyards at this time of night, so if Kale wants to go down on me right here, I'm perfectly fine with it.

He smiles as his hands push my dress up my legs. It's just a summer dress, flimsy and light, but I wanted to wear something nice for him tonight, our first real night together as husband and wife.

My hand finds his on my thigh, and I lace our fingers together. This is the realest thing I've ever felt in my life.

Somewhere in the distance, I hear a noise that captures my attention, if just for a moment. A familiar slam. Kale kisses the inside of my thigh, and I try to focus, try to ignore the world around us, but then I hear a soft voice calling my name.

Grabbing onto one of Kale's horns, I shove him away from me and almost stumble back into my bedroom through the window. Kale reaches out to catch me with a hand behind my back. I turn and slide into my room, but when Kale moves to follow me in, I push him back out into the yard.

"It's Alice," I hiss, just as Alice calls my name again, this time much closer. She's coming down the hallway. She has a key, and she must have let herself in. And now she's coming to my room, and she's going to see Kale, and...

"Annaleigh, are you home?" Alice starts to push the bedroom door open slowly.

"Go!" I whisper to Kale, but he doesn't move, and I guess I can't blame him. The last time someone was in my house, it was Trent, and he was attacking me.

I spin around in time to see Alice step into my bedroom. Her eyes go to my bed first because where else would I be? And then she scans the room and sees me by the window. My heart hammers in my chest, banging in my ears so loud that I can barely think.

"What are you...?" Alice starts, and then she sees him. I see her eyes shift and focus on Kale on the other side of the window.

She screams.

"Alice!" I shout over the sound of her shrieks. "Wait! It's okay!"

But she doesn't hear me. She turns and runs from the room, and I almost feel relieved. If she runs away now, I can let the matter rest for tonight and explain what's going on in the morning.

I hear Alice's footsteps pad down the hall, and I turn back to Kale. "Maybe you should go," I tell him regretfully, but he does the opposite. Gently nudging me aside, he climbs in through the window.

"I think I should stay," he says, his voice much rougher than I'm used to hearing it. "If your friend is upset–"

Before he can finish, Alice reappears in the doorway. But this time, she's holding a knife, the biggest knife I have. Beside me, Kale's entire body starts to flame, a slow and insistent burning.

"Kale, no," I say to him before taking a step toward Alice, my hands up like I'm placating a rabid animal. "Alice, just listen."

"What is that thing?" she shouts, holding the knife up in front of her.

"It's just Kale. He won't hurt you."

Her panicked eyes turn to me, wide and white. "You're possessed!" she shouts. "You're possessed! We have to get rid of it!"

"Alice, no." I try to stay calm, but Alice stalks forward, the knife at the ready. Behind me, Kale shoves me aside, out of Alice's way. I fall onto my bed and shoot back up. There's Alice, coming at Kale with a knife, and there's Kale, his body bright like the sun now, and without thinking, I jump between them.

And the kitchen knife slides smoothly into my stomach.

I'm aware of so many things at once: the pain where the knife has begun to destroy my insides, the horrified look on Alice's face as she realizes what she's done, the earth-shattering roar that erupts from Kale's mouth.

His hands come around me, nothing but smoke and ash now as he lifts me into his arms.

I can't breathe. I can't think. My mouth opens, but all that comes out of it is blood.

"I must get you to Isiriel," he says, turning for the window. My head lulls back, and the world is suddenly upside down. But before Kale takes me out through the window, he pauses and the world swings as he turns back to Alice.

"If she dies," I hear him say in a distant voice, my ears starting to go muffled, "I will return to kill you."

"No," I try to choke out, but I just cough.

And then the world goes black.

EPILOGUE

I wake up in darkness. I have no idea where I am. I can feel something soft underneath me, a bed most likely, but in front of my eyes, it's only black. I reach out with one hand.

Stone. A stone wall.

I roll over and there he is. Kale sits beside the bed, his head down, his angular horns pointed right at me.

And it all comes back. Alice, the knife, Isiriel.

Isiriel. Is that where I am?

"Alice," I whisper, and Kale's head jerks up. He's immediately on me, his hands on my face and then my stomach and then my face again.

"You are awake," he says, and I nod.

"Alice, is she okay? You didn't...you didn't hurt her, did you?"

He shakes his head. "I would have only hurt her if you had died. But you are very much alive." He smiles as he says this, his voice coming out a little breathless.

"It wasn't her fault," I say, but when his eyes blaze with anger, I figure it's best to not try to win this one. He's not going to hurt her, and that's all that matters. At least, I think he won't. He said he won't unless I die, and I'm not going to die, right?

I press a hand to my stomach and sit up, examining myself. I'm naked, and where I should have a fatal wound, there's only my perfectly intact skin. "I don't understand," I say, looking up at Kale. "What did you do?"

"I brought you to the Healing Waters. It is a pool here in the caves of Isiriel. No one understands its magic. It cannot heal every wound, but it healed yours, and now you're safe and well."

I touch my stomach, poke and prod at it, feel the solidity of my own body. It's a comfort, for sure.

"The king is eager to meet you."

"He is?"

Kale has a strange look on his face, his mouth twisted into a grimace. "There is something I should have told you about earlier, something we have to do."

Anxiety pulls my chest tight. It's not like I thought this whole thing was going to be a piece of cake. I knew there would be an adjustment period, but I wasn't ready for him to spring anything on me this quickly.

"Okay..."

Kale sighs, wilting a little. "You asked me if there was a marriage ceremony, and I told you there wasn't. And technically, that was true. There isn't a marriage ceremony. But there *is* a mating ceremony."

"Okay..."

He tilts his chin away from me, like he's avoiding my gaze. He looks like a dog with its tail between its legs. "The mating ceremony requires that we mate in front of the king."

My brain sputters to a halt. "Wait. We have to have sex in front of the fire monster king?"

For a moment, Kale doesn't move, and then he smiles. "Fire monster?"

Oops. I guess I haven't really let that little nickname slip out in the time I've known Kale. I know he's not just a fire monster. He's an Isiriel captain. "I'm sorry. It's just what I've taken to calling you in my head." I pull the blanket on the bed up over my chest, suddenly feeling very exposed at the thought of someone other than Kale seeing me naked. "Everyone in Isiriel has to perform this mating ceremony?"

Kale nods. "Everyone who is married to an Isiriel. I believe other races have their own mating traditions. This is ours." His eyes sweep down my body. "We can perform the ceremony another time if you are not physically able yet."

"No," I say quickly. "I feel completely and entirely healed. Not even a headache. I'd like to complete the ceremony, so that we can be married in Isiriel." A thought creeps into my mind, and I scowl at him. "The king won't be *joining* us, will he?"

Kale's eyes burst into high flame, and he takes my face in his hands. "No. You are *my* bride. No one but me will touch you from this day forward."

My stomach fizzes pleasantly. "Okay," I say, breathless.

Kale gives me a nod, like the matter is final, and then stands. Going to a trunk in the corner, he opens it and pulls out a white dress, plain and simple. He looks at me questioningly and then reaches into the trunk for another one. This one is blue, with little beads along the hem.

"I purchased several outfits for you from the humans in the village. If you don't like any of them, I can take you into town tomorrow and we can buy new ones."

I crawl out of the bed, not missing the way his eyes flare higher at the sight of my naked body, and reach for the blue dress. It's shorter than the white one and has thick straps instead of long, lace sleeves. It'll be more comfortable to wear in this hot cave.

As I pull the dress over my head, I ask, "Is this where you

live?" The stone room we're in is quite small, big enough just for his bed and a small table, which sits beside the trunk. It's really not a living space big enough for two people.

"It is, but now that we are married, we will be given a home big enough for us and a family, should we choose to have one."

I settle the dress into place and look up at him. He's waiting patiently for me, and as soon as I'm ready, he places his hands on my shoulders and bends down to kiss me. What starts as something gentle quickly turns into me trying to climb him, but he laughs and sets my feet back on the ground.

Holding my face in his hands, he says, "It is a dream that you're here."

———

The cave the Isiriel live in is very intricate. We take several turns and corners, passing by openings and rooms as we go. I feel the eyes of people, their presence, but we move so quickly, and I have to keep my eyes forward not to lose Kale in the maze.

We pass a room with a giant pool in it, and my feet stutter to a halt. I wonder if that's where Kale brought me, if those are the Healing Waters he spoke of that saved my life.

When he sees that I've fallen behind, Kale reaches out his hand to me. "Come, my love. We've kept the king waiting long enough."

I take his hand and he leads me, finally, into a huge room. Where the ceilings of the cave have been just tall enough for Kale to fit up until now, this room has massively tall ceilings and a river of lava flowing through the center of it. As we walk through, I see a glimmer of something, and I realize it's a portal. Kale passes by it like it's not even there, but I stare at it as we go past. Is that the portal back to Earth?

And then my eyes fall on the throne in the center of the room, and I stop walking. Because on that throne is a creature even bigger than Kale. Like Kale, he has ashen skin and veins made of fire running along his body. But his horns are different from Kale's. Where Kale's come from his head and then bend up in a sharp ninety-degree angle, the king's twist like a corkscrew and seem to go on forever toward the ceiling.

When he sees us approaching, he stands from his throne and lowers his chin to nod at Kale. And when he speaks, his voice seems to boom loud against every crevice of the cave. "Captain, I'm glad that you've returned." He settles his gaze on me and presses one large, claw-tipped hand to his chest. "And Annaleigh, I'm happy to see that you're well, though I sincerely wish we were meeting under better circumstances."

I've never curtsied before, never had reason to, but I attempt a bow now and immediately feel ridiculous.

As if to confirm how silly I look, the king laughs, a gurgling noise low in his throat in concert with the fire that joyfully flares up in his eyes. "Oh, that won't be necessary," he tells me, putting a single finger under my chin to raise my face. "You are married to the second-most powerful man in Isiriel, which makes you the highest-ranking female, and the highest-ranking female bows to no one."

I just gape at him. "Me? Highest-ranking?"

He shrugs, and his mouth pulls into a deeply handsome smile. I don't know how the Isiriel define beauty, but between his smile, his extremely muscled body, and his deep voice, the Isiriel king is pretty sexy in my book. So when he leans forward and flashes his sharp teeth at me, I can't help but blush. "I have no queen and no daughters. And as you are the highest-ranking female, I hope you'll agree to be an ambassador for the humans in the village. It would bring great help to everyone in the kingdom."

As if he knows what I was thinking a moment ago, Kale's

hand circles my upper arm, and he yanks me back against him. I feel a rumble against my back that I'm fairly certain is Kale growling.

The king chuckles again. "No need to be defensive, Captain. I would never dream of laying a hand on your bride." He seems to sober then. "Speaking of which, I do believe a ceremony is called for." He tilts his chin toward me. "Kale told me that the two of you mated in your realm. While you are, for all intents and purposes, married, we do have a way of doing things here in Isiriel. Do you feel well enough to perform your mating ceremony?"

Anxiety ripples through me. I wasn't prepared for this, didn't know it was coming, and now it's here, and I have to do it, or I can't be married to Kale. Trembling, I nod. "I feel healthier than I ever have. I'm ready."

The king nods and turns back to his throne. As he settles, two Isiriel males appear and lower a large rug onto the stone floor in front of me. I suppose everyone wants me to be comfortable while I have sex in front of them. I glance over my shoulder at Kale who bends and takes my hand in his.

"It will only be the three of us when we begin. You need only pretend we're back in your room, just the two of us."

I roll my eyes. "Easier said than done."

His other hand finds the hem of my dress, the tips of his claws lightly raking up the inside of my thigh. "Would it be easier if I were to blindfold you?"

While the idea is actually fairly appealing, I shake my head. I want to be strong enough to do this for him. He crossed realms to be with me. This is the least I can do in return.

"Before we begin," the king says, his voice booming, "Annaleigh, I must ask you, are you here of your own volition? Have you chosen this male as your husband of your own free will?"

I smile, some of the anxiety settling quietly into something more peaceful. "Yes. I chose Kale. I love him."

Another growl escapes Kale, but this one is different. It isn't meant to threaten. It's almost...a surprised noise.

The king nods, seemingly satisfied, and then motions toward the rug on the ground. I'm not sure what I'm supposed to do until Kale presses his mouth to my ear and says, "On your hands and knees, my love."

Despite the fact that a person I've known for all of three minutes is watching, I get excited at the command in Kale's words. For someone who lost his virginity yesterday, he seems to know exactly what he's doing. I wonder how many of these ceremonies he's witnessed.

I'm shocked at the way my pussy responds when I kneel down on the rug. I've never done anything like this before, and it feels so deliciously forbidden. All of my nerves have melted into curious desire. By the time Kale crouches behind me and grabs onto my hips, I'm wet and ready for him.

Kale slides my dress up, baring me to him, and despite my better judgment, I can't keep myself from glancing up at the king and seeing the mild interest in his eyes as he watches Kale take my ass in his hands.

When Kale's cock, completely hard, presses against my backside, I whimper. I remember the way he felt inside me, the way I came harder than I ever have before, faster than I ever have before, the way those ridges pressed against every good nerve ending inside me. I'm desperate to feel it again.

Kale presses the tip against my opening, but then he stops. I turn my head to look at him, and he smiles. And then he wraps a hand around the back of my neck and pushes me down toward the ground, until my cheek is pressed to the rug, my hips still in the air.

He slams into me.

I scream, squirming on my knees at the pain and the pleasure of it. I feel torn in half, but it feels so good, like this was exactly what my body was made for. My mouth falls open, and my eyes are barely able to focus, but for a brief second, I see the look on the king's face. He's watching me closely, a worried expression looking back at me, probably unsure whether or not Kale is hurting me.

But when Kale pulls out and pushes back in, the ridges on his cock gliding against my inner muscles, I moan with ecstasy, and the king smiles and turns his face away just slightly.

"You are mine before the king of Isiriel," Kale says. "No other will ever touch you, or they will meet death."

"Yes," I whisper, eyes falling closed. "Yes, Kale. I'm yours."

He fucks me hard, brutally, so different from what happened between us last night. I love every second of it. When I feel my orgasm starting to build, I reach between my legs, searching for my clit, but Kale pushes my hand away, replacing it with his own. He takes me, pounding into me so hard that all of me trembles with each thrust. My teeth rattle, and my skirt billows around me like harsh waves on the ocean. Kale's fingers locate my clit, and I explode.

Slamming my eyes closed and crying out, I feel like I'm being set on fire, like Kale is covering us both in a blaze so bright, even though I know it isn't true. Before it's over, before my muscles have stopped clenching over and over, Kale pulls out of me and turns to spill onto the rug. Somehow, it doesn't burn a hole in it.

I know I should move. I literally have my entire ass and pussy in the air for anyone to see, but I can't get my limbs to uncurl. As soon as he's caught his breath, Kale crawls over to me and lowers my dress, covering me back up. He helps me onto my feet, though I'm wobbling so much that he has to support me with a hand at my back.

The king smiles at both of us. It feels ridiculous to be standing in front of him with my own juices sliding down the inside of my leg, my pussy still spasming every few seconds, and my lungs struggling to breathe normally.

"I'm very happy for the two of you. Truly." His gaze flickers over to me. "Kale has hardly spoken of anything else since he caught sight of you in the portal. I hope you'll be happy here in Isiriel, and I hope we will be good friends. If there is anything you need, please ask."

Even though he told me not to, I bow, just my head, the way Kale did when we first arrived. "Thank you, Your Majesty."

The king chuckles again. "Get some rest. Kale, I'll see you back at your post in two days' time. That should be enough time to get your bride settled into your new home."

"Yes, My King." Kale bows, and then he bends and lifts me into his arms. I don't fight him. I'm exhausted. I suppose almost dying and then having your brains pounded out by your enormous husband can really wear you out.

As Kale walks me through the cave, I nestle in against his chest, my mind racing with everything that's changed now. I've started a completely new life, literally overnight.

One thought keeps coming back to my mind. "Alice, is she alright?"

"I promised not to kill her if you survived, so I can only assume she's well."

I tilt my head back to look up at him. His eyes are ablaze, lighting our way. "I just mean, she doesn't know whether or not I'm okay. All she knows is that I vanished in the arms of a giant monster after she stabbed me. She's probably sick with worry."

"Once you're settled, the king will give you leave to visit the human realm to see her."

I press my hand to his chest, and he stops walking. "Really? He would let me do that?"

Kale smiles down at me. "The king is very generous. You

won't be permitted to travel back and forth, but he will let you go back to inform your friend that you're safe."

I sigh, feeling the worry melt away. And then everything else hits, the knowledge that I'm married to this person, that I'm going to spend the rest of my life with him, that I have a chance at something new with him, here in Isiriel.

"I love you, Kale."

He bends to kiss me. "I love you, too, Annaleigh."

With a smile, he keeps walking, and I may not know these halls yet, but I'm fairly certain we've gone much further than we did to get to the throne room. We should be back to our room already.

"Where are we going?" I ask.

But Kale doesn't answer. He keeps walking, and somewhere in front of us, I see light. Not firelight, like the rest of the cave, but sunlight.

Kale walks right out into it, and I have to shield my eyes. The sun is...blue, and the light it's giving off is an odd color, like a permanent solar eclipse, casting odd shadows. We're standing on the edge of a cliff that overlooks mountains and a long valley that stretches out in front of us. Kale sets me on my feet and points across the valley, to a little town that's tucked into the side of one of the mountains. It's far away, but I can make out houses and roads.

"That's the village where the humans live." He gestures behind us. "This is the High Mountain. There are other mountains and other villages, but this mountain and this village are ours. Welcome to Isiriel."

King of the Fire Monsters

King of the Fire Monsters

I came to Isiriel looking for happiness.

What I found was a cranky fire monster king.

He wants to marry me to repair the relationship between humans and Isiriel.

But I don't like him, even if he is hot.

I'm about to learn the truth about what it's like to be married to the king of the fire monsters.

Chapter One

There's a burn mark in the middle of Annaleigh's bed, and I can't stop staring at it. It's like someone stuck a cigarette into the mattress. The last time I saw my best friend was two weeks ago, when she came back through the portal to Isiriel to tell me that she and her fire monster boyfriend, Kale, are officially trying to have their first baby, a process that's apparently complicated because his cum is lava.

I stare at the hole in the mattress. Did...did Kale come on the mattress, and that's why there's a hole? I exert a full-body shudder and jump back up off the bed.

Ever since Annaleigh went through that portal to another realm that's mostly inhabited by fire monsters, I've been keeping an eye on her house. She told me a while ago that I could move in because she isn't really planning on coming back now that she's happily shacked up with her boyfriend—who has *horns* and *fire instead of eye balls* and *LAVA CUM*. But I digress.

I told her I didn't need to stay in her house because I was living with my fiancé, Matt.

Well…now Matt is fucking some woman he met in his robotics class, and I guess I'm moving into Alice's house.

Just maybe not into the room where her boyfriend got his lava cum on the mattress.

My eyes flicker to the window, to the portal in the backyard. The last time Annaleigh came through, she showed me where the portal is. From this distance, it's just a shimmer, like someone sprinkling fairy dust from the sky. But she told me that if I get closer to the portal, I'll be able to see into the realm on the other side, Isiriel. She described the place she lives as a mountain cave.

Going to the window, I shove it open, immediately feeling stupid because the house does, in fact, have a back door. I don't have to crawl out the frickin' window. But here I am, climbing out the window and approaching the portal slowly. Annaleigh seems so much happier since she went through. She's found a guy who loves her—even if he is a fire monster—and a purpose, which is something she swears she never really had here on Earth.

Maybe if I go through that portal, I'll find purpose, too.

I'm standing in front of it now, and it's almost like looking through a keyhole, if the keyhole was shaped like a very large vertical eye socket. I can see fire and stone, and possibly the end of one sharp horn.

I look back at Annaleigh's house. If I stay here, I could be happy. I would have a place to stay that's one hundred percent paid for. I have a pretty good job, and I'm working on getting a bachelor's degree. I wouldn't even have debt after school is over because I got a free ride to the university I'm attending.

But I'm curious.

I turn back to the portal. Something flashes across it, and before I know it, I've stepped forward.

The sunlight fades immediately, swallowed by darkness. My eyes are trying to adjust to the shadow, but before they can, something warm and sharp settles against my neck, and I freeze. My eyes slowly scroll to the left to see a very familiar fire monster, eyes alight with fire. A fire monster who's holding a sword to my neck.

"Kale?" I'm only about fifty percent sure it's Annaleigh's boyfriend. He's the only fire monster I've ever met, and I don't know if they all look the same, or if there's some way to tell them apart. Maybe this is some other fire monster that just looks like Kale.

"Alice," the monster growls out, and I feel my shoulders fall in relief. It *is* Kale. But he's still holding a sword to my throat... "I'm sorry to have to do this, but you came through the portal without leave to do so. I must take you to the king."

He sounds so regretful of that fact that it strikes fear into my chest. "What will the king do?" I ask Kale as he takes the sword away from my throat and then turns me in the direction of a large doorway cut into the rock of the mountain. He wraps his very large, ashen hand around my arm, and I have a flash of the first time I met him, when I caught him and Annaleigh together and thought he was a demon trying to possess her. That was nearly a year ago, and now it all seems so ridiculous.

We walk by a throne made of stone in the middle of the room, sitting before a river of magma. The heat of it makes me sweat as we pass by it and into a room on the other side of an arched doorway. We stop just inside the room, which isn't covered in the orange-tinted shadow of the other room. This room is dark and blue-hued.

Kale turns his head and speaks to another guard standing by the door. "Send word to the Ambassador that she's needed in the king's dining hall immediately."

Dining hall. That makes sense. Stretched out before us in the shadow is a long table with one chair situated at the head of it. And just as I'm wondering where the king is, a large, dark form steps into the room, his fire eyes finding us immediately. He stops inside the door and reaches over to something attached to the wall. I'm not entirely sure what he's doing until a flame appears at the end of his hand. He touches his hand to the long stick he's holding, and the room is suddenly much brighter. A torch. He reattaches it to the wall.

Now that there's light in the room, I have to hold in a gasp at the sight of the monster before me. Just like Kale, his skin is the color of ash, and those veins cover the length of his body, glowing orange with the heat of fire or whatever is going on inside them. But unlike Kale, the king's horns aren't sharp and geometric. His steel horns spiral straight up out of his head, and where Kale's body is slim and sinewy, the king's is broad and shockingly muscular.

"Captain," he says, his voice deep and his fire eyes flaming up just a little higher when he addresses Kale. "What has happened?" His chest is bare, showing off surprising muscles, pecs and abs well defined. All he's wearing is a pair of lose-fitting linen pants, and when my eyes fall compulsively to the bulge between his legs, I look away quickly, my face heating.

"My king," Kale says, "This woman came through the portal unbidden. I have sent for the Ambassador to speak on her behalf."

It's weird the way I can tell the king's gaze has shifted to me even though he doesn't have actual eyeballs. Something about the shape of his eyebrows. He moves to the table and sits down, never taking his gaze off me. "Coming through the portal without authorization is punishable by death."

My heart seizes up hard in my chest. "But I didn't know–"

The king's hand comes down hard on the table in front of him, causing everything on it to rattle ominously, and the fire in his eyes crackles high, engulfing most of his head. I jerk away, doing my best to put Kale between the king and me, on the off chance that Kale would choose protecting me over his loyalty to his monarch. I'm thinking chances are slim.

The king points one long, clawed finger at me. "You will not speak in my chambers unless you have been asked a question."

"My king!"

I spin around in time to see my best friend, Annaleigh, come through the stone doorway. Her eyes flicker over to me, and even though I want to run to her, she gives a subtle shake of her head as she steps up to Kale's other side and lowers her chin in the direction of the king.

"My king, please allow me to speak on behalf of our visitor."

"Visitors request entrance. This human is trespassing."

"My king," Annaleigh says again, and I wonder why *she* gets to speak whenever she wants, and I don't. Did Kale call her an *ambassador*? "Please consider that this woman doesn't understand the laws and customs of Isiriel. Those on Earth don't even know of the portal's existence, so they don't understand the political importance of receiving clearance to travel through it. I beg you, my king, let her speak. She means Isiriel no harm."

The flame in the king's eyes has fallen to a mere flicker, like the flame of a large candle, and I get the distinct feeling that the king is very fond of my best friend. He lowers his chin in a nod and then looks away from her to turn to me. He leans one elbow on the table, regarding me. "Alright, human. Speak. Tell me who you are and why you came here."

I glance over at Annaleigh, and she smiles at me, which brings me a lot of comfort. She won't let anything bad happen to me. I feel sure of it. I turn back to the king. "My name is Alice, and I came here because Annaleigh told me that she's been really happy since she came here, so, I don't know, I thought I might be happy here, too."

For a long time, the king doesn't say anything, just stares at me. And then he looks away, down at the table, like he's reading something there. "You weren't happy in your own realm?"

The memories hit me like a mallet: walking in on my fiancé fucking someone else, the way he tried to apologize, the ring I left on his kitchen table.

"No," I say confidently to the king. "My fiancé, the man I was supposed to marry, I caught him with someone else."

I hear the slightest gasp of breath come from Annaleigh's direction.

The king seems to have a confused wrinkle to his brow. "Caught him doing *what* with someone else? Planning war? Did he betray his country?"

Despite the precarious situation in which I find myself, this makes me laugh. "No. I caught him having sex with another woman."

At this, the king's flaming eyes climb higher. "What fool would think he could find a human female more desirable than you?" He asks this question so seriously, like he's expecting an actual answer, but all I can do is sputter. When nothing actually manages to come out of my mouth, the king just waves me off.

"You're free to leave." He tilts his chin in my direction, and there's a slight upturn of one side of his mouth. I get a weird feeling in my stomach. Is this giant fire monster...cute? "Alice," he says, my name coming out almost like a purr, "welcome to Isiriel."

CHAPTER TWO

1 MONTH LATER

I'm tending my garden in the strange blue light of the Isiriel sun when a shadow falls over me. I put a hand up to shield my eyes and look up at the Isiriel male that's just approached my cottage. He's small compared to the other males I've seen that come from the High Mountain, but his eyes are still glorious flames in his head.

"Hi," I say, dusting my hands off on my pants. It's a strange thing, but I discovered when I settled into life in Isiriel that I like to garden. It's something I never really considered when I lived on Earth, but Isiriel is a much more simple place than Earth, and things move slowly here. When faced with how I wanted to spend my time and what kind of job I wanted to take on to benefit the community, I chose gardening. I don't grow vegetables like some of the other gardeners here, but I grow flowers, beautiful flowers that I barter on the weekends for everything I need to survive. A bundle of flowers called Liyriatha got me the pants I'm wearing right now.

"The king requests your presence." That's all he says, and

then he just stares at me, his clawed fingers laced together in front of his hips.

"Do you know why?" I ask him, feeling feisty. The Isiriel king, King Cage, sure is bossy. Annaleigh, who doesn't live in the village with the humans but in the High Mountain with Kale, assures me that King Cage is actually very kind-hearted, but all I ever hear is that he summoned this person here and sent that person there. There's a reason America isn't a big fan of monarchy.

"The king requests your presence," the monster repeats.

I sigh and stand. "Should I change?" I'm in dirty cargo pants and a tank top, not exactly attire to visit a king in.

"The king requests—"

"Jesus, I get it. Okay, I'm coming."

It's a long walk to the High Mountain, and by the time we get there, I'm sweating. But inside, it's cool. At least, it is until we get to the throne room. The throne room is way hotter than the rest of the mountain, which I've walked through several times, because it's where the river of magma is, which is probably exactly why it's the throne room, knowing King Cage and his arrogance.

And then I'm standing in front of the empty throne, and when I turn to ask where the king is, the guard that led me here is gone. I'm alone in the room. I glance over at the alcove that leads to the portal to Earth. I wonder if anyone cares that I'm gone.

"Alice."

I turn at the sound of the king's voice. He walks into the room, so big and broad that it seems like he takes up all the extra space, and I forget that I'm supposed to bow until he's already seated on the throne. And then I mostly bow just so that I have an excuse to stop looking at him. I don't really understand the biology of it, but even though he's a fire monster, King Cage is...well...hot. It doesn't seem to matter to my libido that he has fire for eyes and that I can see his lava blood beneath his ashen skin, skin that leaves dark marks behind at every touch, according to Annaleigh.

I dip my chin, and when I look back up, there's a curious smirk on his face. Arrogant bastard. I guess you get to be arrogant when you're the king.

"The Captain of the Guard tells me you're integrating well into society here in Isiriel."

I lace my fingers behind my back. "Oh. Well, that was a kind thing for him to say."

He does that thing with his brow bone that tells me he's giving me a skeptical look, even though he doesn't have eyebrows. "Would you disagree?"

I shrug. "I suppose it depends on your definition. I just plant flowers. I'm not exactly a useful contributor to the community."

He regards me for a moment. "Flowers are nice." I shrug again, and I can tell he doesn't like it because he heaves a heavy sigh. "I asked you here because I have a proposition for you."

I just scowl at him. I'm not really sure what to think. Is he...asking me for a favor? "What kind of proposition?"

He sits up straight, not slouching in that cocky way that he does, and I watch his chest rise and fall as he takes a deep breath. "A political proposition."

"Oh." Now I'm even more confused. How am I going to help him politically? "And you're sure I'm the right person to ask?"

"I'm certain of it."

There's so much confidence in his voice that I start to feel confident as well. Whatever it is, he wouldn't be asking me if he didn't think I could do it. "Okay. What is it?"

"I need a wife."

I feel like someone just splashed me with cold water. I just blink at him, my brain trying to process his words. "I'm sorry,

I don't really understand. What does that have to do with me?" I mean, if he wants a wife, can't he just...go out and pick one? I'm sure any of the Isiriel females would be happy to marry King Cage and have his beautiful fire-breathing babies.

He taps his long, clawed fingers on the armrest of his throne, over and over, a little *click-click-click-click*. "I need to marry a human woman."

"Why is that?"

"There's been a rift between the Isiriel and the humans. Some of the humans believe it's unfair that I should rule over them. They want their own human rulers. I don't want to split the kingdom, but the throne belongs to someone of my line, someone with Isiriel blood."

"Your people were here first, weren't they?"

He smiles, and I'm fairly certain it's the first time I've seen his perfectly white teeth, so stark against his dark skin. "So, you do understand then."

I feel a shock of something in my stomach, something like...pride. That he's speaking to me like I'm on his level, even though I'm as far from his level as anyone in this realm could possibly be. That he's discussing such important matters with me. It makes *me* feel important.

"I feel that marrying a human, allowing a human to take the role of queen, could repair some of the friction between your people and mine. They would feel they have a voice and a place here, a true place."

"So, you'd like me to help you find the right wife then? Be a mediator between you and the humans?"

"No."

I want to groan and demand that he just spit it out then, but I have to be polite. He's a king, after all. "Then what—" I start, but he cuts me off.

"I want *you* to be my wife."

I've heard him wrong. I know I've heard him wrong. That

wasn't what he meant to say. Maybe he mixed up his English. Kale still does that sometimes, even though all the Isiriel speak it fluently. But he's looking at me so expectantly, and I know he didn't use the wrong words.

"I...But...You don't even know me." He does that thing where he raises one eyebrow without actually having eyebrows. "...my king," I add to the end of my sentence, the way Annaleigh and Kale are so fond of doing.

King Cage rises from his throne and steps toward me. I resist the urge to take a step back as he gets closer, towering over me and radiating so much heat that just standing this close to him, close enough that I have to tip my head back to look up at him, is making me sweat even more. He bends, until I'm almost blinded, looking into those two small flames in his head.

"I do know you, Alice. I know that you're stubborn and strong-willed and very bad at being obedient. I believe you'll make a good ruler. You would, of course, always answer to me, but you would be queen over human and Isiriel alike, and I need someone who can put an Isiriel male in his place as easily as disciplining a dog."

My heart thumps in my ears so loud I know he can hear it. He has to be able to hear it. But what irrationally comes out of my mouth is, "You have dogs here?"

His mouth curls up, and I find my eyes glued to his lips. I see Isiriel males all the time, walking around the village or the mountain, but never, not once, have I wondered what it would be like to kiss one of them. Until now.

"I'll give you time to consider my offer." He straightens away from me and turns back to his throne. "You're dismissed."

Chapter Three

"His wife!"

Annaleigh shoves a carrot in her mouth and shrugs. "Is it really that surprising?"

My mouth falls open. "Uh, yeah! He's known me for a month! And in that time, we've spoken, like, three times! And he hates me! I broke his precious Isiriel laws. And I don't like him either."

One of Annaleigh's eyebrows arches. "You don't?"

I scowl. "Of course, I don't. He's so cocky and rude."

She shrugs again. "He's the king. Isn't that a given?"

I sputter. "Why are you defending him?"

She takes the empty bowl that we were snacking out of over to her sink, where she leaves it. She turns and leans against the stone holding her sink aloft. The quarters that Annaleigh shares with Kale are the only ones I've been in, but according to her, they have the biggest quarters in the High Mountain, with the exception of the king. I guess those are the perks of being married to the Captain of the Guard.

"I'm defending him because the king and I are very good friends. He's a good person. He's stern when he has to be, but if you would just get to know him, I'm certain the two of you would get along nicely."

I narrow my eyes at her, a suspicion starting to form in my gut. "Annaleigh..."

She turns her back to me and starts washing dishes, clearly avoiding my eye.

"Annaleigh, did you tell King Cage to propose to me?" Just the thought has my stomach rumbling uncomfortably.

She spins to face me. "Yes, okay? He mentioned to Kale that he thought marrying a human would be helpful for the human-Isiriel relationship, and I just mentioned that you might be open to it."

I feel like a fish, unable to stop gawking. "But why?" I choke out.

She comes back to the table and takes my hand. "Because I'm worried you'll get lonely here. I feel like you came here to be with me, and now I live here and you live in the village. If you marry the king, you'll be permitted to live here in the mountain and you'll have responsibilities. You'll have a job."

"I have a job."

"I know, and you can keep doing that. You can sell your flowers here, too. The Isiriel would love it."

I can't believe we're even having this conversation. I can't believe my best friend, of all people, thinks I should do this.

"When I mentioned you," she says, catching my attention again, "he didn't even question it. He actually seemed...excited. Alice, I think the king really likes you. He wouldn't have asked you to do this if he didn't want you to be his queen. He takes his role very seriously."

She thinks he...*likes* me? I guess I couldn't really fathom what he wanted with me, but could it be possible that he just wants...*me*?

"Wait. Do you think King Cage is a virgin?" Annaleigh told me a long time ago that the Isiriel don't have sex until they're married and that losing their virginity is akin to taking wedding vows.

She smiles. "He's never been married, so I can only assume he is."

Something about knowing this makes my heart race, and I have to look away from the smug look on Annaleigh's face.

———

After I've stayed far too long and realize I need to get back to my plants before sunset, I walk back to the village alone. Annaleigh offered to walk me back, but I honestly just need time to think. The blueish tint of the Isiriel sun paints the dirt a strange purple color, and I stare down at all the little rocks and pebbles as I step over them. The first thing I bought when I came to Isiriel almost a year ago was a pair of shoes made by an Isiriel woman in the High Mountain. My high tops weren't great on the rocks.

I think, to an extent, Annaleigh is right. Since I've moved here, I haven't really felt like I've fit in. I have some friends in the village, mostly other people who trade in the market and have stalls close to mine. But I eat dinner alone every night. I go for my morning walk alone. I stand at my stall alone.

Maybe I should get an Isiriel dog. What are the chances it would set my cabin on fire?

I come to a stop when I reach the edge of the village. There's a group of Isiriel males doing something in front of the door that leads into my cabin. I watch them, trying to figure out if they're a threat. I've never once felt unsafe in the village, but I guess every place has to have its dangers.

Just as I'm about to turn back for the mountain, maybe come down here with Kale in tow or something, one of the males spots me, and I finally see clearly what's happening. It's the guard from this morning. He has a box in his hand, and he and the other Isiriel are unloading more boxes from a small wheelbarrow between them.

"Ma'am," the guard says, nodding his head in my direction. "We were sent to deliver these gifts from the king."

I finally get my feet to move, taking me closer so I can get some idea what's in the boxes, but they're just regular brown boxes. "What are they?" I ask the guard.

"Seeds." When I don't immediately answer, he elaborates. "The king has sent you seeds from every plant that grows here in Isiriel. He wishes you to have the beautiful garden you desire." He hands me the box he's holding, so light it might as well be empty. I'm curious if those were the king's words, or if this person in front of me is just making assumptions about the king's intentions.

Either way, I open the box and stare down at all the little packets inside, brown paper rolled out flat and folded around the seeds, the same packets I buy in the market to grow my own plants.

They finish stacking the boxes by my door and then one of them reaches down for the handles of the wheelbarrow. And just as they're about to walk away, I say, "Excuse me?"

The guard who handed me the box turns back around.

"Can you give the king a message for me?"

He doesn't look surprised to be asked. He just nods.

"Can you please tell the king that I accept his offer?"

Chapter Four

I guess the Isiriel don't have mirrors. It's not something I ever noticed before, not really much concerned with my appearance when I was just going to work in the sun all day, but now that I'm standing in Annaleigh's room, preparing myself for my wedding to the king, I'm very aware that I have no idea what my hair looks like.

There's a gentle knock on the door to the bedroom, and I open it to find Kale on the other side.

"You hardly have to knock in your own quarters," I tell him, stepping back to let him in. Damn, he's big. I know all the Isiriel males are big, and I've seen plenty that are bigger than Kale, including the king, but it's not something you really notice until they're standing right next to you in a small space.

One side of Kale's mouth lifts. I can see why Annaleigh was so attracted to him when he showed up in her bedroom and asked her to marry him. There's something so primal about Isiriel males that's rather irresistible.

Hence why I'm about to go out there and marry the king of the fire monsters.

"I didn't want to interrupt you if you were having a private moment. The king has requested that I come in here and explain to you what will happen during the mating ceremony."

"I already know what's going to happen," I tell him. "Annaleigh explained it to me. We just have to have sex in the throne room, right?" I try to sound casual about this, as if I'm not absolutely trembling over the fact that I'm about to fuck King Cage. I'm about to fuck a guy who has fire for eyes and lava for cum. Yep, totally casual.

Kale's mouth twists in a strange way. "Yes, but the mating ceremony will be different for you than it was for Annaleigh. Traditionally, an Isiriel couple would be taken before the king. The king would ensure that the female is there of her own free will." When I glance sideways at him, he says, "There was a dark time in our history when females were often kidnapped and forced into mating ceremonies. This is to ensure that no longer happens. As the king is the one getting married, during the ceremony, I will be the one to ask. In a traditional ceremony, the couple then mates before the king. However–"

"The king is the one getting married. So, we just have sex in an empty room, right?"

He frowns. "Not exactly. There must be a witness for the mating ceremony. It is tradition that the king mate before the court."

Silence falls on the cave. And then the question bursts out of me. "He *what*? The *whole court*? How many people is that?"

Kale puts up a gentle hand that I know he means to be comforting, but it really isn't. I'm already going to have sex with someone I barely know and be married to him forever, and now I'm learning I have to have sex with him in front of an audience?

"Not nearly as many as you're probably imagining. Annaleigh and I will be there, as well as all the other speakers and ambassadors. If I had to put a number on it, I would say thirty people."

Thirty people. Okay. Thirty people are going to see me naked. Thirty people are going to see me fuck the fire monster king. Thirty people are going to witness the most awkward moment of my life.

"Great."

Kale offers me a gentle smile and then the crook of his elbow, like he's my father, getting ready to walk me down the aisle. "You will do well, my queen."

The way he says it startles me. I've heard him say that to King Cage so many times that to hear it turned in my direction makes my stomach clench. I settle my hand into the bend of his ashen elbow and let him lead me from his quarters.

When we get to the throne room, I feel like I'm going to vomit. There are definitely more than thirty people in the room, a mixture of humans and Isiriel, but I suppose, at this point, it doesn't really matter. It could be ten or a hundred, and I would be equally as petrified.

Kale leads me to the throne. Once I'm standing before King Cage, he sets my hand at my side and takes a step back, taking his place beside the throne. There's another guard on the other side, an Isiriel female that I don't recognize. When she sees me looking, she smiles comfortingly.

King Cage stands, towering over me, and I realize just how much bigger he is than Kale. Taller and with wider-set shoulders. He comes to stand in front of me, and as I tremble, he reaches out and wraps a lock of my hair around his clawed finger. I look right into his fire eyes, flames slowly but surely crawling higher as I look at him.

"You are breathtaking, my bride," he says, and the words send a shiver through me. Is Annaleigh right? Is he really doing this because he *wants* me?

"Thank you, my king," I say back, not really sure what else to do.

And then Kale's voice breaks through the room. "Before we begin," he addresses everyone, "Alice, I must ask you, are you here of your own volition? Have you chosen this male as your husband of your own free will?"

"Yes," I say, without looking away from Cage, and I swear, I see a shiver run through him, too. The next time his fingers touch me, they're sliding slowly over my lips.

And then his hands move down to the robe I'm wearing. I'm not even fully positive where it came from. It might have even been made specially for me. All I know is that it was waiting for me when I got to Annaleigh's room to prepare for the ceremony, a silky thing with a golden pattern across its black fabric. Cage slides his finger under one side and pulls it open. The two sides part, and he lets them fall, until the whole thing slides off my body and to the floor in one quick movement, and I'm left naked before him.

I don't know what to do, other than stand here. I can't really tell if his eyes are taking me in or not, but after a moment, his hand reaches out, and he slides his rough palm down my shoulder and then my chest and then along one of my breasts. I suck in a breath, and Cage's eyes burn a little brighter. The flames are taking up the entirety of his eye holes now, and I can't tell if that's a good sign or not.

"Exquisite," he says, and just before he pulls his hand away, the tip of his claw brushes the hardened end of my nipple. I bite back a moan. He offers me his hand, and I follow him over to the throne. This close, I can't help but glance over at Kale, but his face is pointed forward, deliberately not looking at us. I wonder if everyone else in the room is doing the same thing, but I refuse to look and find out.

Cage sits on the throne and then subtly pats his thigh. Oh,

God. This is it. We're going to do it right here, on his throne. It's time for me to find some courage.

The king doesn't look away from me as I set one knee beside his leg on the throne and then the other beside his other leg. I'm completely exposed now. My boobs are in his face, my legs are spread for him, and I'm trembling. Why did I agree to this?

I feel something brush the inside of my thigh, and I look down to see Cage undoing the knot on the piece of fabric slung around his waist. Every time I've ever interacted with Cage, he's always been wearing pants, just like all the other Isiriel males. But this must be some sort of tradition thing because there are intricate designs all over the clothing he has tied around his hips. And then the knot comes undone, and Cage is completely naked. He lets the fabric fall open onto the throne, and I let my eyes travel down to that part of him that I'm about to have inside me.

I gasp. Holy shit. It stands to reason that if Isiriel males are so much bigger than human males that their reproductive anatomy must be bigger, too, but someone should have drawn me a fucking diagram. Because not only is Cage much bigger than any guy I've ever had sex with, but his dick also has... ridges? It's standing straight up, which is honestly pretty flattering.

"Don't worry," Cage says, clearly mistaking my surprise for worry. "I will make you ready for me. It will fit."

And without waiting for me to respond, he reaches between my legs and settles his fingers right over my opening, already pretty wet, if I'm being honest. When I gasp again, Cage leans forward and takes one of my nipples into his mouth. I whimper, and the flames in Cage's eyes spark high enough that I feel the heat of it on my skin.

This is supposed to be a transaction. It's not like I thought I was going to hate it, but I thought it would be awkward and kind of stiff. But Cage is running his hot fingers back and forth across my pussy, and his hot tongue is lapping at my nipple, and this is definitely *not* awkward. I'm so wet that in the silence of the throne room, I can hear the squelch of Cage's fingers between my legs.

He slips across my clit, and I keen. Cage's mouth tilts into a smile, and he finds the spot again, rubbing it and rubbing it until I have to grab onto his shoulders so I don't fall over. My hands come away black with ash, and something about it is so sexy that I want to rub it all over my body.

Instead, I reach down and wrap my hand around Cage's cock, feeling those ridges against my palm. He groans, and I watch my hand move up and down across the dark skin, interlaced with lava-colored veins.

Oh, fuck. I'm so turned on by King Cage.

"Now," he growls, and I meet his eye again, questioning him silently, but he ignores the look. His hands latch onto my hips, and he lifts me, positioning me right over his cock and lowering me slowly. He sinks into me without effort, and all I can do is close my eyes at the pleasure of it. All those ridges feel incredible sliding along my insides until I'm settled entirely on top of him. My mouth hangs open, and I can feel the way Cage is watching me closely. He seems so interested in my reactions, which is another thing I wasn't expecting. Why should he care if this feels good for me?

"Ride me, my queen," he says, the words rumbling through his chest and mine. I didn't really process the fact that we're pressed together completely. It feels...so good.

Following his lead, I lift up until just the tip of him is inside me and then lower myself back down. I hold his gaze as his flames burn higher. Does that mean it feels good for him, too? Like he's reading my mind, he lets out a sensual groan that pushes my pleasure higher.

I find myself moving faster, bouncing up and down on

him. When his mouth closes around my breast again, I bite my lip and reach out to grab onto the back of his throne to anchor myself. Using it to pull myself up, my movements become rough. It's like I can't stop myself. Maybe I should be embarrassed to be so enthusiastic, but Cage's cock feels so fucking good.

And then Cage tips his head back, and his mouth finds mine.

I gasp against his tongue, and he kisses me deeper, taking my face in his hands even as I clutch the back of his throne tighter and fuck myself on him harder.

Oh, God. I'm going to come.

I break my mouth away from his and cry out. The sound echoes off the stone walls of the throne room. My whole body goes hot and tight, and I don't realize my hands have fallen from where I was clutching the throne until they find Cage's shoulders. I dig my nails into his skin as I ride through the waves of my orgasm.

And then my whole body goes soft and pliant, and I slump against him. I set my cheek against his shoulder, letting him thrust beneath me as I hold on. My eyes meet Kale's, still standing beside the throne, and this time, he's looking back.

Cage thrusts up into me quick and hard, and then he wraps his arms around me to lift me off of him. His cock slips out of me, and he shouts loud in my ear as he comes. I have just enough energy to look over my shoulder at where his lava cum is splattered across the floor.

And that's when I see all the eyes that are still on me. The entire time Cage was inside me, I could forget that all of them were there, but I can't forget now. Especially not when, one-by-one, they begin to cheer and clap.

I turn and bury my face in Cage's shoulder. I feel the rumble of a laugh go through him. I don't suppose I blame him. Seems silly to be bashful now, after everyone in this room just watched me come on his cock.

I hear the commotion of the crowd talking and then moving around, as if Cage and I aren't still naked in front of everyone, and then I feel the touch of something on my back. I sit up and find Cage's eyes as he settles my silk robe around my shoulders. Kale must have retrieved it for us. Cage wraps it around me and then his fingers brush across my chin.

"Come, my queen," he says. His hands maneuver me on his lap so that my legs are to one side, and then he stands, lifting me in his arms, still draped in the silk robe. He's completely naked, but I don't mention it. He carries me slowly out of the room, and once we're in the hall, I set my head against his warm chest and listen to the steady thrum of his heartbeat.

"That was really amazing," I say, feeling warm and bubbly toward him. I slide my hand up the side of his neck, watching the way it turns my fingers gray. It's amazing that there's any part of me that's still my own peachy skin color.

"It was," Cage says, and his mouth pulls into a smirk that sends a shot of desire down into my stomach, as if my body isn't still limp from just being completely railed.

Cage carries me down a hall I've never been down before, and I can't seem to tear my eyes away from him. He's cradling me so gently, and I feel more at ease than I have in months. I settle my head against his shoulder as he walks me through a tall archway and into what appears to be a labyrinth of rooms. A long corridor leads into a room with a bed that we pass by. Another room seems to be a dining room of some sort, and we pass yet another that looks to be a library, filled floor to ceiling with books. Cage carries me past all of it to a room that's almost completely bare, with the exception of a large tub that's filled with steaming bathwater, from the looks of it.

Cage sets me on my feet and removes my robe, letting it

fall to the floor. And then he lifts me again, settling me in the hot water.

"Your queen's maid will be along shortly to help you get clean," he says, crouching beside the tub and swirling his finger through the water that's slowly turning black from the ash on his skin and mine. It sizzles at his touch and begins to boil.

"I'm not that dirty, am I?"

Cage raises a brow at me in that way that he does. He seems to be just as surprised as I am that I'm getting flirtatious with him. This isn't exactly how we do it. Cage and I haven't liked each other since the moment I walked through the portal without permission.

But, well. Maybe I do like Cage, after all. I've never seen him like this before, playful and sweet. It's a good look for him.

He grabs onto the side of the tub and leans in close to me, until I feel breathless at how little space there is between his mouth and mine. When he speaks, his breath is hotter than the water in the tub. "You're absolutely filthy, my queen."

A shiver runs through me, despite the heat, and when I think he'll close the distance between us and kiss me, instead, he stands. "I'll see you in the morning, at breakfast."

Disappointment rises in my throat. "You're not staying?"

Halfway back to the archway, he turns and looks at me. "My quarters are on the other side of the throne room. These are *your* quarters."

"We don't...share quarters?"

He seems to regard me for a long moment. "That is not how it's done here."

I don't know why his words seem to knock the wind out of me, but they do. Wasn't the biggest reason I agreed to this whole thing was so I wouldn't be so lonely? And now, what,

I'll be married to this person but we'll never see each other or spend time together? I guess I'll have my maid...

I don't know what he's seeing on my face, but he's definitely seeing something because he turns his body back toward me and says, "We will sleep apart, my queen, but you are my wife, and I intend for this to be a marriage in every way. If you want me, you need only ask."

Does he mean right now? Right this second? If I tell him that I don't want him to go, that I want him to stay while I take a bath, will he do it?

I can't even decipher my feelings for this person, someone who I thought I really didn't like until he kissed me while he fucked me, and now I feel like a teenager, ready to beg for the affection of a king who has better things to do.

"I'll see you in the morning," I tell him, sinking down into the tub and watching the ash on my skin run off into the water.

I can't read his face, not with his eyes just small flames in the darkness of his head and his mouth a thin line. And after a minute, without another word, he turns and leaves.

As soon as he's gone, a woman comes in from a doorway on the other side of my bathing room. She has a jar in one hand and a towel in the other. She smiles as she crosses the room to me and sets the towel on a nearby boulder.

She bows, that same bow that I've learned to offer Cage, a slight lowering of the chin, quick and painless. "Hello, my queen. It's an honor to meet you." She doesn't look much older than me, maybe in her early thirties, with her hair pulled back in a tight bun. She's the first human I've seen in this part of the mountain.

I smile, but I'm distracted. I wonder what Cage would do if I just went to his room or if I begged him to stay here with me. I'm the queen. Doesn't that get me special queen privileges, like having the king sleep in my bed?

Do I *want* him to sleep in my bed?

Fuck, I don't know what I want.

"Can I ask you a question?" I ask. My maid's eyes go wide. I guess she wasn't expecting me to speak to her while she helps me wash my hair. "How long have you worked for the king?"

Her chin wrinkles, and she pours something into the tub that immediately begins to bubble. "I suppose about six years now. I worked in the kitchen, but when we heard that you would be joining us, I applied to be your maid."

"So, you know the king well?"

She sends me a quizzical look and then nods. "I guess you could say that. I've interacted with him quite a bit."

"What kind of person would you say he is?"

She stops lathering shampoo into her hands and looks at me. "My queen, I believe the king is the kindest, most honorable person I've ever known. He shows empathy to his people and generosity. If it isn't wrong to say so, I think you're the luckiest woman in Isiriel."

I sink down into the bath and consider her words. Should I expect less because I'm already the luckiest person in Isiriel? I should try not to overthink this whole thing. I've been married for all of twenty minutes.

When I've finally gotten all the ash off my skin, my maid helps me get dressed and then leaves me alone to crawl into my bed. It's big and comfortable. And empty.

If you want me, you need only ask.

I've been on my own for a month now in Isiriel and for the majority of my life before I came here. I don't need Cage. I'll be just fine on my own.

Chapter Five

I wake sometime in the night, unsure what woke me up. I stare forward into the dark, waiting for my eyes to adjust, to remind me where I am, when I hear something shift behind me. I flip over onto my back, and it takes me a second to figure out what I'm seeing in the pitch black darkness of my new cave.

A dark form stands beside my bed, two flames burning bright in his face. I sit up, dread settling in my stomach. "Cage? Is everything okay?"

In the light of his eyes, I see him nod. "Yes." He steps forward, planting one knee on my mattress and then both of his hands. He seems to slide across the sheets to me, until his face is inches from mine. "I woke wanting you. I must have you again. May I?"

I'm nodding before the question is all the way out of his mouth, a kind of relief settling into my bones that's completely unexpected. I wanted him here, yes, I definitely did, but I wasn't going to be the one to make the first move. And now he is, pushing the covers off my body and crawling on top of me. His eyes are nothing but small flames, almost not even there, when he bends down to kiss me.

There's a moment when doubt becomes vapor in the air with nothing left to make it concrete, and when Cage's tongue finds mine, my doubt vanishes like a bad dream in the sunlight.

He came to me. I didn't have to go to him. He came to me, he wanted me, even if it's just sex. He has my clothes off in seconds, the ones that were left at the end of my bed, probably some kind of ceremonial sleep garment or something, And then he starts to devour me. He kisses his way down my neck, but it's like he's tasting me, opening his mouth against my skin and licking with every kiss. Down my chest and across both of my breasts and then to my stomach. The kisses aren't urgent. They're slow and sweet, and it's like he's still waking up himself, moving slow and sleepy.

And when he finds his way back to my mouth, covering me with his huge, hulking frame, he gently pins my hands above my head and kisses me deep.

Before, in the throne room, that was him claiming me in front of everyone, but now, this feels like he's claiming me in secret. He's showing me that I'm his.

Pushing my legs apart, he settles between them. He slides into me deep, and I whimper against his mouth. My knees brush against his sides, and when he frees my hands, I can't help but clutch him tighter to me. When I wrap my legs around his waist, he grunts.

It's surprising to me how gentle it is, gentle enough that I almost feel bad for how rough I was with him earlier. He was a virgin, after all, if what everyone says about the Isiriel is true. Maybe this was what he wanted on that throne, slow and steady, instead of the way I took him. But he wasn't exactly complaining when we were up there. I want to make this good for him, though. I want him to know all the different ways that sex can be good.

He buries his face in my neck, lips trailing down my skin. I clench my inner muscles, focusing more on his pleasure than my own, but when he groans, clearly liking it as much as I hoped he would, pain blooms on my neck.

"Ow!" I shout, and Cage jerks away from me. Going up on his elbows, he presses the palm of his hand against my neck, but the heat of his body just makes the pain worse. "Fuck," I hiss, pushing his hand away, and then he's gone completely, sitting on his knees at the foot of the bed.

I press my own hand to the burn on my neck and look at him. It must have been his eyes. I got him too excited, and they must have flared too high.

"I'm sorry," he says, his voice thick. "I'm so sorry, my love. I'm so sorry. I didn't mean to hurt you."

"It's okay." I push myself up and look at him sitting there, his eyes locked on me and his mouth turned down in a frown. Every muscle in his body is tight, and between his legs, his cock is still standing at attention. If it wasn't for the look on his face, I would laugh. "Cage, it's fine."

He bares his teeth. "Fine? I hurt you. I'm meant to bring you pleasure, and instead, I burn you." He stands and paces away from the bed in all of his nude glory. "This was a mistake. We are clearly not physically compatible. I will keep my distance from now on. I will sleep in my room. I will not touch you again."

I stare at him with my mouth hanging open. "What? No. Look, I know you're new to this whole sex thing, but I'm not, and if you tell me that I have to spend the rest of my life married to you without having sex with you, I might die. Especially because-" I cut myself off. Nope. Not going there.

He takes a step back toward the bed, toward me. "Why *especially*?" He looks so pitiful, his shoulders slumped and his mouth turned down at the corners. Isn't this the scary fire monster that threatened to put me to death when I came through the portal? He's known as a fierce warrior and a stern leader, but right now, he looks like a little boy who's in trouble.

So, I throw him a bone. Literally. "Especially because now I know how good it feels to have you inside me."

His eyes burn higher, the tips of the flames poking out enough to touch the top curve of his eye holes. "Does my cock please you?"

I snort. Does his cock please me? His massive, ridged cock? That's certainly putting it mildly. I stand and watch with pride as he takes in my naked body. I'm shocked by how much I want to please him, but I do. I want him to want me. I want him to be miserable without me. I want the idea of not having sex with me to make him feel like he'll die.

I want him to feel about me the way I feel about him.

God, when did that even happen?

"Yes, your cock pleases me, my king, and I don't want to go without it. Without you."

When I'm close enough, he puts his hands out and settles them on my shoulders, like he can't keep himself from touching me.

"Perhaps all we need is to learn each other a little better. Maybe we just need to conduct an experiment."

His flames die down to a small blaze. "An experiment?"

I reach down between us and wrap my hand around him. The flames immediately burst back into twin infernos. I slide my hand up and down, feeling each ridge as I go, wet from me.

"An experiment. Maybe we just need to see where your limits are. We'll try a few things, and I need you to focus on controlling your flames."

"My solis."

I stop stroking for a second. "What?"

"That is what we call them. Our solis."

To reward him for giving me that bit of information, I squeeze him tight around the head of his cock. His breath comes out on a grunt, and his solis burn higher. "When you get to something that's so good that you can't control them anymore, we'll know where your limits are. How does that sound?"

His fingers caress my neck, slowly trailing down to my breasts. He leans forward, pressing his lips to the sore spot on my neck. "I'm at your mercy, my love."

My brain stutters to a stop. *My love.* He called me that before, too, but my mind didn't process it. *My love.* It's just something they say. He doesn't mean it literally.

His tongue peeks out and licks at my skin. I pull my attention back to his dick in my hand. I continue to stroke him, pulling away a little so that I can see his solis. And then I reach down and cup his balls. Like I thought they would, his solis flame high.

"Control it," I whisper to him, and he makes a sound in the back of his throat, like a growl. But the flames burn lower. So I drop to my knees in front of him.

Annaleigh told me that Kale didn't really understand the concept of oral when they first had sex, so it doesn't surprise me when Cage just watches me patiently. He doesn't know what it means for me to be on my knees, and I can't wait to show him.

He runs his fingers through my hair, his claws scratching lightly at my scalp in a way that makes me shiver. "I feel you're at an advantage," he says. "Were you to have solis, I would know what pleases you beyond distraction as well."

I smile up at him. "I could just tell you." I cover his hand with mine, and then I curl my fingers around his, until his own fingers curl in my hair. His face is curious, but I just grin at him. And then I wrap my lips around the tip of his cock.

His solis burst high, like a firecracker, and he shouts up at the ceiling of the cave. The sound booms around us like thunder, and I have to pull my mouth off of him so that I can laugh.

"I take it we've reached the limit of your control."

With the top of his head on fire, he wraps his other hand in my hair. "Please do not stop," he says between his teeth.

As if I would be that cruel.

I take him in my mouth again, and this time, when I see the flames of his eyes burn higher, I just suck harder, take him deeper. I don't usually have a terribly sensitive gag reflex, but the ridges of his cock brushing against the roof of my mouth makes it harder for me to take him. I give him my best though, sucking hard and reveling in the sounds he makes.

I feel the vein against my tongue become engorged, and then Cage uses his hold on my hair to pull me off of him. He turns quickly and, giving his cock a few more strokes, comes on the ground. His cum burns bright yellow and orange on the stone floor, and I watch it in fascination as it slowly starts to cool, turning a dull red and then eventually black.

Standing above me, Cage sucks in heavy breaths, halfway bent at the waist.

I wipe my mouth, feeling particularly proud of myself. But then Cage is bending, grabbing onto my hips and lifting me against his body. He takes three large steps and then drops me onto the bed. I bounce, laughing and feeling very content, like slipping into a warm bath.

"You must allow me to give you intense pleasure," he says, covering my body with his again. Between us, his cock is hot, like something that just came out of an oven. He reaches between us and slips it into me without effort. I'm so slippery that he hits deep with one quick thrust.

I cry out against his mouth. "Do Isiriel males not go soft?" I gasp.

"Oh, they do. But I want you so much that I doubt I will be soft for a very long time."

This makes desire curl deep in my stomach, even more desire than was already there. My hand snakes down, finding his ass and pulling him in tight to me.

He grunts. "Tell me what you like," he says. "I want to make you lose control."

"I want it hard," I say. I loved how gentle he was being with me earlier, but now that I'm so turned on I feel like I might melt, I just want to be fucked. "Be rough with me."

I feel gratified when his solis flame high again. Apparently, he likes the idea of that just as much as I do. He stands, tugging me closer to the edge of the bed and then lifting my legs with a hand under each of my knees. Holding my legs wide open, he thrusts into me hard, and my eyes roll back into my head. With each thrust, he hits deep enough to make me scream, until I'm just lying there with my mouth open, gasping up at the ceiling.

I snake my hand down, pressing it over my clit. I feel lost to the pleasure, and when Cage's fingers collide with mine, eventually sliding my hand away so that he can replicate my movements against my clit, I'm gone. I come so hard that I fear I might black out. My ears ring, and my whole body vibrates, and before it's over, Cage leans forward and devours my mouth with his.

And long after the aftershocks of my orgasm have started to fade, we stay like that, kissing and kissing and kissing. Until eventually, I start to get sleepy, my limbs getting heavy.

This time, Cage doesn't mention a bath, and I'm thankful because, even if I had someone to help bathe me, I would probably still fall asleep in the tub. Cage helps me crawl up to the pillows and then covers me with my blanket before pulling away.

"No," I say, the word bursting out of me. I shoot up in bed, grabbing onto his arm before he can move. "No, please stay."

I can feel his hesitation in the long moment that he looks at me. And then he peels back the covers and climbs in beside me. For a moment, we lay there on our sides, looking at each other, and then he reaches out and strokes a single finger down my cheek.

"Goodnight, my love," he says.

I want to discuss that, address it, beg him to tell me what he means by it, but instead, I get swept into sleep.

Chapter Six

I'm not sure if it's the knock at the door or Cage getting out of bed that wakes me up a little while later. I roll over and watch him walk to the door. I push up onto my elbow and try to listen as Cage speaks to someone on the other side. Their voices are low, but I can hear the tone of Cage and Kale's voices, the way Cage grumbles out a question before closing the door again.

But instead of getting back into bed, he reaches for his pants and pulls them on.

"What's going on?" I ask, sitting up.

"Most likely nothing. There was a slight disturbance at the portal. I'm just going to make sure all is well." Leaning down, he presses a kiss to my forehead with enough affection that my heart aches. His hands slide away from me, and I watch him leave before falling back onto the bed.

This is...not happening the way I thought it would. And in fact, I'm not even sure I know what I thought this would be like. I guess I thought we would consummate the relationship and then maybe meet every once in a while after. I imagined that he would basically ignore me. That he would treat me the way he does all of his other subjects.

But I wasn't expecting the mating ceremony to be so explosive. And I wasn't expecting to miss him when he went back to his own quarters. And I wasn't prepared for him to come to me in the middle of the night.

What the hell am I to this fire monster?

Something shifts somewhere in the darkness of the hallway that leads deeper into my quarters, and I hold very still. If I was back on Earth, I would assume it was an ice maker or an electric air freshener or something. But they don't have those things here. In the silence, I hear the slide of something, like a shoe on the stone floor.

I shoot up in bed, holding the covers to my body as I stare into the dark. I can't see anything now that Cage isn't here with his bright solis. I strain my eyes, trying to make out the shapes of the hall that leads to the bathing room.

Something moves in the dark.

Throwing the covers off myself, I run for the door. But I'm not fast enough. Something hits me on the back of the head, and then darkness fills every crevice of my awareness.

I wake in the dark, but this dark is different. Where there's something warm and comforting about the darkness of the High Mountain, the cave I wake in is cold. My head pounds as I lift it from the chilled stone and look around. I can't see anything, and when I try to sit up, I realize my hands are bound together with rope.

I gasp and tug at the ropes, but they just dig harder into my skin. As my eyes adjust, I can see that the rope around my hands is attached to a metal ring on the cave wall. I pull at it, but it's embedded so deep into the rock that I have a better chance of pulling my arms out of their sockets than pulling the ring out of the stone.

Looking around, I find that I'm in an empty cave. It's relatively small, and across the way from me, there's a dark hallway leading to some other dark part of the cave. And that's it. Just an empty cave with a metal ring on the wall. Totally normal.

I want to call out, but I can't bring myself to open my mouth. What the hell is happening? Who was in my room? How did they even get in there? At least they covered me. I look at my body. Of course, it's with my bathrobe, but that's better than being abducted completely naked.

I tug at the rope again, twisting it to try and get my hand out of it, but it's so tight around my wrists that after a few minutes of maneuvering, I start to panic. I can feel tears rising in my throat, my situation finally really setting in. Someone kidnapped me. And Cage doesn't know where I am. I'm in a cave somewhere, but I don't know where or how long I was unconscious. Annaleigh once told me that there are other mountain ranges outside of Isiriel that are inhabited by other fire monsters. What if I was kidnapped by one of them? What if they're not as nice as the males in Isiriel?

Setting my bare feet against the cave wall, I pull at the rope, but the ring still doesn't budge.

"You're wasting your time."

I scream, spinning around and pushing my back up against the wall. There's a man standing in the middle of the cave, holding a flashlight. Not a fire monster. A human.

"What do you want with me?" I ask immediately. If he's going to try to assault me, I kind of want to know now so that I can face the situation head-on. The man comes closer, until eventually, he takes a seat in front of me, a few feet away. He's small, scrawny, or maybe I've just been spending too much time with giant fire monsters. He's sweaty and dirty, dark stubble on his chin and his head shaved down low.

His face isn't familiar. I rarely pay attention to everyone in

Isiriel, even from behind my booth at the market, so maybe I've seen this guy before and just don't remember.

He sets the flashlight on the ground between us and folds his hands in his lap. "I know why King Cage married you. He thinks that he can marry a human and suddenly all of us will just accept him as king, right? Well, that creature is no king of mine. Isiriel deserves a democracy, and the rebellion is going to make sure it happens."

"This is his home," I snap at him. "If you don't like it, why don't you just leave?"

He chuckles. "And go where? Have you been outside of Isiriel? It's nothing but wasteland for miles. This is where civilization is."

I set my head back against the rock behind me. "Seems pretty cut and dry to me."

"What's cut and dry is what's happening here," he says, but I don't look at him. I look up at the stalactites hanging above us. "By now, the king knows you're gone. We've made it very clear to him that if he wants you back, he'll agree to a fair election for the throne."

I look straight at him. "You're an idiot," I sneer.

"And you're a disgusting slut for fucking a monster."

I throw my head back and laugh. "This is clear jealousy. You're mad that you're not man enough to stand beside one of the Isiriel males. Mad that they're stealing your women and satisfying them like you never could."

The impact comes quickly. He doesn't even bother to hit me with his own hand. He swipes the flashlight hard against my cheekbone. The pain slices through me, and my head throbs. For a minute, my vision is white, and then the world comes back into focus. I blink down at the stone floor.

"Sickening whore," the man hisses at me and stands. "Your husband can give us what we want, or you'll die. Better hope he's smarter than you are."

I grit my teeth until he's gone, taking the only light with him, and then I start to cry. My cheek hurts, and the back of my head, where he knocked me out earlier, throbs. I settle my face against the cold stone, and it's a relief.

Wherever Cage is, I hope he's safe. I don't know how easy it is to kill an Isiriel male. They have flesh and bones just like the humans do, but they're bigger and stronger and are basically walking infernos. He's safe. I have to believe he's safe, or I'll lose my shit.

I don't know what to do. I work slowly at the ropes on my wrists. I read somewhere that rope stretches over time. Maybe if I just keep tugging at this stupid thing, I'll eventually be able to stretch it enough to slip my hands out.

My stomach starts to roil from the pain in my head, and I lean over and vomit on the ground. The world is spinning. To get to it to stop, I lay down on the ground and focus on breathing to battle the nausea.

What am I supposed to do now? There's nothing in this cave but the ring I'm attached to, so it's not like I'm going to be able to strategically use something sharp to get myself free. I stretch out a hand and run it along the wall. It's smooth. No sharp edges on which to create fiction and break ropes.

I sigh. I really should have seen this coming. I didn't know there was an active rebellion against Cage—he may not even know that himself—but I should have at least known that it would be dangerous to get married to a king. Aren't a king's loved ones always a target?

Loved ones. I'm not about to delude myself into thinking I mean more to Cage than I do. His whole *my love* spouting was just sex talk. The guy was a virgin twenty-four hours ago, so he would probably call any person who made him come his love.

My eyes grow heavy, the pain in my head inescapable, and eventually, I fall asleep.

———

I jerk awake, staring into the dark. It takes me a second to realize that what woke me up is a cold, wet cloth being held to my swollen cheekbone. Turning my head, I catch sight of a flame, and my heart jumps.

"Cage," I gasp, trying to push myself up into a sitting position. I'm somehow even dizzier than I was before, and in the confusing shadow, I try to make out Cage's face, but my mind can't seem to form a complete picture in the dark.

"I'm sorry, no," a woman's voice says, and I jerk away from the hand touching my face. It's not the comforting warmth of Cage. Instead, as I'm able to finally get my head to stop spinning, I see the shape of a woman's face. I scramble away from her, until my back hits the cave wall.

"Hey, hey," she says, and now that I'm looking right at her, I see the fire that she's started on the floor in the center of the room and the hand that she still has reached out toward me with the cloth on it. On the floor in front of her is a bowl of water. She's a human, young but clearly still older than me. "I'm not going to hurt you."

I scoff. "Yeah, sure. You just kidnapped me and are holding me hostage. Oh, and your friend hit me. But for sure, now the abuse will end."

Her hand falls by her side. "I apologize for him. He's angry. We all are."

"Right. Angry that you couldn't come to this realm and take over."

She dips the cloth in the water and tries to bring it to my face again, but I shift away from her. "It's a little more complicated than that," she says quietly.

"I don't care how complicated it is."

She nods, setting the cloth in the bowl. "Listen, I don't think—"

A roar erupts from somewhere in the cave, cutting her off. She immediately scrambles to her feet, and I start to tug at the ropes on my wrists. Some very concerning sounds are coming from down the hall, in the part of the cave that I can't see. Someone screams, and I stop moving, stop breathing. The woman who woke me has pressed herself against the wall, as far from the opening to the hallway as she can get. I watch her watch the mouth of the cave.

And then that roar sounds again. I turn toward the opening in the cave just in time to see the entire hallway light up with fire. The woman and I both gasp as the flame floods into the room like there's been an explosion. I duck my head, but the flames blow in and then immediately die back down, leaving nothing but smoke and darkness in their wake.

The cave is suddenly so hot that I start to sweat. I yank at the ropes and listen as the woman starts to whimper in fear. If I'm being honest, part of me enjoys it. The bruise on my cheek throbs.

"Alice!" Cage's shout is so loud that it feels like the entire cave shudders.

I tug recklessly at the bindings, like now that he's here, I'm no longer tied to the wall. "Cage! I'm back here!"

As soon as he comes around the corner, long horns spiraling up toward the ceiling and eyes burning so high that they almost completely engulf his face, Cage turns toward me. He seems to find me with his whole body, and then he runs to me. His arms surround me, holding me tight to his chest. I can feel a tremor moving through him, and the heat of his solis burning up the air around us.

"My love," he says into my ear, and then the flames of his eyes die down to small enough embers that he can lean forward and kiss me. His hands come up to hold my face, and I wince.

He jerks back from me, his eyes immediately flaming high

again. "What's wrong, my love?" In the dark, he tilts my face up until he can see it clearly. The flames erupt so high that the heat of them is almost unbearable. "They hurt you."

I don't deny it.

"They are dead now for what they've done to you."

From somewhere in the depths of the room, the woman—who I completely forgot about—whimpers again. Cage stiffens and turns toward her. I can see him directing his anger already. The other people have already been punished for taking me. But now he's seen the bruises and there's someone around he can take it out on. Fresh meat, as it were.

He takes a step toward her, but I hold on tight to his arm. "Cage, no."

He turns to me, and I see the way the anger sparks higher. "They hurt you," he says in a growl between his teeth.

"She didn't," I tell him, nodding toward the woman. "She was trying to help me." Sort of.

For a long moment, he doesn't move, and then he turns back to her. "I want you to send a message to the rebellion. They'll have one chance to leave my kingdom. Tonight, at dusk. Whoever doesn't take that chance will face consequences."

The woman, pressed completely to the wall of the cave, nods. "I'll tell them."

"Go. Now."

She runs across the room and down the hallway. I hear her scream, and I can only imagine that she just ran into another fire monster—probably Kale—on her way out of the cave.

Cage easily breaks the rope tying me to the wall. He takes a moment to free me from the knots and then he lifts me into his arms, and I'm thankful. Now that all the excitement is over, I'm very aware of the throbbing in my head, the way that the room doesn't quite come into focus.

"My head," I say, as Cage walks me from the cave.

"Rest now, my love," he says. "I will make you good as new."

I press my face into his chest as we descend into the darkness of the cave, and let my eyes fall closed.

EPILOGUE

I wake in my bed. The torches on the walls burn bright, and all the pain in my head is gone. I turn my head and find Cage. He stands at the open door of my quarters, speaking quietly to Kale, who stands in the hallway. Kale seems to notice me first, and when he turns his chin in my direction, Cage spins to face me.

"My bride," he says, coming quickly to the bed. "How are you feeling?"

I take a deep breath. "Good. Much better than I've felt in days. What did you do?" I sit up. In fact, the only pain in my body is the hunger pains stinging my stomach.

"I took you to the Healing Waters. You had a very bad head wound." He hesitates, and when he speaks again, his voice is thick. "You were bleeding."

I put a hand on his firm jaw. "I'm okay. I'm fine."

He presses his forehead to mine, his hot breath puffing out across my mouth. "You were gone for two days. I was afraid they had killed you. I thought I would never see you again."

I don't know what to say. Not really. I wasn't ready for

this. To feel all of this so soon. To feel it at all. To know that he feels it, too. "I knew you would come for me."

He sighs. "I'll always come for you."

"My king?" Kale says from the doorway.

Cage pulls away from me and looks over at the Captain of the Guard. "I'm coming." And then he's lifting himself from the bed, pulling out of my embrace. "I am set to speak with all of Isiriel in a moment. I would like it if you came with me. I'm not ready to let you out of my sight."

I smile. "Of course. Let me get dressed."

I step out of the bedroom and into the area where all of my clothes are kept. And there's Annaleigh, moving my clothes around like she's my maid. She must not hear me coming because when she turns and sees me, she jumps, putting her hand to her chest.

"Oh, my God, you're awake!" She rushes over and throws her arms around me. "We were so worried." When she pulls away, still holding onto my shoulders, there are tears glistening in her eyes. "When Cage found you missing, I thought he was going to burn the whole mountain down."

Hearing that does something to my stomach. I take her wrists and lift her hands off me. "He wants me to go with him to address the kingdom. Help me find something to wear."

———

When we come out into the sun, the valley extends before us, and standing in it are all the people of the kingdom. They stretch far, all their faces pointed toward us.

I look over my shoulder, where Annaleigh offers me a reassuring smile.

Taking my hand, Cage leads me out into the sun, where I immediately feel the rocks under my shoes. When he speaks, his voice is loud, carrying out over the valley that spans between the High Mountain and the human village.

"Thank you all for joining me," he says to the crowd. "As you all know, two days ago, there was an attempt on my life."

I squeeze his hand, fear slicing through me. No one mentioned this. No one said that Cage was in any danger. I must have been the back-up plan. Plan A was to kill Cage, but if they couldn't manage it, they took me as a bargaining chip.

Cage ignores my reaction to this news and continues. "Those responsible for the attack and the fools who kidnapped my wife are all dead." A murmur goes through the crowd, but Cage ignores it, too "I am now aware of a rebellion in Isiriel, a group of humans upset that their king is and always will be one of my own. I will say this only once." He pauses, and when he speaks again, his voice is louder, firmer, his solis flaring high and powerful. "This land belongs to my people. We were here long before the humans came through the portal and settled here. I have married a human in hopes that our union would bring the humans and the Isiriel together. We will have heirs—"

From somewhere in the crowd, someone yells, "Disgusting, half-blood filth!"

Cage drops my hand and roars. His entire body lights up. He is a raging inferno. "This will not be tolerated!" he shouts, voice booming out across the valley. "We will have peace in Isiriel." The flame dies down, flittering away until it's all contained inside his eyes again. "Isiriel will be home to my people, to humans, and to the descendants that come from the union of the two. I will not stand for hate or for prejudice or for war. So, I'm offering a solution. The portal will be open to Isiriel and humans alike for the rest of the day. Anyone who does not wish to reside peacefully in Isiriel may leave with my permission. And any hint of rebellion against your ruler or against the merging of our two people will be crushed beneath my heel."

His gaze sweeps across the valley. Everyone is silent, watching him with mouths fallen open and eyes filled with fear.

I feel nothing but pride. Pride that Cage cares enough to end the rift between humans and Isiriel before it can begin. Pride that he wants peace in his kingdom. Pride that I get to stand by his side while he fights for the right of his own kind... and mine.

"And lastly," he says, his voice lowering and yet somehow dripping with something far more terrifying than before, "if anyone touches my wife again, I will burn the entire human village to the ground."

"Cage," I whisper to him, and when he turns to me, he bends, finding my mouth with his. His kiss is urgent, possessive, and I whimper against his mouth, tasting all of his rage and fear.

When he pulls away, his voice is quiet, just for me to hear. "No one will ever take you from me again."

My heart pounds in my chest, and all I can do is nod.

———

Cage asks Kale to oversee the mass exodus of the humans involved in the rebellion. According to Cage's sources, the rebellion was merely a spark and was made up of a very small group of angry humans. All the ones who were named are either dead or going through the portal. Hopefully, that means Isiriel can be a peaceful place again.

Cage leads me down a dark hall in the High Mountain, his solis the only light, until we're in the largest cave I've seen in the mountain so far. I gasp, amazed by what I can only assume are the king's quarters, on the opposite side of the throne room from my own. His quarters are all one large room, and just over his lush, giant bed is a long beam of sunlight.

I laugh and rush over to it, climbing onto the bed to get better access. The small hole in the side of the mountain is almost exactly the size of my face, and when I look out, I can see the valley between the mountain and the village. I feel a giggle rumble up in my stomach. I've always thrived on sunlight, craving it the way some other people don't, and... well...now I live in a dark mountain.

"Does this please you?" Cage asks. I spin around, aware that I'm standing on the king's bed without asking permission to do so. I immediately drop down onto the mattress.

"Yes, my king," I tell him, feeling like I just got caught with my hand in the cookie jar. But when I look up under my lashes at him, Cage is smiling.

He reaches out a hand to me. "Come. I have something to show you."

I crawl off the end of the bed and take his outstretched hand. And that's when I see the open wardrobe on the other side of the room. A pile of my clothes lay on top of a long table, like they were abandoned, but the rest of my things hang inside the wardrobe beside Cage's.

"What's going on?" I ask him.

He's poised to tug me further into the depths of his quarters, away from the bedroom, but when I ask this, he turns, following the path of my eyes. "I've asked Annaleigh to oversee the moving of your things to my quarters."

I blink at him. "But I thought you said—"

"Come. I want to show this to you before the sunlight is gone." He takes my hand again and leads me further into the cave. We pass through a long stretch of darkness, and I'm surprised when we find the sun at the end of it. We're standing on some sort of cliff, a mouth into the cave that's high above the valley. A large stretch of rock hangs over us, so that we're still covered. It's a huge room, almost as big as the bedroom in my quarters. Are they even my quarters anymore if I live with Cage now?

"Wow," I say.

Cage crosses the room and turns to me, the length of the cliff between us. He spreads his hands out before him. "I will have beds cut into the rock and filled with soil. Here, you can plant whatever you want. It receives enough sun throughout the day for almost any plant to thrive. And there will be room for furniture, so that you can sit in the sun with your plants and your flowers." There's a slight tremble to his voice. Is he... nervous? He tilts his face up, looking at me. "Does this please you?" he whispers, so quiet I barely hear him.

I have to take a moment to catch my breath. He's so beautiful, standing in all his glory before me and offering me gifts. "Yes," I finally breathe.

He nods, his voice coming out a little louder this time. "It is my wish that you would be happy here, my queen. That you would be fulfilled and live out your life with joy—"

"Do you love me?" The words burst out of me. I don't even know where they come from.

Cage stops speaking, and his solis burn high for a moment before settling again. "What do you mean?"

I walk toward him, slowly, feeling the cold rock under my bare feet. As I get closer, the air gets hotter, until I'm right in front of him, almost in a sweat. "You call me *my love*. You killed to get me back. You *married* me, for fuck's sake. Annaleigh told me that she told you to propose to me because she suspected you had feelings for me. Is that true?"

It's amazing how much you can read on someone's face when they don't actually have eyes. I see his hesitation. And then I see the moment that he surrenders. "Yes," he says, the word a growl. "I have wanted you since you came through the portal. You were so insolent, so unafraid, even though I had the power and authority to end your life. It intrigued me. No human has ever looked at me without fear, even the ones that wanted me dead. I watched you as you settled into the village. I had the guards keep an eye on you and report back to me. They told me how you would give away flowers to those who couldn't afford them. They told me how happy you looked to work the ground. And I just wanted to be close to you.

"I asked Kale for his suggestion as to who I should make queen because I knew he and Annaleigh would suggest you. I wanted them to help me convince you. I–" He cuts himself off and takes a breath, his broad, lava-veined chest rising and falling. "I planned the whole thing because I was desperate for you. And I can only hope you are not disgusted by that."

"Disgusted?" I say, moving until I'm close enough that I have to tip my chin to look up at him. "Tell me you love me, Cage."

"I do," he says, gently. "I love you."

Going up on my tiptoes, I press my mouth to his and speak against it. "I'm yours, my king."

Where our chests are pressed together, I feel the rumble of a growl go through him. "Are you sure you are well, my love?" he asks, and I feel a shiver move through me at the question.

"Positive."

With rough hands, he grabs my arms and spins me away from him. Quickly, he walks me to the other side of the cave, where a ledge sticks out of the wall. Bending me over it, he doesn't waste time lifting the hem of my dress and shoving my underwear down my legs. I press my cheek to the cool stone and close my eyes, focusing on the feel of his hand on my hip, the other hand positioning his cock against my entrance. When he sinks into me, my mouth opens on a silent scream.

"Please, don't hold back your screams. I want everyone in Isiriel to know you're mine. I need them to know that I'll kill anyone who touches you. You're mine to touch. Mine to ravish. Mine to own."

"Yes," I whimper.

And then Cage lets loose on me. His gentleness from the last time we were together like this is gone. He's ruthless now. He pulls out of me and slams back in, forcing a harsh cry from my mouth. The ridges of his cock stroke inside of me as he fucks me rough, and it feels so good that all I can do is hold on, crying out everytime he impales me on his huge cock.

His claws dig into my sides. I feel certain they're close to puncturing my skin, but I don't tell him to stop. I want him to mark me. I cover his hands with mine and push them deeper into my skin, giving a relieved cry when he breaks the skin.

He shouts behind me, matching my desperation, before fucking me so hard that my teeth rattle. I know I'll have bruises where my ribs are pressed into the stone ledge, and I love it.

Cage roars and tilts his hips, and one of his hard ridges rubs right against my G-spot. "Yes!" I cry. "Right there. Harder!" His solis flame so high they lick the ceiling, and when he throws his head back, the whole thing engulfed in flames, I come. My legs shake as I try to stay upright, but eventually, I sag, and Cage removes his claws from my hips to hold me up.

He fucks up into me a few more times and then rips away from me with a high-pitched moan. I lean against the ledge and watch the lava erupt from him. He hunches over, head bowed and broad shoulders obscuring his face. His back heaves as he gasps for breath, and then eventually, his shudders stop, and he looks over at me, smiling.

Like someone blowing out a candle, his solis go from a raging fire to small flames inside his head. He steps over the puddle at his feet and wraps his arms around me. He lifts my dress and finds the spots of blood on my hips where his claws dug in hard.

"Did I hurt you, my love?"

I shake my head, feeling heavy and sated and loved. "No. I liked it."

He nods and leans in to place a soft kiss on my mouth. And then he lifts me into his arms and carries me back to our quarters, the quarters we'll live in together. Forever.

Touched By The Shadow Creature

Touched by the Shadow Creature

I booked the cabin for a week to finish my novel.

But I discover pretty quickly that I'm not alone.

There's someone watching me - something.

Gabriel is a member of the Shadow People, and he's trapped in this cabin.

Only I can set him free.

Chapter One

The cabin that I just rented for the week is an ominous figure against the black sky. The owner said they would leave the lights on for me, but the only light in this creepy forest is spilling from the full moon overhead. Branches deep in the trees flutter, sending a chill down my spine and spurning me to finish the rest of the walk up the path to the little cabin.

I punch the code the owner gave me into the lockbox and take out the key. I really wish they were here to walk me through the place. My eyes wander over to the windows on either side of the front door. It's just so...dark.

Last week, when I came up with the idea to rent a place to get some writing done in peace, it seemed like a great idea. But I didn't really think this one through. Peace means *secluded*, and secluded means *fucking scary*.

There's rustling in the leaves behind me, and I quickly stick the key in lock, step into the cabin, and slam the door shut behind me. As scary as a dark, empty cabin in the middle of the woods is, being *outside* a dark, empty cabin in the woods with mysterious wild animals is worse. I turn slowly, shocked by the starkness of the dark inside the cabin.

And yet somehow, the darkness doesn't quite feel...*still*. It's like the shadows are alive. With trembling fingers, I reach over to where a light switch makes the most sense and am relieved to find one. I flip it on, satisfied with the sight that greets me: a warm-looking living room, with a charming floral couch, antique furniture, and a soft yellow light.

Suddenly, it all just seems less scary.

Dropping my bag by the door, I decide I won't write tonight. Not right away, at least. I deserve dinner first. I fish in the bag of groceries I brought for the pasta and sauce and head for the kitchen.

Everything is updated and very nice, which almost makes me feel guilty about how much I'm paying to stay here for the week. I definitely got a deal, and I'm not exactly sure why.

It was an impulsive decision, booking the cabin and taking a week off my day job to go into the middle of nowhere Montana to focus on my novel. So when I saw the price on this cabin come across my social media page, I jumped at it. But now that I'm here, I know I severely underpaid.

I make myself dinner, using the expensive dishes and cooking utensils provided and then decide to go back for the wine I bought. I didn't intend to open it my first night here, but the creepiness of the darkness outside of the windows and the quiet of the cabin is making me think this whole experience might be a little more enjoyable if I was too tipsy to worry about whether or not I'm going to get murdered in this forest.

I read a book while I eat my pasta, and before I know it, I'm three glasses of wine in and feeling warm all the way down to my bones.

I push aside my dinner plate, completely engrossed in my book. I plant my elbows on the table, my stomach just as warm as the rest of me now. I bite my lip as the couple in my book starts taking their clothes off.

I can't remember the last time I was naked with a man. It's

easily been over a year. Between work and the dismal state of men in New York, I haven't had the energy to really put myself out there, no matter how many times my friends have tried to convince me to set up a Tinder profile.

Out of the corner of my eye, something shifts. I stop breathing. My eyes shoot to the corner of the dining room, where the warm light of the lamp above the table doesn't quite reach. Right where the two walls meet, shadow bathes the wall.

There's nothing there. Of course there's nothing there. Did I think a serial killer was standing in the corner of the room the whole time I've been sitting here, and I just didn't notice? I stare into the shadows until my eyes begin to water, and then I shake off the weird feeling and go back to my book. I'm just spooked. I should have known this was going to happen. It's one thing to be alone in your apartment when you know you have neighbors on either side of you and walls so thin that everyone can hear you scream. It's something else entirely to be in a cabin in the woods alone.

I'm just drunk. I've made it through almost half the bottle of wine, so it's no wonder that things in the room are starting to move when they shouldn't be.

On the page in front of me, the couple has started to go at it. I forget all about my fear and just start to feel horny instead. In the book, the hero starts to go down on the heroine, and I bite my lip. What I wouldn't give for a little oral right about now.

The blood has started to pulse between my legs, and I immediately feel stupid for not bringing any toys with me. I was so excited about getting here and getting to work that I didn't even think about the possibility that I might get here and feel the need to get off, a serious oversight on my part. I'm always desperate to get off these days, but I don't have the time or the patience half the time, and the other half of the time, it's terribly unsatisfying.

I just want some fucking *dick*.

I pour myself another glass of wine and focus on the scene unfolding before me. But with every passing sentence about this fictional couple, who are so sexually in-tune that she's had about four orgasms already, I'm getting hotter and hotter. Of course, that might also be because I've now had three glasses of wine. I look at what's left of the bottle. It's not much, a quarter of it or less.

And then I take in the shape of the bottle, the long neck of it.

I look away from it quickly, as if it was just looking back at me. Holy shit, I can't honestly be considering...

But now that I've given myself permission to even entertain the thought, I can't seem to drown it back out, even when I start reading my book again. I mean, it's not the most insane idea I've ever had. How different is it, really, to stick the neck of a wine bottle up in you than to use a dildo?

Guess I'm about to find out.

Tossing my paperback onto the table, I empty what's left of the wine into my glass and then hold the bottle up. I'm getting wet thinking about sliding it inside of me. Something about the idea has me positively *aching* for it. Aching so much, in fact, that I don't even bother to move somewhere more comfortable. Right there at the dining table, I shove off my pants and underwear, kicking my way out of them with so much enthusiasm that I almost tip right out of my chair.

My eyes go to the big windows on either side of the room. I know I'm in the middle of nowhere and that there's absolutely nobody around, but I still feel like I shouldn't be doing this in front of uncovered windows. I feel like someone is watching me.

I get a chill up my spine, but I'm honestly so hot and

bothered with my hand wrapped around the neck of this wine bottle, that if someone wants to watch me then I guess they're going to get a free show because I'm not stopping.

Hiking my feet up on the edge of the table, I spread my legs wide and position the end of the wine bottle against my entrance. I'm so turned on, I'm trembling. God, what is wrong with me? Who gets this hot over the idea of being impaled by a wine bottle?

As I sink the bottle into myself, I let my eyes fall closed, but I honestly don't even know what I would fantasize about at this point. I don't have some sexy ex or one that got away that I get off to. I usually just watch porn, but I don't have internet access, and I'm sure my cell service isn't good enough to stream videos out here.

So, I imagine a faceless man between my legs. I imagine that we're somewhere extra naughty, like maybe an alley behind the bar where we just met. I imagine him shoving my skirt up and finding me bare underneath. He bends me over, planting my hands on the building and pushing his cock into me from behind.

I let my head fall back, plunging the bottle in and out of me hard and fast. It feels even better than I expected, just from the sheer knowledge that it's an object that probably shouldn't be inside me. I push it deeper, until the neck starts to widen at the base, stretching me.

I'm rocking my whole body now, still imagining the faceless man fucking me. An orgasm starts to build, making my thighs tingle. I moan loudly, reaching up to knead one of my breasts and pinch my nipple.

A sensation whips across my clit, and my eyes spring open, shocked by how good that just felt. Glancing down my body, I realize how ridiculous I look, with my legs hiked up on the table and a wine bottle sticking out of myself, but...

What was that that just made my clit pulse like that?

Maybe I hit a spot inside me that nobody has ever hit before. I push the bottle back in, gasping, but I don't feel it again, that sensation like fingertips across my clit. I slide my hand down between my legs and rub at my clit, going at myself hard with the bottle before my orgasm hits.

I cry out, throwing my head back. The orgasm doesn't last long, acting more like a lightning strike than anything else, and then I'm left feeling weird as I tug the bottle out of myself slowly. I don't know if I should be ashamed or not about how badly I need to be fucked and that I would take pretty much anything inside me at this point, but I'm going to choose to ignore it.

I put my dishes in the sink and leave my book on the table as I get in the shower. When I get out, wrapped in a big towel, I also ignore the prickle up my neck from that sensation of feeling watched. It's just because of all the windows, and I'm going to have to learn to live with it if I'm going to manage a whole week in this place.

I dress and get in bed, and now that my libido is sated for the moment, falling asleep is easy.

Chapter Two

In the morning light, the cabin is homey, a far cry from its intimidating presence in the darkness. I'm feeling rather charmed as I take a seat at the desk in the spare room and set my coffee beside me.

Okay. I'm ready.

Back in the city, I can't focus. Yes, I moved to the big city for my dream job, but I figured out pretty quickly that a high-speed executive job in the city wasn't really my dream at all. I still love living in New York, and I wouldn't want to live anywhere else, but I knew that if I stayed there twenty-four/seven, I was never going to write this damn book, so I rented this cabin, took a week off work, and made a run for it.

And now that I'm here, I have to actually do it. So, I open the notebook I brought with all of my notes in it, and I get to work.

———

When the headache sets in, I finally stop writing. The sun has long since set, the only light coming from the tall lamp beside the desk that I turned on hours ago. I've been writing for ten hours. I only stopped for food and bathroom breaks, even though I can recognize now that I probably should have taken a walk or something. Well, there's always tomorrow. The forest will still be there once I've had a few hours of sleep.

My sore limbs protest when I unfold myself from the desk chair. Who knew that writing all day would take such a toll on my body? My legs hurt from sitting at a ninety-degree angle; my back hurts from being in that computer chair; and my eyes are burning from focusing on a screen for way too many hours. I may work an office job normally, but I rarely spend that much time focusing so hard on what I'm typing.

So by the time I pry myself away, I don't even have the energy to make myself dinner. I stumble into my bedroom and collapse in the center of the bed. At least I had the foresight not to change out of my pajamas all day.

I fall asleep quickly in the peaceful darkness.

———

Beautiful girl...

I jerk awake, staring into the shadows. My body is on fire, covered in sweat, like I have a fever. But it's not a fever. My body is primed for sex. I look down at myself, surprised to find that I've pushed my shirt up over my breasts in my sleep. I've got one hand wrapped around the plump weight of one of them, and my nipples are rock hard.

The hollow between my legs pulses, as if I've already begun the ascent to orgasm. I'm panting. The air around me feels thick, and I close my eyes again and reach between my legs, mindlessly pushing myself toward satisfaction.

I arch my neck, feeling the imaginary pressure of hands along my skin. I imagine a man with rough hands, touching and stroking and *feeling* me. I swear the weight of his hands are there, even though I know they aren't, but it's like a caress along my breasts and my belly and the inside of my thighs.

I moan and shove my underwear down and stroke myself, not surprised when I find just how wet I already am.

Yes, just like that...

I gasp. I know it was my imagination, that voice in my head. My own fantasy. But it feels so real. It's then that I wonder if I'm not still mostly asleep, floating in and out of a dream even as my toes curl into the mattress, and I hook my fingers inside myself. I feel that if I just stopped moving right now, I would slip right back into sleep, and maybe back into whatever dream is making my body react this way.

Keep touching yourself...

It's like a whisper in my head, and I'm certain it's coming from my own mind, even if it doesn't sound like the voice of my inner monologue. No, I've clearly conjured a male voice in my head, a voice that's telling me what to do so that I can find release.

That's it. Pleasure yourself, pretty girl...

The voice is enough to shove me over the edge, one hand fisted in the sheets and the other slamming hard into the space between my legs as I come.

When it's over, my body goes limp, and even though I'm sweaty and covered in my own juices, I fall right back to sleep.

———

Later, when I wake again, it takes me a moment to remember it all. The sun drifts in through the window, and I find myself mostly naked in the crumpled sheets. I turn over and burrow down deeper into the blankets, my mind still slipping in and out of sleep.

Last night was weird. I can't even adequately describe what the hell happened. It was like a fever dream. It felt so real, but I know that the voice I heard had to have been remnants of a dream. I couldn't have conjured that on my own. But I can't clearly remember even *having* a dream.

Good morning...

I shoot up in bed, coming fully awake. I know what this is. I've experiences it before. It's a very specific delusion that comes with not having been held or kissed or touched by someone of the opposite sex in too long. I've had dreams before where I was in love with a stranger and then woke up with a chasm of loss in my stomach because that person wasn't real. That's all this is. Dream fragments. My mind has been so thoroughly convinced that someone existed in the depths of my dreams last night that I've dragged those fictional emotions into the light of day.

Pathetic, really.

I take a quick shower, scrubbing away the evidence of my indiscretions, and then head into the kitchen for my breakfast.

My skin still tingles from everything I felt in the middle of the night, an intense sexual experience even if it was entirely fantastical.

I hum as I move into the kitchen to start my coffee for the day. I slept later than I meant to so I consider skipping break-fast altogether. I go to the cabinet to grab a coffee mug and my eye catches sight of the dining room table, just on the other side of the counter.

There's a bouquet of flowers in the center of the table that wasn't there before.

I gasp. The mug slips from my hand, but before it can fall to the ground, darkness sweeps across the floor and envelopes it.

I scream and race for the front door, feeling the presence of whatever that thing was at my back as I run through the house. I throw open the door and rush down the steps to my car.

Wait!

I scream again, my steps stuttering on the cobblestone path. I know that wasn't my subconscious. There was a voice *inside* my head, as loud as my own thoughts.

Please, don't go!

My vision goes blurry as I scramble to get my car door open. I'm so scared that I'm actually *crying*. I've got one leg hitched up into my SUV when that voice in my head speaks again.

Please, I swear I won't hurt you. Please.

It's the way it seems to be pleading with me that finally stops me. I've got my steering wheel in my grip and one foot on the ground, my chest heaving in fear and exertion. I look around, but it's not as if anyone is there. Not anyone I can *see* anyway. If that voice is inside my head...

"Where are you?" I finally manage to choke out, my voice tiny with fear.

I'm here.

And in the late morning light, I watch as a shadow attached to absolutely nothing slithers along the ground in front of me. It raises itself from the ground, becoming something more than a shadow. It's like it's black smoke and shadow mixed together, not solid but not *not* solid either. Once it's raised to its full height, I can almost make out its face, the slope of cheekbones and the shape of eyes, there but not really there, all at the same time.

My breath trembles as the shadow finally stops moving, clearly waiting for me to react, but I can't bring myself to speak, now that I'm looking at it.

My name is Gabriel, the shadow says, but the curve of his mouth doesn't move. He's definitely speaking directly into my mind. How the hell is he doing that? *What is your name?*

"Calista," I say.

The shadow's eyes widen. *That is beautiful. Calista, I'm so very sorry that I've frightened you. It wasn't my intention. I know I shouldn't have spoken to you at all, but you're the first really beautiful thing I've seen in so long. I couldn't help myself.*

I have no idea how to respond to that. For a long moment, we just stare at each other, until finally, he says, *please, come inside. I'd like to speak with you.*

"We're already talking," I say. My pulse hasn't slowed yet, my breathing still ragged. Sure, he seems to be kind. He seems like he doesn't want to hurt me. But how can I know for sure? What if he lures me back into the house and kills me? Or possess me or something? Is he a demon? A monster?

I know you're still frightened. But may I point out that if I wanted to kill you, I could have done it already? We have been alone in these woods for two days.

I clench and unclench my hands. "So...you've just been *watching* me?"

His arm drops to his side. *I have no choice. I am tied to this house. Where we stand now is as far away from it as I can go. Yes, I could have retreated as far into the woods as possible while you were here, but you came in the night, shining bright like the sun, and I couldn't tear myself away.*

There's too much to process. I have so many questions, but I don't even know where to begin. I steady my breathing and shut the car door behind me. A strange shimmer goes through Gabriel, like a sprinkle of joy. I guess he's satisfied with the fact that I'm not leaving.

"I need to understand *everything* by the end of this conversation, or I'm leaving."

He doesn't say anything. Instead, he scatters into the air, like someone blowing on a puff of smoke, and I'm left staring at the cobble-stoned path, awash with sunlight.

Chapter Three

I find Gabriel in the sitting room at the front of the cabin, waiting for me. Sunlight spears in through the window, but he sits in a loveseat in the darkest corner of the room. In the sun, he seemed to barely be there at all, but here, where the sun isn't on him directly, I can see the shape of him better, the cut of his jaw and the broad slope of his shoulders. His eyes are still dark as midnight, no whites around them at all, in a way that's unsettling.

I sit on the couch, as far from him as I can get, still not sure how I feel about this whole thing. I feel like I'm in a horror movie, but the horror movie apparently wants to be friends with me.

His eyes shift, moving back and forth, black moving over black. *How much do you know about the Shadow People?*

I blink at him. "Am I *supposed* to know about the Shadow People?"

His mouth shifts, revealing shockingly white teeth as he smiles. *I suppose not, though some do. The long and the short of it is that sometimes, when people die, they leave behind shadows.*

And those shadows –he gestures down to himself– *get stuck here in the land of the living.*

I scowl. "Wait. So, you're the shadow of someone who died?"

He nods. *But we're two different people. The man who left me behind–Gabriel–he's gone. His soul has passed on. I am not him; I was simply made in the moment of his death. There are Shadow People everywhere. We cannot leave this plane and therefore must spend eternity roaming the earth.*

That sounds...lonely. But I don't say so. If he's sad then I certainly don't want to make it worse. There's no reason to be an asshole. "So, you can just go anywhere? You can enter anyone's house, even if they don't know it?"

I can feel him hesitate. I guess the way I worded it wasn't particularly generous.

Well, yes. But we don't generally stay in one place too long. If any human encounters one of the Shadow People, they're usually just passing through. It's easier for us to travel through the shadows during the day, so we'll often duck into buildings just to keep moving.

I'm struck by the image of him here on that chair, in the middle of this cabin. He couldn't look more out of place if he was an eight-limbed water alien. His shadow seems to stretch, curling along the fabric of the chair and up the wall behind him.

"If you were just passing through, why are you still here?"

At my question, he seems to shrink, the shadows pulling in tight around him again. *I am not just passing through. Several years ago, I visited a woman here who knew and under- stood the Shadow People. Maybe she was even seeking us out; I'm not sure. She seemed to be waiting for me. She cursed me some- how. I'm not sure how she did it exactly, but she made sure I would be stuck here. I can't travel very far beyond the confines of this house.*

He's trapped here. Maybe I could believe this was some sort of trick, some sympathy trap, if it wasn't for the way his entire physical being seems to have altered in the face of his sadness. Where his joy showed in shimmering waves before, his despair pours off of him in obsidian waves.

"I'm sorry," I find myself saying.

His onyx eyes meet mine, and it's less frightening than it was a moment ago. My body has calmed at the idea of his presence.

He holds my gaze, and having his voice in my head is made all the more intimate when I'm looking him in the eye. It's like he's sitting right next to me, whispering in my ear. *I've been attached to this house for over a decade. People have come and gone, hundreds of families on vacations and couples on their honeymoons. I try to stay out of sight, but every so often, someone catches sight of me. Sometimes they leave, and sometimes they just huddle together under their covers in fear.*

His voice holds such regret. *I've thought many times about reaching out to someone in hopes that they would try to free me, but I could never bring myself to strike such terror into someone.* He pauses. *Until you.*

Warmth spreads in my belly, like someone just told me I was beautiful. Is it really a compliment to have a spirit from another plane of existence tell you you're different?

"Why me?" I ask. "I mean, you *did* strike terror into me."

Like a gust of wind, he moves, going from his spot across the room to the cushion right beside me so fast that I gasp. He doesn't touch me, but I can feel him beside me, like wet vapor across the surface of my skin.

I am very sorry that I frightened you, but since you walked into the cabin two days ago, I've had this feeling in my gut that you would be able to help me.

Sitting this close to him, I can make out the texture of him, like black sand, glittering faintly with rainbow specks. I can make out more of him, the shape of his face, the line of his bottom lip, his eyelashes as he blinks, slowly.

And then an image pops into my head, a memory from two nights ago: my legs propped open on the dining room table as I plunged an empty wine bottle deep into myself.

My face flames, and I raise both hands, covering myself as best I can. "Oh, my God," I whisper. I remember the way it felt like I was being watched, like there was someone in the room with me. It was him. It had to have been him.

His nearness is suddenly far from comforting. I catapult myself off the couch, putting the width of the room between us and spinning around to face him. I can see the startled confusion in the tilt of his eyebrows. "Oh, my God. Were you watching me the other night? Did you...did you touch me?" I think about that strange sensation I felt that I tried to recreate and couldn't. Was it him? And last night? When I woke up so horny, with that voice in my head?

Gabriel's shoulders slump, his shimmer disappearing so all that's left is flat shadow. *I will admit that I did watch you, but I swear I didn't have contact with you. I...* He trails off, and a shimmer goes through him. I imagine him recalling the entire ordeal, and I have to turn away.

"Oh God, I can't believe you saw that. Both times! I can't believe–"

A gust of wind surges around me, and then I feel his hand on my shoulder. I spin back around to face him. He's so close, even closer than he was on the couch. I can make out every single pigment of his shimmer, moving through him like ocean waves.

Please, don't be embarrassed. What I saw, it was truly... transcendent. I didn't touch you, but...I did...something. I'm not even sure how to describe it. I put a sensation into your mind. It was almost as if I wanted to touch you so bad, right in that spot that makes you feel so good, that my thoughts...made it happen.

I've never had anything like that happen before. And then, last night while you slept, I did it again. I projected my thoughts into your dreams, and you woke up full of desire.

I know I should be appalled. I should be disgusted that he did that to me, that he somehow manipulated the way I was feeling until I was so horny that I *had* to touch myself. I felt his touch, or whatever it was that he did to me, like it was real, like it was physical. The memory of his voice as he talked me through the act is enough to make me clench my thighs together.

"I think maybe I need some time alone." I can't process this when he's here, staring at me like that.

Gabriel blinks slowly at me. It's disarming the way there's almost no change between the color of his eyes and the color of the rest of him. The only indication that he blinked is the shimmering edge of his eyelid moving down and then back up.

I cannot leave you entirely.

"No, I get that." I take a step back, putting distance between us. "But I need some space to think. Can you...can you maybe go as far away as you can?"

He nods, a slow dip of his chin. *Of course.*

And then he's gone. Just like that. The only thing left is a puff of black smoke that dissipates almost immediately.

Chapter Four

I wish I had brought more wine. I only brought the one bottle because I'm generally not much of a drinker. But finding out I'm stuck in a cabin with a shadow creature–or whatever he is–for a week is a call for wine.

I try to get back to work, but how can I possibly focus on this book when I know Gabriel is somewhere nearby? I told him to go as far away as he could, but that doesn't mean he's not watching me. It doesn't mean he can't see me right now.

A tingle travels up my spine, and I spin around, looking out the window behind me into the trees beyond the property. I stare long and hard into the shadows, but I can't see him. Of course I can't. He can blend in with the shadows. He *is* a shadow. And he has decades worth of experience making himself invisible to humans.

Even thinking the word *human* makes me shudder. To think that there are things in this world that *aren't* human, just walking around amongst us, makes me a little queasy. What else exists in the world, if Shadow People do? Ghosts and monsters and creepy crawlies?

I feel bad as soon as that thought hits my brain. Gabriel

isn't a creepy crawly. He's been nothing but nice to me. It's not like he tried to possess me or murder me or anything.

I take my empty teacup to the kitchen, where I spot the flowers sitting in the middle of the table. Hyacinths. I didn't really look at them before, but I see them completely now. They're shades of pale blue and soft purple. I walk over to them, brushing the tips of my fingers against them.

That's it. Please yourself, pretty girl...

The memory of his voice plays through my mind. He said he somehow made me feel good with his thoughts. Does that mean he isn't able to touch me?

I roll my eyes and let my hand fall away from the flowers. It doesn't matter. It's not like I'm going to let him touch me. I should go. I know I should. I should pack up my stuff and get out of here.

But I spent so much money on this week at the cabin, and it's only been two days. I want my money's worth. Maybe it's not so bad, having someone around. He won't bother me as long as I ask him to stay away. I can keep working, and he can just hang around in the trees outside. Right? Or does he have to eat? And go to the bathroom?

I feel so stupid. I don't know anything about a creature like him. Maybe I should have asked him more questions instead of kicking him out. That might have been more productive.

My eyes lift, going to the window, where the sun is setting on the other side of the glass, the light shifting to something aquamarine through the trees. If I wanted him to come back, how would I let him know? Would he hear me if I said his name? What if I just *thought* it?

"Gabriel?" I whisper, and a chill moves from one side of my body to the other, like someone has run their hand up under my hair. I gasp, planting a hand on the table and feeling the way my nipples harden under the sensation.

Gabriel stands in the corner of the room, the outline of him stark against the natural shadows cast by the sun. I can feel his eyes on me, and I hold myself perfectly still, not even really sure why I called for him. I have no idea what I'm doing.

Yes, Calista? he asks, his voice almost a purr.

I have a hundred questions, but I can't bring myself to ask any of them. I don't even know why. It's like they're caught in my throat, like if I open my mouth and speak, I'll choke on them. I take a deep breath, feeling the thick presence of him in the corner, and then I say, "I think I'm going to go to bed early. Goodnight."

A shimmer goes through him, but he just says, *Goodnight, Calista.*

I turn to leave the kitchen, but at the last minute, I turn back. "Thank you for the flowers."

All of him shimmers and spreads, like someone throwing a rock into a pond, and I bite back a smile as I rush out of the kitchen and down the hall to my bedroom.

———

A few hours later, I'm still laying awake in bed, staring at the ceiling. I keep thinking I see movement out of the corner of my eye, keep turning quickly to check, seeing nothing but shadows. How well can Gabriel blend in with the shadows? Would I be able to tell he was there, no matter what, or could he make himself undetectable?

I guess I thought it would creep me out to know he's out there, but I feel oddly...safe. I feel certain he's not going to hurt me, so maybe he could keep away anyone who *would*. My eyes scan the windows on the wall on the other side of the room, and I start to feel a tingle low in my belly that's almost embarrassing.

My mind has gone...interesting places. I can't help

thinking about the way I felt last night, when I woke up with Gabriel's voice in my ear. It was like having him in this bed with me. It was like having him whisper to me while he touched me. *Can* he touch me?

Gabriel? I think his name, wondering if it'll bring him near the way it did when I spoke his name out loud. But the room is still, quiet, none of the shadows shifting.

Movement outside catches my attention. I can barely make it out in the darkness, but I think I see a slight shimmer among the trees. As I watch, one of the shadows in the woods begins to spread, that black smoke that I now know is somehow tied to Gabriel's emotions. Does that mean he's happy? Or excited?

I bite my lip, reconsidering my plan. I must have lost my mind. But honestly, that orgasm I had last night was the best orgasm I've had in a while, and well, if Gabriel can do that with just his mind...? Do Shadow People have dicks? Shadow dick?

The shadow outside shifts, and I think I can make out his eyes, those onyx globes, but I might be just imagining that I can see them, as I know generally where they would be located in relation to the rest of him. Shoving my blanket down to my knees, I lift my shirt up just enough to run my hand along my bare stomach. I sigh, immediately feeling heat between my legs.

My last boyfriend told me I needed sex too much. He told me women shouldn't be so horny all the time, and the fact that I wanted it every single day meant there was something wrong with me.

But it doesn't *feel* like there's anything wrong with me. It just feels like my body is ready to *feel* all the time. Not even just sexual things. It's everything. A cold breeze, the ripple on the surface of the water, the burn of a crackling fire. I've just always been so *sensitive*, and it's never felt like something bad.

Shoving my shirt up to my neck, I bite my lip at the feel of the open air on my nipples. They harden, and I reach up to pinch one, tugging it in my fingers and bucking my hips at how good it feels. *Touch me*, I tell Gabriel in my head, but that's clearly not how this thing works because the shadow outside the window never moves. He doesn't come to me. He doesn't reach out with his mind and slide along my skin the way he did last night.

But I can't bring myself to open my mouth and ask him to. So, I decide to entice him instead. Keeping my eyes firmly locked on where I think his are, I slide my panties down my legs and toss them aside. From where he's standing, I don't think he has a very good view. So I shift, turning enough that when I let my legs fall open, I know he has a perfect shot of my pussy.

Just knowing he's watching, being certain of it this time, makes me wet. I slip my hand between my legs and find my clit, moaning as I start to circle it.

Something washes over me like a cloud. It settles against my skin like raindrops, but when they land, all I feel is happiness, eagerness, desire. It's him. Somehow, I can feel everything he's feeling.

And it's making me wetter.

An intelligible sound escapes me, like a whine, but even I have to admit it's his name. "Gabriel," coming out of me in a high-pitched noise.

He's there beside me in a second, the shape of him stark against the other shadows in the room.

Beautiful girl... he whispers into my mind, and my mouth falls open on a gasp. It's not like a whisper. His words, they're like a caress to my mind.

"Please," I finally force myself to say out loud.

He doesn't ask me what I want. He doesn't have to. That thing he does with his mind, it touches me, sending a shock-wave from my nipples down to my clit. God, I don't know how he does that, but it's like he's touching me everywhere, setting me on fire from the inside out. The pressure curls around my clit, and I dig my toes into the mattress, my body bowing off the bed.

Is that good?

"Yes," I practically shout, all insecurities gone with the wind. "Yes, right there, you're doing so well." I don't know where the words come from, but they spill out of me.

When I turn my face toward him, I see the shimmer of him, like prickles of starlight against the darkness. What I've said has clearly made him happy. His desire is almost palpable.

"Is that what you like?" I ask, aware of the almost painful pleasure between my legs as much as I'm aware of his delight spilling over me in waves.

He nods, his eyes locked on mine. *I'm doing a good job?*

The way he asks, his voice shaking with nerves, makes me grin up at the ceiling. Does Gabriel need to be praised? If so, I can definitely make that happen for him. "Such a good boy," I whisper, and he lights up. Well, as much as a Shadow Person can light up. He glitters with rainbow colors.

Can I...Can I touch you? he asks, sounding breathless, which doesn't even make sense because he's in my head. Can thoughts lose their breath?

Between my legs, I'm dripping, my clit thrumming like every ounce of my blood is pulsing there. If he can touch me, will it get even more intense?

"Yes," I whisper, uncertainty curling into the pit of my stomach. What am I doing? This is a person I don't even know, and he's not even human! He is literally a living shadow, and I'm going to let him pleasure me?

His arm snakes out, black as charcoal, and his hand moves between my legs, covering mine. I gasp, shocked by how solid he feels. Part of me thought he might go right through me like a ghost, but he doesn't. He's warm like a human, and his soft fingers graze mine like a human. I move my hand out of the way, and when his fingers find my clit, I throw my head back and groan. I grab onto his arm and rock my hips against his hand. It feels so good, having someone's hands on me after such a long time.

With my grip around his wrist, I push him a little lower, until two of his fingers are sinking into me, the heel of his hand pressing hard against my clit.

Am I doing it right?

My eyes fly open, meeting his in the dark. There's a sprinkle of color across his face. Is he...blushing? And then it dawns on me. Has he never done this before? Maybe just not with someone who isn't like him. Do the Shadow People have sex with each other? They must, right? Suddenly, I'm not so sure.

I nod and smile up at him, trying to encourage him. "Go faster," I tell him. "Harder."

A wave of black smoke comes off of him, and then his other hand settles on my stomach. He presses into me. He's *holding me down.* The hand between my legs starts to pump furiously, hard and fast, and I scream. I wrap my hand around the wrist holding me down. I don't want to lose the upper hand here. And I don't think he wants me to lose it either.

"You're doing so good," I manage to choke out. "Keep going. Don't stop. Be a good boy and make me come."

His eyes spark, and then, to my surprise, something warm and wet splashes across my stomach. My eyes shoot to the gray liquid on my skin. Did he just...?

Seeing his release on me, watching his hand hold me down while the other pumps between my legs. It's too much. I come, fighting against his hold so I can writhe against his hand. Oh fuck, oh fuck, oh fuck, it's so good.

My body goes limp, and as I lay there, Gabriel slowly takes

his hands away from me. I turn my head quickly, wanting to catch a glimpse of his cock, now that I know he definitely has one and is definitely using it, but all I can see are swirling shadows.

I think about asking him to show me, but I'm feeling exhausted and boneless, so instead, I curl into my blankets and close my eyes.

And from somewhere in the depths of my mind, I hear him say, *Sleep. I'll watch over you.*

Chapter Five

The sun is bright and high when I wake. My mind plays back the events of last night, and I smile into my pillow. I don't know what the hell I was thinking, but I certainly did enjoy myself. Gabriel stands in the corner of the room, holding my book open in his hands, the one I brought with me, doing his best to blend in with the shadows. But he stands out like a splash of black paint on a fresh canvas.

For a moment, I just watch him, his head bowed over the page. Everything I've been taught is telling me not to trust him. He's a monster. A stranger. A man who sat outside the cabin where I'm staying and watched me without me knowing, touched me without me knowing, even if it was with his mind.

But when I'm close to him like this, I don't feel fear. I just feel...safe.

I shift on the bed, and his head comes up, his pitch-black eyes meeting mine.

Do you...write books like this? he asks, and I see that slight hue on his face again, like he's blushing. I assume he's referring to the very graphic sex scenes in that book. The book that got me so worked up at the kitchen table the first night I got here. It's anything but mild. It just makes me wonder again what Gabriel's sexual experience looks like.

"Yes," I say, even though I haven't gotten to the point of my book where the couple actually has sex. They will, though, and when they do, it'll be very explicit. Maybe it'll even be inspired by what happened last night with Gabriel.

He puts the book down on the little table beside the reading chair and looks at me. *Did you sleep well?*

I nod. I did sleep well. I usually toss and turn, waking up several times in the night, but last night, I slept hard, like my whole body was exhausted. "You don't sleep?"

A slight smile curls up the corners of his mouth. *No. But I enjoyed watching you. I enjoyed...being here with you.*

Now that I know he's here, I wonder how I didn't notice him hanging around before he made himself known. "I think I'm going to go into town today," I tell him.

His shimmer dims, turning him into the color of coal, and I sit up, immediately feeling guilty that I took away his joy. The blanket falls to my waist, and his dark eyes drop to where my breasts are pushing against my tight shirt. "I'll be back. I just want to see if there's anyone in town who can help me figure out how to get you severed from this place."

He does that thing where he moves so quickly that he's just a gust of wind. And then he's sitting beside me on the bed, his eyes running over my face. *You would do that?* he asks, his voice nervous. I think about last night, about how much he needed to be praised and guided. He's made himself so vulnerable to me.

"Of course, I would. You're stuck here. You deserve better than that."

I gasp when he reaches out to take my hand in his. It's still strange to me that he feels so solid against my skin when he just looks like smoke. His hand caresses mine, his long fingers running over mine gently.

I'm glad I met you, Calista, he says, and I'm about to answer, to tell him that I'm glad I met him too, but before I can, he leans forward and kisses me.

His mouth is so careful against mine, and in the back of my mind, I'm reminded of my first kiss in high school at the winter formal, the way the boy who kissed me wasn't sure of himself. I smile against Gabriel's mouth and reach up to wrap a hand around the back of his neck. The feeling of plunging my hand into the mist that surrounds him is strange, leaving tingles along my skin.

I open my mouth against his and feel him do the same, following my lead. When I let my tongue run along his bottom lip, he groans, the sound nothing but a loud vibration in my head. It's so shocking that I falter, losing my place in the act for a second, but Gabriel doesn't miss a beat. He lifts both of his hands to my face, opens his mouth, and kisses me so deep that all I can do is melt against him.

I don't know how long we stay like that, just kissing and kissing, until eventually, I'm aware of the light around us changing and the ache in my body. I pull away, trying to catch my breath, and Gabriel uses the opportunity to kiss along my jaw, down my neck, until his lips find my collarbone.

I smile. "I should go. The sooner I get moving, the sooner we can get this all figured out. Plus, I still have work to do."

Gabriel pulls away from me, nodding adorably, like a soldier to their commanding officer. *I will miss you while you're gone.*

I bite my lip and stand, going to my suitcase to pull out some clothes for the day. When I turn around and find that Gabriel hasn't moved even an inch, I consider asking him to turn around, but in light of everything we did last night and everything he's already seen, it certainly can't hurt to let him watch.

I pull my shirt off over my head and bend to push my underwear down my legs. And then I watch Gabriel's eyes sweep over me from head to toe. He's all shimmery now, his black smoke flooding out of him in waves, covering half the room in darkness. It's like he's exploding.

I have to look away from him so that I can concentrate enough to get dressed, and when I'm done, I say, "I'll see you later, okay? I won't be gone long."

His shadow is taking up the entire room. It's so dark that I feel like I need to turn on a light or something. The knowledge that it's out of his own excitement sends a shiver through me.

Take your time, he says into my head.

———

There are two bookstores in Lewistown, Montana, but only one of them has books on ghosts and the occult. I get goose-bumps walking through the section because I was raised by parents who taught me to *never under any circumstances* mess with things like Ouija boards and tarot cards. It always seemed like sage advice, and it's not like I've ever really been into those things anyway.

At least, not until I found a Shadow Person in my cabin rental. I pull out every book they have on this sort of thing, sitting down on the floor and flipping through them to see if I can find something on how to get Gabriel unstuck from the cabin. I'm not even really sure where to begin.

"Shadow People, huh?"

My head snaps up. Hovering over me is a woman about my mother's age, her eyes glued to the pile of books around me. The one that's open in my lap is currently displaying several very creepy (and inaccurate) photos of Shadow People.

I don't think any of them are real photos, which tells me this book isn't going to do me much good.

I give a nervous laugh, shutting the book. "Yeah. Someone told me about them recently, and I guess I just thought they were interesting."

The woman tosses her long, blonde hair over her shoulder and reaches down for one of the books I chose. I can see the streaks of gray in her hair that match the lines around her eyes. "Shadow People are quite dangerous, from what I've heard."

I try not to let anything show on my face. "Oh, I don't know about that. They seem to be fairly harmless." I realize how that must sound and roll my eyes playfully, trying to throw this woman off the scent. "It doesn't really matter. I don't believe in all this stuff. I'm just working on a book." Ah, there. A nugget of truth. That's helpful.

The woman regards me, her eyes scanning me up and down. "Well, you can not believe in it all you want, but it's all real, the ghosts and the ghouls. And these particular ghouls will drag you into Hell."

I think about Gabriel, the way he can't hide his pleasure and the way he came last night just from touching me and being called a good boy. Am I really supposed to believe that he wants to drag me into Hell?

I smile politely. "Thanks for the input."

I'm hoping that's enough to get this woman to leave me alone, but all she does is step closer to me. My eyes fall to the brown leather of her shoes. "I don't mean to be nosy," she says, in that way that people warn you just before they're about to say something awful, "but are you staying in that cabin at the top of the hill?"

Something uncomfortable twists in my stomach. How the hell does she know where I'm staying? I look up at her slowly, glad now that I wasn't open with her about the truth. I clearly need to be cautious.

I'm not sure how to respond, but she doesn't wait for me to. "You know, several people have claimed that place is haunted. It's sort of local lore, actually. More than one person has mentioned a demonic presence."

Anger rises up inside of me. "He's not–" I don't cut myself off in time. Jesus, my caution lasted all of ten seconds. I clamp my lips together and meet the smug expression the woman is wearing with a fierce one of my own. "I don't mean to be rude," I say, throwing her own words back at her, "but what goes on in that cabin while I'm there is really none of your business." I stand, reaching down for the books and then piling them onto a table at the end of the aisle. I'll find somewhere else to get answers.

I turn for the front of the bookstore, but the woman rushes out in front of me, stopping me in my tracks. "Please." She puts her hands up, as if to show her innocence. "I'm just trying to help you."

"Please, move out of my way."

People are starting to turn in our direction, but the woman doesn't pay them any attention. "You were looking into Shadow People. Is that what's in the cabin with you? They'll convince you to have intercourse with them, and that's how they bind themselves to people forever. You're not safe!"

As much as I hate to admit it, I full-on shove the woman out of the way at that point. I'm so mad and so desperate to just get the hell out of here that I don't even care when she stumbles back into a table of books, knocking down the display that was masterfully perched there. Several people gasp, and I make a run for it before someone calls the cops on me.

Chapter Six

Some of the adrenaline has worn off by the time I get back to the cabin, but my hands are still shaking. What the hell was up with that woman?

I've been running her words through my mind over and over, trying to figure out if there's even a chance that any of it could be true. Because if it is...

As soon as I climb out of my SUV, Gabriel is there, bringing with him that gust of wind that he always does. I shut my door and lean against it. I think he can tell immediately that things didn't go great. A crease forms between his solid black eyes.

What happened? he asks, and I feel bad that I didn't offer him a warmer greeting. I'm sure it's miserable for him, waiting around for me to get back.

"Gabriel, I need to ask you a question."

He just nods, his shadows moving around him in restless ripples.

"Before, when that woman trapped you here, did you have sex with her?"

For a moment, he doesn't react, just stares at me. And then he lifts his chin. *Yes, I did.*

That answers a lot of my questions about his sexual experience where human women are concerned but not all of them. "Did the woman...I don't know...do something weird?"

He seems to shrink in on himself a little, like he's trying to make himself smaller. *I'm not sure what you mean. Weird?*

I'm starting to wonder about this woman. What did she do to Gabriel to make him react this way?

"Listen, I met someone in town who told me that if you have sex with someone, it could bind you to them forever. Do you know anything about that?"

His eyes look past me, like he's thinking through things, and then shoot back to mine. *But if that was true, I would be bound to her, the one who tied me to this place.*

Obviously, I thought about that, too. "Did she do something maybe before or after the two of you slept together? Something out of the ordinary?" This time, when his eyes leave me, they fall to the ground, and I see that sadness in them that I saw before. "I'm sorry," I tell him. "I hate to ask. This is clearly–"

It's okay. The words burst into my mind, and then he sighs. I just want to see him all spread out with joy again. This is agony. *It's hard for me to talk about. It was...quite a difficult time. Her name was Julie. She was kind and beautiful. I was passing through, and I stopped in the woods while she happened to be outside, watching the sunset. She didn't seem to be afraid of me. It was almost like she was waiting for me.*

I didn't show myself at first. I stayed hidden, but then she called out to me. She said she knew I was there and that I didn't need to hide. So...I didn't. I came out. She invited me to sit with her. She spoke to me like I was a real person. I'll admit...it was intoxicating.

"You *are* a real person," I say, taking a step closer to him.

His eyes shoot to mine, and a little shimmer goes through him. *We talked for hours, and then eventually, we ended up in her bed. I had never been with a human before, only other Shadow People like myself. It was...amazing. So, so lovely.*

He stops talking for a moment, his eyes looking far off into the distance, and I'm surprised when a burst of jealousy flashes through me. I don't want to think of him with some other woman, especially not a woman who hurt him.

We made love, and I could feel that something shifted. It was like...I don't know, it's so hard to explain. It's like I suddenly needed her so much that I felt I would die without her. It was like she was food, and I was so hungry I would waste away at any moment. And then she, well, she tied me to the bed. I don't understand how she did it, but when she put the chain around my wrists, I couldn't become shadow. I was completely solid, unable to move. And then she left.

"Oh, Gabriel." I take his face in my hands, shocked to find that his kin has gone cold. This woman, whoever she was, wounded him, and her betrayal clearly still has a hold on him.

He doesn't meet my eyes. *I don't understand it, but I think that when she left, the bond broke somehow, like it was corrupted, and I ended up tied to the house instead. That's the only way I know how to explain it. If I'm honest, I didn't think the sex had anything to do with it. I thought she put some kind of curse on me.*

I can't rule that out, but there's really only one way to know for sure.

"If we have sex, there's a chance that we can break your tie to the cabin."

He looks at me with that confused expression of his again. His hands come up to settle on my waist, and suddenly his shadows are reaching around me, covering both of us like some kind of midnight bubble.

But then we would be tied to each other. You would have to live your life with me in tow. I can't ask you to do that.

"You're not asking me. I'm offering. This is the only way you'll be free. That is, if that's what you want. I don't want you to be tied to me against your will anymore than I want you tied to the cabin when you don't want to be."

A slight shimmer goes through him again. *I don't think I would mind being tied to you. I would like to go where you go.*

I shrug, trying to hide the pleasure I feel low in my stomach at his words. "Maybe it won't be so bad, being followed around all the time by someone who can make me come with just his mind."

A sly smile spreads across his mouth. *I can make you come with more than just my mind.*

Heat flushes all the way down to my toes, and I lace my fingers through his, pulling him toward the cabin. "Come on."

He doesn't fight me. As soon as the door is shut behind us, I turn Gabriel and press him to it. Pushing up on my toes, I find his mouth with mine. Just like this morning, just the touch of my lips seems to send him into a frenzy. He takes my face in his hands and kisses me deep, sweeping his tongue into my mouth.

It's comforting to know this won't be his first time. The last time I had sex with a virgin, I was still a virgin myself. And really, with a situation like this, I'm the one who has no clue what they're doing. It's not like I've ever been railed by a Shadow Person before.

When I wrap my arms around Gabriel, his shadows stretch around us, like they did before, covering us in darkness, like we need privacy, here in this empty cabin. I can feel him growing hard between us, and I'm beginning to feel desperate to see it, to hold it, to feel it inside me.

I pull back, looking into his black eyes. I can't believe

anyone could ever be afraid of him. Looking into his eyes, all I feel is...safe. "Can I touch you?" I ask him.

He gets this look on his face, like I've just surprised him with some kind of gift, and then nods. *Yes.*

I reach my hand up between us, approximating in the dark where his dick is, and gasp when I come into contact with it. A flush rushes up my cheeks as I run my hand up the length of him.

I can make it bigger, he says, *if it's not big enough to please you.*

I'm about to protest, to tell him that it's far bigger than it needs to be to get the job done, but then he's growing longer, and I realize the shadows are collecting on the tip, hardening to add length.

"Hang on there, buddy," I say with a nervous chuckle. "You were fine with what you were working with before."

It's been my experience that women like rather large penises.

I bite back a laugh and give his dick a flew long strokes from root to tip. "You're perfect the way you are."

His little shimmer goes through him, and then he pushes me back into the cabin, leading me over to the couch. He gently lowers me to it and then falls to his knees in front of me.

I want to please you, he says into my mind. His voice in my head always feels intimate, but now that all my blood is pulsing between my legs, it's practically a caress. I bite my lip as he starts to tug at the waistband of my pants. But even with his nimble fingers, he can't get them down because of the knot at my belly button.

I giggle and push his hands away. "Let me."

He sits back on his heels and watches as I peel away my shirt first and then my bra. He's already seen me naked, so this isn't exactly an unveiling, but when the cool air hits my breasts and my nipples harden, he sucks in a breath. His shadows creep past his body and slide up my stomach, covering my breasts with that strange mist.

I feel devoured by him, and he's not even touching me with his hands.

The pants, he says, and I absentmindedly stand to push my pants and underwear down to my feet and step out of them. As soon as they're out of the way, Gabriel gives me a gentle push. Or maybe it's the shadows that push me. Is it all him, or are the shadows separate from him?

In this moment, I don't know that I care as long as he doesn't stop touching me.

Gabriel walks forward on his knees, and the sight of him crawling to me makes me throb between my legs even more. He pushes my legs apart, and when the air hits where I'm so extremely wet, I shiver.

The first night you were here, I smelled you, Gabriel says, eyes flickering up to me and then back down between my legs. *You were at that table, doing delicious things to yourself, and I could smell the scent of your arousal from outside the cabin. That's why I came. That's why I watched, even though I knew I shouldn't.*

He doesn't wait for me to answer. He holds my eye and then leans forward and swipes his tongue up the wet, hot center of me. I drop my head back on a gasp. Instinctively, I reach down to take his head in my hands, and I'm shocked when I encounter horns.

My eyes fly open, and I look down between my legs. There was so much shadow around him that I didn't notice before, but I can see them now from this angle, two horns that curve around the back of his head.

Like he can tell I've lost focus, Gabriel slips his tongue inside me, and I have to grab onto his horns to anchor myself. He feasts on me, and all I can do is enjoy it, closing my eyes and letting him explore every inch of me. I suddenly feel ridiculous for thinking this might be his first time. He clearly knows what he's doing.

I'm on the very edge, one hand curled around a horn and the other gripping the fabric of the couch, when I open my eyes and gasp.

The room is black. Gabriel's shadows have wrapped around us completely, blocking out everything but us. They move over us like mist, and I feel every single separate particle on my sensitive skin.

And here, in the protective bubble of his shadow, I feel safe. When I glance down at Gabriel, our eyes meeting, I tip right over the edge, shouting out my release as he relentlessly licks and sucks and worships my pussy.

When my orgasm subsides, and the touching begins to be too much, I nudge one of his horns until he lets up. We're both panting, and even as he moves back to sit on his haunches, Gabriel strokes himself. I want him inside me. Now.

Like he can read my mind, he leans forward, his hands going to my thighs to push them open again.

The world spins, and he's suddenly sitting beneath me on the couch as I straddle him, both of us still shielded by his dark globe. I've never been completely against him like this, somehow solid and not at the same time. His cock nudges against my ass, and I bite my lip.

Please use me, he whispers to me. *Use me for your pleasure.*

I take his face in my hands, gratified by the shimmer that moves over him, lighting up my vision for a second. His hands find my hips, gripping tightly, as if he can't help himself.

"Is this what you want?" I ask him. "You want to be my little toy?"

He quivers against me. *Yes. Yes, please. I'm begging you.*

Oh, he's begging alright, and I'm shocked by how wet it makes me.

I run a finger along the ridge of his bottom lip and then dip it into his mouth. He immediately closes around me, his wet tongue tracing my finger. "Good little toys don't come until their masters do."

He moans around my finger, and I use the opportunity to lift my hips and then lower myself onto his cock. His mouth drops open, and my hand falls to my side. Oh, God, he feels so good inside me. I can't believe he thought for even a second that he needed to be bigger than he already is. His dick is so big that it's almost painful, nudging deep deep *deep*.

But then something changes inside me. He's not getting longer, but he's getting thicker, and I think the shape of him is...shifting. I gasp when a knob forms on top of his cock, pressing hard and rubbing against my G-spot.

A rough, desperate noise bursts out of me, and I dig my nails into his shoulders. It feels so good that my legs tremble. "Oh, fuck, yes." My head falls back, my body entirely focused on that spot where he's rubbing against me with every rock of our hips.

When he groans loud, I open my eyes to focus. He has his head thrown back, and I smile watching him. I can barely see him in the darkness that surrounds us, his body and face blending with the shadows, but the shimmers flashing through him and the chaotic swirl of the black smoke tell me he's enjoying this.

I find his hand and press it to my breast, satisfied when he curls around me instinctively. "Please me," I tell him. His eyes pop open, almost like he forgot I was here in the first place. He was so lost in what he was feeling.

Yes, he says, his thumb pressing into my nipple as his other hand finds my clit.

I shiver, slamming down onto him hard. Any hope that this might have been something sweet and gentle is gone. And I don't want that. He doesn't seem to want that either, if the steady groans bursting from his mouth with each of my movements is any indication.

Does that please you? he asks, but I'm too distracted by it all: the depth of his cock inside me, the bounce of my own breasts as I ride him, the intoxicating feel of his nakedness pressed to mine. I lean back on my haunches, pressing my palms to his knees. The shift must really feel good because he starts to make a low, whining noise.

"Don't come," I tell him, certain he's right on the edge. "Don't you dare come until I do."

He nods, and I go at him faster, chasing my orgasm, all the while aware that he's keeping his own at bay. I hold his gaze, fighting back my instinct to look away during something so vulnerable, but when his hand shifts, settling right over my heart, and he looks at me like I'm made of starlight, I shatter.

I shout up at the roof, the orgasm pulling me in all different directions as the dark mist around me caresses my over-sensitive skin.

When I'm aware again, I slump against Gabriel and find him trembling. I look up at the sharp jut of his jaw and smile. "You can come now, baby."

He groans loud and long, hands each taking a big handful of my ass. He slams me down on him, his shout muffled into the side of my neck. And when it's over, and I'm completely boneless against his chest, I feel more at peace than I ever have in my life.

Chapter Seven

I don't get to enjoy the peace for very long. As soon as we're able, Gabriel and I untangle ourselves from each other, and he pulls all of his shadows back into himself, until it's just the shape of him sitting on the couch.

I stand in front of him, completely naked, and watch. "Do you not wear clothes?" I ask. Last night, when he came on me while touching me, he never took off any pants or anything like that. And this time, too, he had just been magically naked, though I had assumed he had just disrobed while I was recovering from the oral he gave me.

The shadows cover anything that should not be exposed, he says, and I take a moment to examine him. He's right, I suppose. His skin is black, and the shadows that constantly swirl around him cover his body. Everything is so dark that it's almost impossible to tell his shadows from his actual figure, but maybe it doesn't matter since it's all part of him anyway.

"Do you feel different?" I ask him.

I guess I thought once we were done, I would be able to feel that he's connected to me, but I don't really feel any different.

Yes. There's that shimmer. To my surprise, a smile spreads across his mouth, bright white teeth visible against the inky black of the rest of him.

"Hmmmm." I reach for my clothes. "I guess we could go for a walk to see if it took."

Oh, it took. There's no getting away from me now, Calista.

Butterflies start low in my stomach at the command in his voice, and I'm just about to crawl right back into his lap to demand he fuck me again when I hear footsteps behind me.

Gabriel's black eyes move to something past me, and he shoots up off the couch as I spin around. There, with a handful of some kind of herbs held above her head, is the woman from the bookstore. Her eyes are wild, and she shakes the smoking herb stick at me and shouts, "You invited it into your bed! It's attached itself to you!"

"Stop!" I shout, trying to reach for the burning stick. But she dodges me, moving toward Gabriel, and I realize it's not me she's trying to get with all that gray smoke; it's him.

"Go back where you came from!" she shouts, and Gabriel turns into black smoke, scattering backward to avoid the woman. She reaches into her pocket and pulls out something that she holds in the center of her palm. When she lifts it toward Gabriel, I see that it's a black crystal. "Go back to Hell, demon!"

Gabriel's shadows become thinner, like smoke dissipating after a candle has been blown out. As she gets closer to him, he looks like he's caving in, getting smaller and smaller.

"No!" I scream. "Leave him alone!"

I lunge forward and step between them, shoving the woman back as hard as I can. She stumbles, landing on the couch with enough force that it slides back a few inches under her weight.

The woman's wide eyes meet mine. "I'm trying to save you," she says, her face so innocent that it's almost enough for me to feel bad for her. But then I remember that she broke into my rental and threatened my new boyfriend. That she accosted me in a bookstore. That she keeps calling him a *demon from Hell*.

"He's not a demon," I grind out between my teeth, my hands balling into fists at my sides. "Gabriel is not from Hell, and he's not here to hurt me. You have no right to barge into this house and–"

"He's possessed you!" the woman shrieks, holding up her hands again, pointing her supplies in my direction. "You don't know what you're saying. He's influencing you. He's *controlling* you!"

I take a menacing step toward her, and she shrinks deeper into the couch cushions. "He's mine, and if you come anywhere near him again, I will kill you, I swear. Now, get the hell out."

She looks like she's about to argue again, but then her eyes go over my shoulder, and her face goes pale. She looks like she might shit herself.

I turn to look over my shoulder, surprised when I find myself looking into a midnight cloud. Gabriel is so big that he stretches from the floor to the ceiling, his eyes like twin pieces of coal against his smoke form. He looks scary, and...well...if I'm being honest, I'm a little turned on.

But I'm sure from this lady's perspective, he looks like the end of her life.

GET. OUT.

The woman screams so loud that I flinch. She scrambles off the couch and sprints for the door, throwing it open so hard that it hits the wall with a *crack*. The woman is gone.

From behind me, I hear a sort of sigh and feel Gabriel's breath against the back of my neck. When I turn, he's back to his normal size, a smile playing at the corners of his mouth.

I apologize if that was frightening, he says, and a little blush-colored shimmer goes over him.

"Not at all. In fact, I think I might need you to *possess* me again."

He laughs, and it's a beautiful sound.

Epilogue

"I've read a lot of books about Shadow People, but this one is by far my favorite."

I smile up at the last person in my signing line, a woman about my age with stars in her eyes. "Thank you so much," I tell her. "I appreciate that."

The woman blushes and takes her book from me, signed and personalized, the book that only took me a month to write after I got back from the cabin with Gabriel in tow. "So many books paint them out to be devious little devils, but I think Shadow People are just minding their own business."

My stomach flutters at hearing her speak this way. I can't help but wonder if she's met any Shadow People of her own. I think of Gabriel, of how we met, and wonder how many people would even be open to the kind of relationship I have with him. I'm guessing not many.

"Well, be careful who you invite into your life. Some Shadow People *are* devious little devils." I learned that pretty quickly. Gabriel is tied to me, but he's still able to travel as much as he wants now that he isn't tied to a building, and that means meeting other Shadow People. Sometimes they're great, and sometimes not so much.

The woman in front of me gives me a little salute and then turns to leave. The bookstore is empty now, the event over, and I gather my stuff. After thanking the event coordinators and signing a few more books for them to put on their shelf, I head out into the night. My hotel is just a short walk away, and besides, I'm not alone.

As soon as the door to the bookstore falls closed behind me, Gabriel appears, shimmering rainbow colors. *How was your event?* he asks as he falls into step beside me.

"You didn't come inside at all?"

He shakes his head. *I didn't want to frighten anyone.*

I think of all the people who have read my book and who come out to my events. I get the feeling they're not the types to be easily frightened, but I decide not to say anything. Instead, I lace my arm through his as we walk down the street.

He chuckles and then turns to smoke, letting my arm fall back to my side.

We must be more careful than that, he says, and I roll my eyes, even though I know he's right. We've done a good job keeping Gabriel hidden for the last year. I don't want to blow it now.

Will you ever get tired of hiding? he asks now, reappearing in the shadows under the awnings of the shops we're walking beside. *Don't you want to be with a man who can stroll arm-in-arm with you in the sunlight?*

"I want you," I tell him, stopping and turning to face him. "I don't care if it's inconvenient or strange or whatever. I just want to be with you."

I don't want to keep you from living a normal life.

"Never really been interested in a normal life." I smile at him and then continue down the road with my shadow at my side.

About the Author

Winter Randall is the alter ego of B. Randall, which is also an alter ego, but that's a story for another time. She lives in Dallas with her husband. In her free time, she rides her bike, does puzzles, and watches a lot of Formula 1.

ALSO BY WINTER RANDALL

Snowed In With The Mountain Monster

Minotaur Sugar Daddies

My Gargoyle Protector